It suddenly dawned on Kate that she would be spending the night in the same room with Slade.

She turned and saw him sitting on the bed, his back toward her. The sharp, intense longing she'd felt earlier stabbed through her body.

She wanted his kiss again, she acknowledged, as need ran hot through her veins. She wanted the comfort of his arms, the security of his touch. She wanted, just for a little while, to forget her fears and her worries. She wanted him to take her in his arms and help shut out the image of her frail son, alone with a dangerous man in the vast unfriendly desert.

Kate was hurting, and she wanted to be comforted. She wanted to be *loved*.

She had actually taken a step forward when Slade pushed himself off the bed and turned. Startled, she jerked her gaze to his face, hot guilt flooding her cheeks.

His eyes widened when he looked at her, and he went very still. His lips formed one, soft word. "Kate."

Dear Reader,

Happy New Year! We're starting off twelve more months of great reading with a book that many of you have been looking forward to: *Times Change*, Nora Roberts's sequel to last month's *Time Was*. Jacob Hornblower aimed his ship into the past, intending to bring back his brother, Caleb, who had inexplicably decided to remain in the twentieth century to stay with a *woman*! Little did Jacob know that his own heart was about to be stolen by Sunny Stone, Caleb's sister-in-law and the only woman anywhere—or any*when*—capable of making him see the light of love! Love a little, laugh a little, as these two mismatched lovers discover that time is no barrier at all to romance.

Dallas Schulze's *Donovan's Promise* was a big favorite with readers, and now Donovan's son, Michael, has grown up. He's ready for a romance of his own, so prepare to lose your heart to *The Vow*. Like father, like son, as the saying goes, and when it comes to matters of the heart, that definitely seems to be true. Michael Sinclair is every bit as wonderful as Donovan, and his story of love is every bit as compelling as his parents' was.

The month also includes *Catch of the Day*, by Marion Smith Collins, a suspense-filled tale with a tender heart, and *Desert Heat*, by Doreen Roberts, whose luscious prose and very real characters will carry you away.

Read to your heart's content—but don't forget to come back next month for more of the best romances in town, only from Silhouette Intimate Moments.

Leslie J. Wainger
Senior Editor
Silhouette Books

Desert Heat

DOREEN ROBERTS

Silhouette Intimate Moments

Published by Silhouette Books New York

America's Publisher of Contemporary Romance

SILHOUETTE BOOKS
300 East 42nd St., New York, N.Y. 10017

ISBN: 0-373-07319-4

First Silhouette Books printing January 1990

Printed in the U.S.A.

DOREEN ROBERTS

was hooked from the moment she opened the first page of a Mary Stewart novel. It took her twenty years to write her own romantic suspense novel, which was subsequently published, much to her surprise. She and her husband left their native England more than twenty years ago and have since lived in Oregon, where their son was born. Doreen hopes to go on mixing romance and danger in her novels for at least another two decades.

To my husband, Ron.
For all the groceries picked up,
all the meals cooked,
all the errands run.
For giving me time to be a writer.
I love you.

And to Erin.
For caring about my characters
as much as I do.
My grateful thanks.

Chapter 1

The dust filled his nostrils as he joined the riders waiting at the chutes. The wind, warmed by the dry heat of an Oregon summer, snatched at the wide brim of his black hat but failed to dislodge it.

He felt the sun searing his shoulders through the fabric of his shirt and welcomed it. It reminded him of his days in the Arizona desert, and any reminders of his childhood aroused the cold, merciless concentration he would need in the next few minutes.

Impatient for his turn he exchanged no more than a curt nod with the cowhands who sat astride the fences on either side of the bulls.

He heard the announcer's voice reverberating from the loudspeaker system, and rested his booted foot on the bottom rung in readiness.

"The next man up in the bull-riding event is the reigning champion, Slade Montana..." The rest of the words were lost as a roar erupted from the crowd.

The cheers echoed in his ears as Slade swung himself up the fence, his coiled rope dangling from his arm, and straddled the chute above the restless bull. Excitement rippled through the spectators crowding the stands and washed over him like an electric current. Braced by his hands and feet he paused, waiting for the right moment to drop onto the tough, bony back and begin his struggle.

Beneath him the bull pawed the ground, its head tossing in impatience when it sensed the man poised above him. Silence settled over the arena as the crowd waited in anticipation for the coming battle.

Slade lifted his head and scanned the spectators with narrowed eyes. This was the charged moment he looked forward to; every eye concentrating on him, challenging him to face again the brutal test between man and beast.

He enjoyed a challenge. His whole life had been one, with his fighting to escape the stigma that had threatened to follow him the rest of his days. He had finally made it. He was respected and sought after. He'd shaken the shackles of his inglorious beginnings and had achieved a certain, uneasy peace with himself.

Only here in the ring, battling two thousand pounds of raging animal, could he loosen up on the iron control he kept on his temper, the explosive fury that had nearly ruined his life.

The bull snorted and raked the fence with a hoof. Slade looked down and emptied his mind of everything but the fidgeting animal. It was between him and Red Tornado now. The luck of the draw had given him one of the fiercest bulls on the circuit. He liked that; it meant a better chance to show off his skills and score points.

Uncoiling the rope, he dropped cleanly and tightened his thigh muscles as the animal shifted from side to side. With a deft movement he passed the rope under the bull's belly and felt the tug as the cowhand on his left leaned over and caught it.

Slade grabbed the end from him and twisted his wrist until his hand was strapped securely on the massive back. With his free hand on the fence, he slid his hips forward until his roped fist nestled firmly against his crotch.

Tugging his hat down over his eyes, he pulled in his stomach muscles, dragged in a breath and braced himself. His eyes on the smooth spot between the bull's horns, he gave the nod to signal he was ready.

Kate Templeton leaned forward in her grandstand seat, adjusting her sunglasses as she peered through the shimmering heat at the man astride the bull. She couldn't see his face beneath the brim of his hat, and she had to be content with watching his long, lean body.

The aroma of hot dogs overpowered the potent smell of horses and sawdust as a vendor paused by her side, his eyes glued on the chute.

Tension throbbed in the heated air, silencing the crowd. Kate raised a hand to lift damp tendrils of blond hair off her forehead. Now that she was here, her confidence was fading fast. She'd been certain she could handle it—until she'd had her first good look at him.

The chute opened, letting loose several hundred pounds of kicking, bucking, writhing animal bent on dislodging the agile body from its back.

Kate's fingers dug into her palms as man and bull leaped into the air and then crashed to earth with a shuddering impact of hooves. In spite of her anxiety, the old excitement stirred as she watched Slade's lithe body lean backward in his attempt to keep his seat for the full eight seconds.

He was still magnificent, she thought with a surge of nostalgia. Even after all these years, that hadn't changed. The sight of him exerting his incredible control over the powerful animal still gave her goose bumps.

She held her breath as she waited for the whistle that would proclaim the ride over. She hadn't expected this. She fully believed that she'd erased every trace of emotion as far as Slade Montana was concerned.

When she'd seen the announcement in the paper, stating he was coming to town for the rodeo, her reaction had been relatively composed. She'd stared at his blurred picture, and dismissed the faint fluttering in her stomach as surprise. She'd thought he'd left the circuit years ago.

She would never have come near him, she told herself, if it hadn't been for the ad campaign. It was fate that had delivered the perfect answer to her problem, right into her lap, so to speak.

Once more Kate leaned forward, and tried to ignore the acceleration of her heartbeat. He would be perfect, she thought, watching the fluid movements of the champion as he battled the bull. All she had to do was persuade him to agree to pose for the ads, and they'd both reap the benefits.

She was conscious of a twinge of guilt, then immediately dismissed it. What he didn't know couldn't hurt him. He need never know that Michael existed.

It was doubtful, she thought fiercely, that he'd given her a second thought after she'd walked out of his life. He certainly hadn't wasted any time getting out of town.

He probably wouldn't even remember her when he saw her. She had no reason to feel guilty, she assured herself. She had done what she thought was best for all of them.

She wondered if he would agree with that if he knew the truth. She thought about what she planned to do, and wished she didn't have the uneasy feeling that it could all blow up in her face.

The whistle shrilled at last, followed by a wildly cheering ovation from the stands. It threatened to deafen Kate as she watched Slade swing down and grab at the horn of the saddle streaking past him. The rider leaned down and grabbed Slade's arm, hauling the champion up easily behind him.

A clown with wild red hair flipped a balloon at the bull's nose and raced out of the ring with the panting animal in hot pursuit. The announcer bellowed across the dust-clouded ring that Slade Montana was the winner of the event. The champion responded by taking off his hat and waving it at the delighted onlookers.

Kate got a glimpse of lengthy dark hair and a deeply tanned face before he replaced it. She kept her gaze on him as he slid off the horse, slapped his benefactor on the leg in thanks, then strode through the passageway between the chutes and disappeared from view.

The vendor moved on, and the voices around Kate subsided to a low murmur. She stood, her gaze on the narrow passageway where she'd last seen Slade Montana.

She knew he wouldn't be out again until the final parade around the ring. If she was going to talk to him it would have to be now. Once the rodeo was over he would be gone before she could get to him in the crush of people leaving the stands.

Her heart pounded when she thought about facing him again. She had no wish to be reminded of the soul-searing, gut-wrenching agony she'd gone through after she'd left him. If the ad campaign hadn't been so important to her, if it hadn't meant the chance of a secure future for Michael, she reflected bitterly, wild horses wouldn't have dragged her to this place.

She had to pause and draw in a long, deep breath before she could force herself to move. Stepping over crumpled paper cups, empty popcorn cartons and several pairs of feet, she made her way to the stairs and climbed down to the ring. A burly cowboy wearing a Stetson and a red checkered shirt put out an arm in front of her as she approached the gate.

"Sorry, miss, I can't let you through. Only rodeo personnel allowed." He touched the brim of his hat with his fingers and gave her a regretful smile.

"I have to speak to Slade Montana," Kate said, putting a note of authority in her voice. "It's a business matter of some importance to Mr. Montana."

The big man hesitated, then shrugged. "I guess it'll be all right. Just go on through, he'll be around somewhere."

Nodding her thanks Kate hurried through the enclosure, wrinkling her nose at the intensified smell of horses. She'd already rehearsed in her mind the words she would use to persuade the champion to consider her offer.

No matter what he said, she was determined not to accept a refusal. Slade Montana was her son's passport to security, she reminded herself silently, and that much at least he was going to give her. Whatever it took.

Slade saw her enter the compound, his gaze flicking over her with mild interest. She stopped a few yards away from him when Carlos, the man in charge of horses, asked her what she wanted.

It was several seconds before Slade realized whom he was looking at. He felt as if a giant hand was squeezing his heart in that blazing moment of recognition, then his control automatically reasserted itself, shutting down all emotion and sensation. He had time to study her without appearing to do so, his eyes hidden by the brim of his hat.

The years had been good to her, he thought, eyeing her slim figure. She looked cool and composed in a blue top and white slacks. He caught himself remembering what her bare legs looked like, and smothered the image.

His eyes narrowed as he watched her talking. She waved her hand in a slightly imperious manner that touched a nerve. Somewhere along the line she'd acquired a self-assured confidence that seemed out of place with the woman he remembered.

Good dresser, attractive, makeup perfect, not one strand of her smooth blond hair out of place, she'd come a long way from the wide-eyed girl with wind-ruffled curls who'd once fired his blood.

It was an image that had stayed with him long after he'd learned she'd married someone else. He might have taken it a little easier if it hadn't been for the man she'd married. Vic

Wheeler, too old, too dull; what had a woman like Kate Templeton seen in a man like that?

Maybe he hadn't known her as well as he thought. He wondered if she'd become as hard as her image implied. Turning away, he nursed a faint hope that her being there was simply coincidence, a hope that was dashed when he glanced back and saw her walking toward him.

Kate saw him turn to face her, and had to force herself to keep walking until she reached him.

He gazed down at her, his black brows drawn together in a frown. He wasn't the tallest man she'd ever known, he just made it look that way. Dark brown eyes, so dark it was difficult to detect where the irises began, glinted against his sun-scorched skin.

He still wore his straight black hair long on his neck, though it had been neatly trimmed over his ears. His harsh features were uncompromising as he waited with the air of someone annoyed at being disturbed.

"Hello, Slade," Kate said quietly. "It's good to see you again." She saw a flicker of remembered pain before he masked it with the cool indifference she knew so well.

"Kate. It's been a long time." His deep voice stirred shadows from the past, making the trite phrase seem almost meaningful.

She stared up at him, trying to concentrate on the reason she was there, and striving not to notice the rugged maturity that intensified his raw good looks.

Could eight years really have made all that much difference, or had she forgotten just how attractive he was? Hard living had etched lines of experience on his forehead and at the corners of his eyes. He had that weathered, untamed look that was pure sex appeal.

She felt a tremor of awareness and took a small step backward in unconscious retreat. The silence had gone on too long and she stammered, "I—I've come to offer you a business proposition I think you'll be interested in."

Appalled at the way she'd blurted it out, she opened her mouth to speak again then shut it when Slade said abruptly, "Where's your husband?"

Kate's lips tightened. She might have known he wouldn't let it rest. She'd been prepared for his attitude, but she hadn't anticipated the intensity of her reaction to it.

"Vic and I are divorced," she said with quiet dignity. "I haven't seen him in three years."

The news seemed to shock him. His eyes widened for a second, then the impassive mask returned. "And your son?"

She hadn't imagined that she could feel so cold and hot at the same time. "How...?" She ran her tongue over her dry lips.

"News travels fast in a small town," Slade said, his face showing no emotion. "Several people couldn't wait to tell me the moment I got back to Prineville."

Kate swallowed. He couldn't know all of it, she assured herself. Surely he would have contacted her, asked to see Michael...something.

She took hold of the panic fluttering in her chest. It was just her guilt fueling her imagination. He couldn't possibly know Michael was his son.

"What about you?" She managed a faint smile. "Are you married, or does the rodeo still rule your life?"

She'd seen the glint in his eye too late to soften the sarcasm in her voice. Where had all that bitterness come from? she wondered. She'd thought she'd banished it from her system long ago.

To cover her agitation she plunged on. "I heard you'd left the circuit. Didn't you have an accident or something some time ago?"

"Yeah." He lifted his hat and settled it more firmly on his head, shading his eyes so she couldn't see the expression in them. "I landed on the wrong end of a bull's horns. I was out for almost a year, but I made it back. That was three years ago."

Three years ago. She'd been engulfed in her own horror then; it was no wonder she'd lost track of his career. After that nothing had seemed to matter much for a long time.

Suddenly she'd had enough. All the emotions she'd been holding so carefully in check were beginning to rise to the surface, and she couldn't afford that. This whole deal had to be conducted in a professional manner, with nothing between them except the business at hand. It was the only way she could get through the assignment.

"I would like to talk to you about this proposition," she said, assuming a brisk tone.

"Unless you're here to tell me I've inherited a fortune I'm not interested."

She'd expected that, and she was ready for it. She summoned a polished smile, although a tiny ripple of apprehension stirred in the back of her head. "No inheritance. Just a business deal that could amount to a considerable sum of money."

His dark eyes stayed on her face, assessing without apology.

She waited for long, tense moments and when he still didn't speak she said irritably, "Are you interested or not?"

For an anxious moment she thought he was going to reject her out of hand. Then he shoved his thumbs into the pockets of his jeans and said, "Where there's money concerned, I'm always interested."

She let out her breath. He was predictable after all. Nothing aroused curiosity quicker than money. She cast a look around her. She knew he wasn't going to be easy to deal with. She needed the right place to put her proposal across, and this definitely wasn't it.

The smell was beginning to disturb her stomach, and the loud chatter from the group of young girls who had just entered made meaningful conversation impossible. She glanced over at them, and when she looked back, she caught an expression on his face that made her skin prickle.

For a split second she'd seen naked hostility in his eyes. So he hadn't forgiven her. The revelation shocked her. Hiding her discomfort she said carefully, "Is there somewhere a little more…convenient where we can discuss this?"

She watched him raise his arm to look at his watch. The slow, deliberate movement suggested he was using the time to phrase his words before speaking. "How long is this going to take?"

She wished he'd stop looking at her with that blank expression. Some kind of emotion, even the hostility, was better than that cold indifference. "Not too long," she said, trying not to let her anxiety sound in her voice.

He lifted his hat from his head and smoothed his hair back before replacing it. "I'll be at the Redwood tavern from ten until around midnight tonight. You can talk to me there."

Kate felt her heart skip in dismay. "I don't think I know where that is," she said faintly.

"I didn't think you would." A muscle began twitching in his cheek. "It's on the corner of Seventh and Main. Ask anyone around here, they'll know it."

"I live in Portland, Slade. I don't know this town. I can't just take off and leave Michael on his own. Isn't there somewhere we can talk after the parade, before the evening performance?"

She saw his sudden tension and again she felt a moment of panic, cursing herself for mentioning her son. The loudspeakers blared with the voice of the announcer and she was distracted by the flurry of movement from the girls as they mounted their horses for the barrel race.

"Can't you tell me what this is about now?"

She looked back at Slade, disturbed by his note of impatience. "I'd rather wait until I have time to explain," she said quickly. "I'll find the tavern."

"It's only a twenty-minute drive from Portland. Can't you find someone to stay with your son?"

He sounded genuinely concerned. Confused, she dropped her gaze to look at her watch. "It's all right, I'll find a sitter. I'll see you tonight."

She spun around and hurried back to the stands before he could change his mind. The idea of spending time in any kind of establishment with Slade Montana would be an ordeal. She could just imagine the kind of tavern he frequented. He'd probably chosen it on purpose, just to demoralize her.

However, she told herself grimly, if that was the only place she could corner him long enough to talk to him, then she had no choice. She needed him. Or more to the point, she needed what he could do for her. He could give her career the boost she'd been waiting for, and she had to go through with it now.

Besides, she comforted herself, he stood to gain by it, too. When she explained everything to him, he'd probably thank her. Wishing she could believe that, she found the exit and headed for her car, trying to concentrate on her choice of appropriate attire for a country tavern.

Slade watched her go, his dark brows furrowed in a frown. He was already beginning to regret his spurt of curiosity that had made him agree to meet her later. He should have turned his back on her, the way she'd done to him eight years ago.

Seeing her again would only stir up trouble, rub old wounds that should have healed long ago. He swore out loud, kicking at the dirt with the toe of his boot. The scars still smarted like open sores. He'd known that the minute he'd recognized her.

What else could he expect? Did he really believe, he asked himself savagely, that he could wipe out all that bitterness, all that burning resentment?

How could he have been so stupid to agree to listen to some harebrained proposition she was babbling about? It was the mention of money that did it. The one thing he needed. But what kind of deal could she possibly offer that would make him the kind of money he needed?

He had his life mapped out, his plans set. He'd had one goal in mind since he'd climbed on his first bull twenty years ago, and nothing was going to sway him from that path.

He'd learned from hard experience that the only sure way to get money was to work for it. He'd found the quickest, if not the easiest, way to do that and still be able to enjoy what he was doing. It wouldn't be long now before he had enough put away to buy the ranch of his dreams. He wanted nothing else. Least of all from a woman who'd burned him in the worst way possible.

The announcer broke into his thoughts with a call for the final parade. Slade strode over to the horse he'd been given to ride and released the reins from the wall.

He hooked his boot into the stirrup and swung his leg over the saddle. The best thing he could do was send Kate Templeton packing, or Kate Wheeler, whatever she called herself now.

Tugging on the reins he guided Starlight to the passageway. The minute he set eyes on her tonight, he decided, he'd tell her he wasn't interested. Period. Then he'd put her out of his mind as completely as he had before she'd waltzed back into his life and raked up a lot of bad memories.

He wasn't really surprised when he found he was still thinking about her after the parade finished that night and he was free to go.

Kate had made several calls before she finally located a teenager who was willing to come out that late. Putting down the receiver in relief she smiled at Michael, who was hovering near the phone with anxious eyes.

"How come you're going out so late?" he asked as soon as she'd hung up. "Can't I go with you?"

Kate ruffled his blond hair. "Sorry, pal. This is a place for grown-ups only."

"Are you going on your own?" He followed her out to the kitchen and stood watching as she washed lettuce leaves under the faucet.

Kate shook the leaves and laid them on a paper towel. "Yes, but I'm meeting someone."

"A man?"

She sighed. In Michael's opinion every male she met was a prospective father. Her stomach jolted when she wondered what her son would say if he knew who Slade Montana really was. "Yes," she said. "He's a man."

She saw his eyes light up, and hurried to explain. "It's strictly business, Michael," she said gently. "It's to do with my work."

"What's he like?" Michael demanded, ignoring the negative aspect of that statement.

Kate picked up a cucumber and started slicing. "He's tall and dark…" *And handsome*, her mind added. "…and he's a champion bull rider in the rodeo," she finished in a hurry.

Too late she realized what she'd done. Michael's eyes, the same sea-blue color as her own, stared at her in delight.

"A rodeo champion," he breathed, in the same tone he'd used the time he'd sat on a horse at the county fair.

Kate cursed inwardly. How could she have forgotten her son's fascination for horses? She'd become so accustomed to the posters covering the walls of his bedroom she didn't see them anymore. And she'd learned to ignore his constant hints about wanting to move so that he could own a horse.

"Can't I come with you, please?" Michael tugged at her arm. "I'll be so quiet you won't know I'm there."

How she hated disappointing him. He never asked for much, sensing perhaps that she wasn't able to give him much in the way of luxuries. She was constantly reminding herself that quality was worth more than quantity, but there were times when she wished with a quiet desperation that she could give more to her son.

She wrestled with indecision for several moments while the temptation nagged at her. What harm could it do? she thought, feeling her heart bump at the prospect. It would mean so much to Michael. And to her, her conscience added spitefully.

Ignoring it she laid the knife on the counter. "I'll tell you what," she said. "There's another performance tomorrow. It's a Saturday and since you don't have to go to summer school I'll take you to see Slade Montana ride the bull. Okay?"

Michael smiled and wrapped his arms around her hips. "Okay!"

She gave him a quick hug. It was the most enthusiasm he'd shown for anything in quite a while. She just hoped she wouldn't live to regret it.

She tried to calm the frantic fluttering of her pulse. After all, she reasoned, if she was going to work with Slade, Michael would undoubtedly be aware of it. What difference did it make, even if they did happen to meet? Slade knew only that she had a son who resembled her. Looking at Michael, he would never guess that the blond blue-eyed boy could belong to him.

It was worth the risk, she thought as she turned back to her salad. This was the chance of a lifetime. She hadn't been with Betcher and Crown long, and this ad campaign could make her name.

She smiled as Michael went out of the kitchen chanting quietly, "Slade Montana, Slade Montana," over and over again. Her smile faded as she thought about going to the tavern later.

She should have insisted he meet her between shows, she thought, chopping the red cabbage. She could only hope the tavern would be crowded and well lit. The last place she wanted to be was somewhere dark and intimate with Slade Montana.

A tiny shiver chased up her body and she paused, her knife in midair. No, she thought, not that. She didn't need that. Whatever had been between them had been laid irrevocably to rest a long time ago.

In any case, she thought, there had been no mistaking that hostile look on his face. She was surprised he still carried a grudge, since he'd never pretended to feel any real love for her.

It had taken her a long time—too long—to accept the fact that he didn't love her. Not the way she loved him. By the time she'd realized it and let him go, it had been too late. If it hadn't been for Vic—

She shut off that train of thought before it could get out of hand. What had happened, had happened and nothing could alter that. As far as Slade Montana was concerned, maybe it was just as well he felt that way. It would make her job that much easier.

So why, she asked herself later, was she taking so many pains with her choice of outfit? Simple slacks and a shirt would be fine; anything else would be out of place.

That decision made, she dressed quickly in coffee slacks and a cream silk blouse. As a finishing touch she added a smoky-brown scarf and fastened it with a gold pin. All that was missing, she thought, studying her image in the mirror, was a cowboy hat and boots. It wasn't the professional image she usually presented, but it would have to do. The last thing she needed was to draw attention to herself.

Trying to ignore the churning in her stomach, she said good-night to a sleepy Michael, issued final instructions to the studious-looking teenager and went out to her car.

Slade sat at the bar staring moodily into his beer. One more day and he could have a couple of weeks' rest before the next round of competition. He shifted his hips on the stool and pulled one foot up to the rung.

He was getting too old for this punishment, he told himself wearily. His muscles ached from the stress he'd put on them that day, and his body was constantly reminding him of the injuries he'd suffered over the past twenty years.

One more fall would probably do him in. He raised his glass and swallowed down half the beer. It was a nightmare that was always with him—the possibility of doing some permanent damage before he had the money he needed. So far he'd been lucky. Apart from the one bad goring that had left a jagged scar, he'd had a couple of broken bones, one concussion and a trick knee that went out on him when he least expected it.

He'd seen far worse happen to better riders than he. It was only a matter of time, he reflected soberly. His odds got shorter every time he lowered his butt on a bull.

He swallowed another mouthful of beer and sent a glance down the bar. A voluptuous redhead in a skintight T-shirt smiled at him, and he shifted his gaze away.

There was a time when he would have strolled up to the stool next to her and sat down. It was another reminder of the beating his body was taking. He couldn't even get a spark of interest out of it.

He dropped his foot to the floor, and felt the twinge from his protesting muscles. Even the rides didn't hold the same excitement they once had. The challenge had gone out of them. Eight seconds and they were all over.

He needed more than that. He seemed to have spent half his life standing around waiting for an eight-second ride. Once he got the ranch, he told himself, things would be different. Maybe then he'd find the peace he was searching for.

He lifted his glass and drained the rest of his beer. When he lowered the glass again, Kate Templeton was standing in front of him.

He took his time setting the glass on the counter. He'd been wrong about one thing. The sight of her had produced a definite spark in his body.

Kate met the dark gaze with a certain amount of trepidation. Without his hat his scowl was plainly visible. His straight hair was swept back form his forehead, revealing his furrowed brow. He looked disagreeable and totally unapproachable. She hoped that wouldn't come across in the pictures.

"Well," Slade said, drawing the word out in a lazy drawl, "I thought you might have changed your mind."

"I always keep my appointments." Kate looked around her, reminding herself she almost hadn't kept this one. It had taken considerable courage to push open the door and walk into the bedlam of laughter, loud music and smoke. Not to mention the meaningful stares from the men lounging at the bar.

She spotted an empty corner booth through the haze and nodded at it. "Can we sit over there?"

"You think you can trust yourself in a corner with me?" Slade picked up his hat from the counter and swung his leg off the stool

Kate flushed. He was more perceptive than she'd given him credit for. She hadn't admitted, even to herself, how uncomfortable she was feeling. It was because she was so anxious about getting his acceptance to her proposal, she told herself as she led the way over to the booth.

She slid onto the seat and tucked her feet under her. Even so, his knees brushed hers as he edged in opposite. The contact started a new wave of quivers in her stomach.

"I'd like to buy you a drink," she said, looking around for the waitress. "Is it still beer or do you prefer something stronger these days?"

When he didn't answer she sent him a quick glance. He was studying her with narrowed eyes, his expression wary.

"I'm not used to ladies buying me drinks," he said, laying his hat on the table.

She smiled. "Don't worry, it's not going to obligate you."

He lifted his right eyebrow a fraction. "I'm glad to hear it." His soft drawl seemed to creep all over her skin.

To her relief the waitress strolled over to them. "Hi, big boy, what's it going to be?" She put her hand on her ample hip and grinned at Slade.

Kate shifted her gaze to his face, and swallowed when she found him watching her.

Without taking his eyes from hers he said, "The lady's buying. Make mine a beer."

The waitress took her hand from her hip and stared down at Kate. "So what's yours, then?"

Kate saw the disapproval in the black-rimmed eyes and returned the look. "Gin and tonic. With a twist of lemon."

The waitress blew air through her nose and stumped off.

"A twist of lemon?"

She ignored his dry tone and shrugged. "I don't like lime."

"Don't be surprised if you get neither. They're not used to people like you in here." His gaze flicked over her.

Stung by his insolence she retorted, "I'm perfectly aware of that. That's why you asked me to meet you here, isn't it? You wanted to make me feel uncomfortable."

She was instantly furious with herself. She'd played right into his hands. She waited, knowing he wasn't going to let the opportunity slip by.

He didn't disappoint her. "Do I make you feel uncomfortable, Kate?"

His voice was raw with sarcasm and she couldn't answer. She jumped visibly when the waitress, who had arrived unnoticed, slapped two glasses down on the table. Feeling like a fool, Kate scrabbled in her purse for her wallet, found some bills and handed them over to the scowling woman.

She left the change lying on the table, afraid that if she attempted to pick up the coins she'd drop them all over the floor. Closing her fingers around the glass helped. It was halfway to her lips before she realized the lemon was missing. At least they hadn't substituted lime.

She took a sip of the drink and braced herself to look at Slade. She was hoping he would give her the opening she needed, but he still sat watching her, his beer untouched.

She cleared her throat. "As I said this afternoon, I have a proposition—"

"Did you get a sitter?"

She blinked. "Pardon?"

He sat back and folded his arms. "For your son."

Wary now, she nodded. "Of course. I wouldn't have left him alone."

"I'm glad to hear it."

She saw something in his eyes, no more than a faint gleam, but her heart began beating a slow, rhythmic tattoo against her ribs. She waited, wondering what was coming.

"How old is he now?"

"Six," she said quickly, and was instantly aware he knew it was a lie.

"That's funny," Slade murmured with an exaggerated frown. "I thought he was closer to eight."

In a desperate attempt to change the subject she raised her voice. "I came here to offer you a deal—a very lucrative deal I might add—not to discuss my private life."

"Which is none of my business. Is that what you're saying?" Very slowly he leaned toward her, his brittle gaze shattering the last shreds of her composure. "I think it is my business, Kate. I'd say that anything to do with *my son* is my business. Wouldn't you?"

Chapter 2

She felt as if she were suspended in midair with nothing but space beneath her. "How long have you known?" Her voice was barely above a whisper.

He reached for his glass and lifted it to his lips. His movements were slow and calculated and tightened her nerves to screaming point. She waited while he swallowed a mouthful of beer.

"It wasn't hard to figure out." He thumped the glass down on the table, sloshing the brown liquid up the sides. "I heard he was born in December. I didn't leave until May. Unless you were two-timing me, and I find that hard to believe, it doesn't add up any other way."

He kept his eyes on the glass cupped in his hand. "It was me you spent Easter with, not Vic. That's one thing I do know."

Thoughts twisted and spun through her mind in a whirlwind of memories and pain. Easter. March in the mountains. A vision of swirling snow, a roaring fire, warm brandy and a heated passion too potent to deny.

She should have known he'd find out. She wondered now how she could ever have thought otherwise. She lifted her glass and swallowed some of the gin.

Her hand still shook as she set the drink down on the table. Now that she'd had time to recover, the full implication of what she'd just learned was beginning to sink in.

He'd known he was a father, and he hadn't cared enough to even try and see his son. He'd cared so little that if she hadn't insisted on this meeting, he would have come and gone like a summer wind, without acknowledging his presence.

Resentment flared and, unable to deal with it, she started to slide out of the booth. "I've changed my mind," she muttered. "I shouldn't have come here. I made a mistake."

His hand shot across the table, pinning her by the wrist. Stunned by the speed and strength of his grip, she stared at him, and saw her anger mirrored in his eyes.

"You bet you made a mistake," he said harshly. "You made a mistake when you married someone else, without telling me you were pregnant. Didn't you think I had a right to know?"

She tugged at her arm, knowing it was a futile gesture. "I didn't think you'd want to know. You weren't interested in settling down, you made that painfully clear. That's why I let you go. You were trying to be something you couldn't be. You weren't capable of giving me the kind of love and security I needed."

She heard her voice break and cleared her throat. "If you knew," she said, a little steadier, "why didn't you say something? Weren't you even a little bit curious? Didn't you want to see your son?"

"Tell me one thing," he demanded, his ferocity making her jump. "Did you know you were pregnant when you told me to get lost?"

She worked the lump in her throat down to where she could speak. "No," she whispered. "I didn't find out until after you were gone. I didn't try to find you. You couldn't handle a commitment to me, much less a baby."

The muscle in his jaw twitched. "You didn't give me a damn chance. By the time I got the glad tidings you were already someone else's wife."

He let go of her wrist and she leaned back, eyes filling with tears. "It wasn't easy sending you away, but you weren't happy. You were trying to give me something that wasn't in you to give. We would have ended up making each other miserable. I felt it was better to make a clean break."

Slade rubbed his eyes as if he were indescribably tired. "So you married Vic." He looked at her, his expression once more empty of all emotion. "Why, Kate? Why Vic Wheeler?"

"He was there," she said simply

It had seemed natural that she should turn to Vic when her world once more turned upside down. Four years earlier, soon after her eighteenth birthday, she'd arrived home from a pajama party to find her entire family had perished in a house fire. Vic Wheeler had been a close friend of her father's and had shared many family celebrations. He'd become her one remaining link to a life that was changed beyond belief.

"When he found out I was pregnant," she went on, wondering why she was bothering to explain, "he offered to take care of me and the baby, with no strings attached. It seemed the best solution. He said it was just a formality, a necessity to protect Michael."

It was an irony that would come back and haunt her. And never more than now, she thought as she tried to collect her scattered senses.

"From me?"

She heard the note of sarcasm and narrowed her gaze. "What if I *had* let you know, would you have married me?"

The seconds ticked by while her stare challenged his. Someone at the bar raised his voice and was answered by raucous laughter, but the sound barely penetrated the tension-filled silence in the the booth.

He was the first to back down, slumping his shoulders against the wall behind him. "What difference does it make?" he muttered. "It's done, and we can't take back the past. I figured he was better off with Vic, anyway. That's why I didn't interfere. I didn't like the man, but I thought he would at least be there for the boy, someone who would stick around. I guess I was wrong."

She saw the emotion then. Finally. And the pain in his eyes matched her own. "There hasn't been a day gone by," he added quietly, "when I haven't thought about the boy, or been reminded of him in some way or another."

She searched for something to say, something to erase that look, and could think of nothing.

Slade reached for his glass. "I figured you were settled and happy. What happened?"

"Nothing I want to talk about." She felt tired, drained. She had imagined this confrontation so many times, had rehearsed every word she would say, each time conjuring up a different scenario. None of them had been close to this.

He was right, she thought wearily. It was too late for recriminations. They'd both made mistakes. How could she expect him to feel any obligations toward Michael? She'd lost that right when she'd married Vic, naming him as Michael's father.

Even if Slade had married her, it would have been through a sense of duty. How could they have built a life together based on that? It would have been only a matter of time before she'd have had to let him go, leaving her pretty much where she was now.

She hadn't known that anything she might have gone through, losing Slade would have been a thousand times better than the nightmare of her marriage to Vic.

Right now she had another problem on her hands. She had banked everything on this meeting. She'd promised her boss, and the advertisers, that she would get Slade Montana, national rodeo champion, as the model for the ad campaign.

She'd been awarded the contract on that condition. She stared across at Slade's uncompromising face. How could they possibly work together now? she thought miserably.

The second thought came in the same instant. How could she turn her back on what could well be the only chance she had to make the kind of money it was going to take to put Michael through school?

She couldn't, she decided. Michael needed new clothes, shoes, a bike, all the things the other kids had and took for granted. Ever since the divorce she'd sworn that her son would not have to sacrifice for her mistakes. She would just have to put her personal feelings aside and do the best job she was capable of doing.

"All right," she said, making an effort to sound detached, "I agree. It's over and done with and nothing we can say will make any difference now. So I suggest we try to forget it and discuss this proposition, which is the reason I am here, after all."

"So, go ahead. What are you waiting for?"

His expression indicated that whatever she said wasn't going to interest him.

She gritted her teeth. "You're not making this easy for me."

He sat for a moment longer, then folding his arms, he leaned back and muttered, "I'm all ears."

Wincing at his sarcasm she made an effort to concentrate. "I work for a company in Portland called Betcher and Crown. We do advertising for various customers and I've been contracted to do a series of photo ads for MacTaffeys Boots." She paused. "Have you heard of them?"

"I've heard of them."

The look in his eyes unnerved her, but she pressed on. "Well, as you may know, their slogan is 'Strength, Daring and Durability.'" She drew in a long breath. "I'd like you to model for those ads."

She couldn't tell anything from his expression. She pushed aside her personal reaction to him and made herself look at him with a professional eye. His nose had a slight bump, she noticed. She'd forgotten that. They would have to watch the angle of his profile.

His mouth was as fantastic as she remembered—full bottom lip, thin upper, pulled down a little at the corners—hard and sensuous at the same time. The dark shadow on his jaw would add to the aura of masculine power.

Her stomach lurched and she jerked her gaze back to his eyes. He sat motionless, saying nothing.

"If we could get some shots of you on the bull," she went on, "and some studio close-ups, it shouldn't take that long. I can offer you . . ." She paused, then named a figure.

Her estimate was conservative; she could probably get him more. Even so, she saw a flicker of interest in the dark depths of his eyes and felt a small leap of hope. Everyone had their price.

Leaning forward he hooked his thumb through the handle of his glass, and lifted it to his mouth. Kate watched his Adam's apple work up and down as he swallowed the entire contents of the mug. He'd left the top button of his shirt undone; she could see a few dark hairs below the hollow in his throat. She tried not to remember how he looked bare chested. They were not likely to shoot him without a shirt, she admonished herself.

"Let me get this straight," Slade said as he lowered the empty glass. "You want me to pose for photos, that will appear in magazines all over the country, wearing Western boots with dolphins and palm trees all over them?"

She felt the warmth creep over her cheeks. "The boots are very popular," she said, trying not to sound defensive. "By the time we've finished with this campaign, they will be famous. And so will you. This could be a whole new career for you, and a very lucrative one.''

He appeared to ignore that. ''Have you *seen* those boots?'' he asked, a note of incredulity in his voice.

Kate nodded. ''Yes. I think they are very attractive and . . . unusual.''

''They're unusual, all right. They're damn well offensive.'' He shook his head in disbelief. ''I'd be the laughingstock of the country.''

Kate tightened her lips. ''Well, if you're more worried about your macho image than the money . . .'' She frowned at him. ''You are a rodeo rider, after all. You're supposed to have an image of glamour and excitement.''

His scowl deepened. He stuck a foot out from the booth and jerked up the leg of his jeans. ''See this?'' He pointed at his cuffed boot. ''Plain, sturdy and dependable. That's me. You know that. There's no way I'm going to pull on a pair of those flashy, vulgar pimp boots and prance around in front of a camera.''

''Slade, I don't think you realize what you're turning down.'' She reverted to her professional powers of persuasion. ''The money I mentioned was only the beginning. If you become as popular as I think you will, you'll have offers pouring in. Television, movies even—''

She was cut off as Slade's voice sliced through the air like a whip. ''Forget it.'' He leaned forward, his knees pressing against hers. ''You've got the wrong man. Go find yourself another cowboy. I don't belong in a studio any more than you belong in a rodeo.''

Kate edged her knees sideways and gritted her teeth. ''You're turning down a great deal of money, as well as a lucrative career. At least sleep on it for a couple of days.''

He shook his head. ''Tomorrow night I'll be on my way to the mountains. I'm going to stay there until the next contest comes up in Nevada in a couple of weeks.''

He sat back and reached for his hat. "You can keep your deal—and your lucrative career. I don't need your money. And I have all the recognition I can handle."

Frustration and anger destroyed her control and she lashed out at him. "Is it the job you're turning down, or me? Are you punishing me for keeping Michael a secret from you? Or maybe you're afraid I'll force you into some kind of obligation, is that it? If so, you couldn't be more mistaken. We've done very well without you so far and—"

She shrank back as he leaned toward her. "That was the way you wanted it, lady. Don't you forget that."

For a long moment his eyes blazed at her, then he seemed to relax. Straightening, he wiped all expression from his face. "It's got nothing to do with what happened between us. You were right about one thing—I would have made a lousy father."

He stuck his hat on his head and pulled it forward. "Thanks for the beer. See you around." He eased his hips out of the booth and looked down at her. "And take care of that kid."

Before she could answer he lifted his hand in farewell, spun on his heel and strode to the door.

Kate stared after him, fighting back tears. She hadn't expected him to be overjoyed at seeing her, but his hostility and bitterness were emotions she didn't know how to deal with.

For just a moment she allowed herself to remember the laughter and the loving they had once shared. The memories were painful and she shut them away. The Slade Montana who had just left was a stranger. The man she had known no longer existed.

It was understandable, considering the circumstances, but it didn't make it any easier to bear. And on top of everything else, she'd probably lost the contract.

Pulling herself together she finished her drink and slid out of the booth. She wasn't beaten yet. She was taking Michael to the rodeo tomorrow; she would have another chance to talk to Slade.

And Slade would have a chance to meet his son. She ignored the stab of apprehension. As long as he knew the truth there was no point in keeping them apart, and she wanted this for Michael, she told herself.

He had a right to meet his father, even if he didn't know who he really was. If and when the day ever came when she decided to tell him the truth, when he was old enough to decide what he wanted to do about the relationship, he'd have something to base his decision on.

She reached the parking lot and took in long, calming breaths of cool air before climbing into her car. Pride would not allow her to let Slade know how much she needed this job. But if he hung around long enough to give her a chance to change his mind, so much the better.

Now it was more important than ever that she talk him into it. For every day he spent at the studio would give him one more day to spend some time with his son.

She turned the key in the ignition and started the engine. Nosing the car onto the highway, she made up her mind. The afternoon performance was the final one. She would confront Slade on his way out.

It was for Michael's benefit in the long run. One way or another she would get Slade Montana to the studio, she promised herself, even if she had to hog-tie him and drag him there. Something told her she might have to do just that. It was not a comforting thought.

She opened her eyes the next morning to the sound of Michael's basketball bouncing outside her window. She guessed he'd been too excited to sleep, and knew how he felt when her own stomach flipped at the prospect of seeing Slade Montana again.

She did her best to calm her jittery pulse as she drove to the small town where the rodeo was being held. Michael sat quietly in the front seat, only the faint flush in his cheeks betraying his anticipation.

A smile tugged at her lips. He didn't get many treats like this. She hoped the day would come up to his expectations.

Her smile faded. She'd accepted the job at Betcher and Crown because of the opportunities it offered. If only it didn't take up so much of her time—time she could spend with her son—it would have been perfect.

She shot Michael another glance. "Are you looking forward to seeing the rodeo?"

"Yeah." Michael gave her his beautiful smile before she looked back at the road. "Especially the horses."

"What about Slade Montana?" Kate asked, her tongue tripping over the name. "Would you like to meet him after the show?" She heard his slight gasp and smiled.

"Can we?"

"I'll try, though I can't promise."

Michael's "Okay" was automatic.

This time, Kate thought grimly, she'd make sure she didn't disappoint him. She had a bad moment when she wondered if Slade would tell Michael the truth, then dismissed it. Even Slade must realize what a shock that would be for her son.

She was relieved to find seats in the shade when they reached the arena. Michael suffered the same problems with sunburn that she did. Her skin already felt tight and sensitive from yesterday.

They were farther back than she'd been the day before, but now they had a better view of the whole area. Michael sat transfixed through the saddle bronc-riding and calf-roping events, though Kate could see him wincing every time the calves were jerked to a halt at the end of a rope.

To her the events seemed endless. The program shook in her hand as she studied it. By the time the announcer had declared the winner of the bareback-riding event, she could feel tension holding her neck like a vise.

She leaned over and said in Michael's ear, "The bull riding is coming up next. You'll see Slade Montana in a moment."

His face glowed with excitement. "Will he be first?"

"I don't know. I'll tell you which one he is." Kate looked over to where the bulls were being led into the chutes, and tried to control the fluttering in her stomach. Irritated with herself she clenched her hands to stop them trembling.

The shiver of awareness that hit her between the shoulder blades when she saw him leaning against the fence was both potent and unexpected. Admit it, she told herself wryly, the reaction was pure sexual appreciation. It was the main reason she wanted him for her model. He positively breathed sex appeal.

It was the haunting seduction in his eyes, the sensual tilt to his mouth, the deliberate body language he was so good at that would make him a household name. She just had to talk him into it, somehow. She would simply have to keep all personal feelings out of it. It shouldn't be that hard, she thought wryly, seeing as how he felt about her.

There were two riders before Slade, both of whom were tossed from the plunging back of a bull. Kate watched Michael's hand fly to his mouth when a clown, in an attempt to distract the bull from a fallen rider, slipped and fell. His frantic wriggle took him out of reach of the bull's gouging horns with inches to spare.

Michael's eyes were wide with anxiety when he looked at her. "That was close," he said in a hushed voice.

Kate gave him a reassuring smile. "It's all right, honey. The clowns are very good at keeping out of the way of those horns. That's why they're there. They make sure the bulls stay away from the riders." She looked back, her breath catching as the announcer called out Slade's name.

Michael clapped hard as the people in the stands sent up a raucous cheer. "They like him, Mom, don't they?"

She nodded, her eyes on the man climbing the fence. "They sure do," she said, her pulse quickening as Slade straddled the bull.

"I hope he doesn't fall off, too."

She glanced down at his worried face. "He didn't yesterday. But even if he does, he knows how to fall. He'll be fine."

She wished she could be sure of that, she thought, beginning to worry her bottom lip with her teeth as Slade lowered himself onto the bull's back.

She watched him twist the rope around his hand and slide his hips forward. When he raised his head to send a look around the stands she had the ridiculous idea he could see her, and felt her pulse jump at the thought.

Everything she knew about bull riding raced through her mind. It was the most dangerous event in the rodeo. Men had been maimed, even killed, in the arena by the pounding hooves or deadly horns of an infuriated bull. It took tremendous skill, courage and strength to stay with that much animal fury for eight seconds, and then slide off without getting trampled or gored.

She watched Slade nod his head. When the chute opened, the bull charged out writhing and kicking. Slade leaned back and she saw his hat fly from his head.

Almost immediately the champion seemed to slip sideways. Unaware she was on her feet, Kate pressed both hands over her mouth as Slade twisted his body in a desperate attempt to regain his balance.

Not a murmur came from the crowd as they watched in agonized silence. It had taken no more than three or four seconds, but to Kate it seemed like minutes. She saw Slade's feet jerk up in the air. Then he freed his wrist and his entire body somersaulted backward over the thrusting hind legs of the bull.

Kate felt Michael leaning against her and put an arm around his thin shoulders, pulling him to her. "It's all right," she murmured. "He'll be all right." *Please,* she added silently.

Both clowns were racing across the ring as Slade landed on his shoulder. He started to get up, then fell back. One clown grabbed at the bull's horns, but it gave a vicious toss of its head and sent the clown flying.

Before the other clown could get to it, the bull twisted its body, turning its great head toward Slade. Kate felt Michael tense at her side and buried his face against her midriff. Sick with fear she saw the bull lower its head.

By now Slade was on all fours. He got to his knees just as the bull charged, slicing its horn at the champion's back. Some sixth sense must have prompted Slade to throw himself forward. The bull barely grazed him before the clown reached for the murderous horns and bravely hung on.

Kate closed her eyes as the crowd cheered. Michael struggled to free himself from her grasp, his muffled voice asking. "Is he all right, Mom?"

Opening her eyes Kate watched Slade walk unsteadily to the passageway, then turn and accept his hat from one of the clowns. "He's all right," she assured Michael, letting him go.

Across the arena she saw Slade lift his hat in a brief salute, then twist around and walk slowly from view.

With knees that shook, Kate sank onto the hard bench. It had been over in a matter of seconds, yet she felt as drained as if she'd run a marathon. She could feel the dampness of perspiration between her shoulder blades, and her stomach churned.

She looked down at Michael's worried face and managed a wobbly smile. "Well, that was exciting," she said, a little too breathlessly.

Michael studied her, his eyes questioning. "He's all right, isn't he?"

Kate nodded. "He's fine. You saw him walk away."

"Can we still go and see him?"

Her laugh sounded shaky as she hugged him. "You bet we'll go and see him. Want to go now?"

His eyes lit up and he nodded.

Kate took his hand and led him between the rows to the steps. Once again a tall cowboy stopped them at the enclosure.

"I'm an old friend of Slade Montana's," Kate explained. "I was with him last night. He wanted to meet my son." Maybe she'd be excused a small lie, she thought as she gave the man a confident smile.

The man looked down at Michael and winked. "Sorry, son, he's left the arena."

Kate knew her disappointment must match the stricken look on Michael's face. "Where did he go?" she said quickly. If she had to go back to that tavern and drag him out of there she'd do it, she told herself.

The man shrugged. "Back to his trailer, I reckon. He'll probably need to lie down after that fall."

"Where's that?" She braved the suspicious look the cowboy gave her. "I met him at the Redwood tavern. He didn't tell me where his trailer was." She knew what it sounded like, but she was past caring.

The man studied her for several seconds, then waved his arm toward the back of the stands. "In the field out back. Blue-and-white station wagon, with a California license plate."

"Thanks." Kate smiled and put her arm around Michael's shoulders. "Come on, honey. Let's go find Slade."

The trailer and wagon were easy to spot; they stood in a corner of the field, away from the rest of the vehicles. Kate picked her way across the grass, followed by a silent Michael.

Surely he couldn't live in that thing, Kate thought as she eyed the shabby trailer. It didn't look big enough to house a rabbit. Her pulse quickened when she saw the door hanging open.

Wishing her stomach would stop churning, Kate tapped on the door. She sent Michael an encouraging smile as she waited for an answer. Seconds passed, with no sign of movement from inside the trailer.

Kate peered into the gloomy interior. Opposite the door a small counter with a sink stood next to a gas range. She couldn't see more than that without stepping up and going inside.

"Hello?" she called out. "Slade? Are you there?" Silence greeted her and she frowned.

"Maybe he went somewhere else," Michael suggested.

"I doubt it." Kate rapped on the door, louder this time. "He wouldn't have gone off and left the door open." She didn't want to say anything to Michael, but she had a nasty feeling in the pit of her stomach.

What if he'd made it back to the trailer and collapsed? He could be lying on the floor right now, and no one would think of looking for him until it was time for the final parade.

Making up her mind she looked at Michael. "You stay here while I take a look inside."

"I'll come with you." He stepped forward but she laid a hand on his shoulder. She wanted to be sure of what she'd find before she let him in there.

"I won't be long, I promise."

He stood back, his face creased in worry and she gave him a reassuring grin before she stepped up and into the trailer. It felt hot and stuffy and she had to blink several times to adjust to the dim light.

Flowered curtains had been drawn across the window at the back of the trailer. Slade sat on the edge of a narrow seat, his head in his hands, his elbows propped on the strip of table wedged between him and the seat opposite.

If he'd heard her he gave no sign. He didn't move a muscle when she cleared her throat. "Slade? Are you all right?"

"What are you doing here?" The mumbled words inferred that she should leave at once.

Kate tightened her lips. "I came to see how you are. I thought you might be hurt."

"Well, I'm not. I'm used to it." He lowered his hands and looked at her, the shadows hiding his expression. "I thought I told you last night I wasn't interested in your damn proposition."

She didn't need to see his face to realize he was in pain. She opened her mouth to speak, but he cut in, his voice harsh.

"I'm not in the mood for company."

It took all her willpower to ignore his belligerence. Taking a deep breath she said pleasantly, "I'll leave, just as soon as you've said hello to someone who wants to meet you."

"I told you, I'm not in the mood to meet anyone."

"Well, he wants to meet you, so brace yourself." She twisted around and bumped into Michael, who had been standing unnoticed behind her.

"Is he all right, Mom?" Michael asked in his clear voice.

She could almost feel the tension emanating from the man behind her. Without turning she said quietly, "He's fine, Michael. Come and say hello to Slade Montana."

Michael's face flushed with excitement as he peered past her. "Hi!" he said in a shy voice.

Kate heard the rattle of curtain rings and sunlight flooded the tiny room. The contrast was so bright she closed her eyes.

She felt Michael's wiry body brush by her and she made herself turn around. Slade had pulled back the drapes at the window and a stab of anxiety caught at her when she saw his dust-streaked face.

Pain had drawn lines of strain at the corners of his mouth, but it was the stunned expression in his eyes that worried her.

She remained silent as Michael stood and studied the craggy features. "Did it hurt when you fell off?" he said. He'd sounded more interested than concerned and Kate sent Slade a nervous glance.

Her body slumped in relief when he actually smiled. It wasn't much of a smile, just a tug at the corner of his mouth, but it was enough to remind her just how devastating his full smile could be.

"Not much," Slade said. "I was lucky the clowns were there. They were pretty brave, don't you think?"

Michael nodded. "I think you were braver. I wish I could ride a bull. Is it hard?"

"Sometimes. I guess it was this afternoon."

"Mom said you didn't fall off yesterday, though," Michael said wistfully. "I wish I'd seen you then."

"Ah, well, my hat didn't fall off yesterday." Slade's expression was perfectly serious as he gazed at the small boy.

Michael squeezed himself behind the table to sit next to the champion. "Can't you ride without your hat?" he asked, gazing up at Slade's face with rapt attention.

"Well, let's put it this way." Slade reached for his hat, which was lying on the table. "When the hat comes off, I know I'm going to follow it." He placed the hat on Michael's head. It slipped forward and Michael pushed it back with one hand and looked up at Kate.

His eyes sparkled when he said, "How do I look, Mom?"

Kate's stomach seemed to be twisting in knots. How often had she envisioned them together? Never in her wildest dreams had she imagined the piercing bittersweet sensation it would give her to watch them.

With a tremendous effort she pulled herself together. She pretended to study her son, one hand stroking her chin. "I'd say you look like a future champion." She glanced at Slade. "What do you say, Mr. Montana?"

Her pulse stirred as his dark gaze met hers. "I'd say you're right on the button, Mom." His voice cracked slightly over the last word and her fingers clenched.

He turned back to the small boy. "Maybe one day you'll be a champion."

Michael shook his head. "My mom wouldn't let me ride a bull. She won't even let me ride a horse. She only lets me sit on it awhile."

Kate heard the wistfulness in his voice and winced.

Slade must have heard it too because he said, "Maybe if you asked her now she'd let you learn to ride."

"He's not old enough," Kate said sharply. "Perhaps in a few years—"

"The longer he waits the tougher it will be," Slade said quietly, still watching Michael's face.

Kate felt her breath freeze in her throat as Michael sent her a pleading look. "We'll talk about it later," she said, hating the evasion and annoyed with Slade for forcing her into it.

Michael shrugged, then looked back at Slade. "Can I use your bathroom?"

Thankful for the diversion Kate managed a faint smile. "Maybe Mr. Montana can tell us where the bathrooms are?" She looked back at Slade, who was watching her, his face expressionless.

"What's wrong with Slade?" he said quietly.

She didn't know. Somehow it felt safer to call him Mr. Montana. "Slade," she amended.

He looked back at Michael. "You can use mine, if you don't mind it being primitive."

"Primitive?" the boy repeated suspiciously.

Slade slid his hips along the seat and edged out from behind the table. "Well, it's probably a lot smaller than what you're used to, but it works. Here, I'll show you."

"Is it all right if I wear the hat?"

"Sure, you can keep the hat on."

Kate stood back and let them pass. She couldn't contain a small gasp when she saw the bump on the back of Slade's head.

He gave no sign that he'd heard her muffled exclamation. He opened a narrow door to show Michael how to use the portable toilet, then came back to her.

The expression in his eyes was unreadable when he said softly, "He's a good-looking boy."

"I think so." She felt as if she were suffocating. This wasn't going to work, she told herself frantically. She had to get out of there.

In an effort to diffuse the tension she said quickly, "That looks like a nasty bump on your head. You should have that looked at."

His wide shoulders lifted in a shrug. "I'll get a shower later, that'll take care of it."

Kate looked around the meager space of the trailer. "You don't have one in here, I take it?"

"No, I don't have one in here."

He'd mimicked her voice and she flushed. "You don't have to be so defensive. I wasn't criticizing your home."

"Weren't you?"

The disbelief in his voice annoyed her. "If your head is cut, you've probably got dirt in it," she said, trying to control her irritation. "It should be cleaned right away. By the time you get to a shower it could be infected."

He gazed at her for several seconds while her pulse accelerated. She hadn't realized until that moment how little space separated them.

She seemed to be reminded of so many things—the strong line of his jaw, the triangle of tanned skin beneath his throat that gleamed with sweat, the way his right eyebrow seemed permanently higher than the left.

How could she have forgotten how much his nearness had always affected her? The air seemed to close in around her. She saw his eyes narrow, and he lowered his gaze to her mouth. She wanted to speak, to say anything that would shatter the sensual cocoon that held her so securely.

She parted her lips and ran the tip of her tongue around them, then shut her mouth abruptly when she saw his jaw muscle tighten.

From behind him came the sound of the toilet flushing. As if it had broken a spell, Slade dropped his gaze. "I'll be moving on to the campground soon. I'll get a shower there," he said.

Michael came through the door, beaming with excitement. "That's real cool, Mom. You should go try it."

"I think I'll wait," Kate said, struggling to regain her composure. Casting around for safe ground she said to Slade, "Would you at least let me examine that cut? We can't tell how bad it is unless we take a look."

"It's fine." He raised his hand as if to touch his head, then stopped with a short gasp of pain. Kate saw him wince when he lowered his hand.

"Your shoulder?" she said, her voice rising with concern. "Is it bothering you?":

"I told you, it's fine." He touched his head with his other hand and winced again.

Irritated by his stubbornness, she said sharply, "Well, your head isn't. Sit down here and let me take a look."

She made the mistake of glancing at him, and saw him tilt his eyebrow. Considering the scant movement, she couldn't believe how suggestive she found that gesture.

"Mom is real good at fixing hurts," Michael said, peering up from beneath the brim of Slade's hat. "She'll make it feel a lot better."

"In that case," Slade said, "we might as well let her take a look." He sat, turning his head toward Kate.

Intrigued that Michael had succeeded where she had failed, Kate gently parted Slade's dark hair. "The swelling will go down eventually," she said briskly, "but there's a fairly deep cut that should be taken care of right away."

"Go ahead."

Surprised at his capitulation she said, "I'll need hot water, disinfectant, and a clean cloth—a handkerchief will do."

Slade stood and reached up to a cupboard over the sink. He opened it, pulled out a small saucepan and held it under the faucet while he turned the water on. "I think there's some left in the tank," he said, and gave a grunt of satisfaction when water gushed into the pan.

He took a book of matches from the same cupboard and lit the gas ring, then set the pan on it. "Hot water," he said, looking at Kate. "There should be clean handkerchiefs in that drawer under the bed."

Following his gesture Kate realized he was talking about the seats on either side of the table. Wondering how on earth he managed to sleep on that narrow bunk she ducked under the table and edged the drawer open.

"I'll see what I can do about disinfectant," Slade said above her head. She saw his boots moving away from her and looked down at the drawer. A pile of clean shirts lay in one corner, next to a heap of skimpy briefs.

Kate tried not to envision him wearing them as she reached for the handkerchiefs tucked in the corner. When she emerged from under the table, Michael said with a hint of ghoulishness, "Is it going to hurt him?"

"I hope not," said Slade, coming out of the miniature bathroom. "You told me she would make it feel better."

"She will," Michael promised, though his conviction didn't carry in his voice.

Slade handed Kate the disinfectant. She took the plastic bottle from him and tested the water with her finger. "It's just about hot enough. Where do you want to sit?"

He hooked his thumbs in his jeans pockets and looked at her. "Where do you want me?"

Why, thought Kate painfully, did everything he say seem loaded with innuendos? Either he was doing it deliberately, or she was being unusually sensitive.

"Sit on the seat here and rest your arms on the table," she told him. She refused to look at him, and concentrated on testing the water again. Finding it hot enough, she turned off the gas ring.

She twisted around with the pan in her hand and saw Slade leaning his elbows on the table, with an interested Michael inspecting his head. "Ugh, gross," he said with immense satisfaction.

"Why don't you sit down there, honey," Kate suggested, nodding her head at the seat on the other side of the table.

Michael obeyed, watching closely as Kate dabbed the wound with the soaked handkerchief and worked to get the dirt out of the cut. Slade didn't flinch.

"I don't know how much good this is going to do," she said, spraying disinfectant liberally on his head, "but it will have to do for now. I suggest you have a doctor look at it if it doesn't improve."

Slade straightened and sent her a long look. "Thanks."

The glow that spread rapidly throughout her body was too dangerous to ignore. She made herself look at him coolly. "You're welcome."

He held the look a second longer, then stood, "I don't have anything softer than a beer," he said, "but I'll be happy to buy ice cream if you want to walk back to the arena."

Michael's face expressed his delight at that suggestion and Kate smiled. "We never turn down ice cream," she said lightly.

"That's what I figured." He looked down when Michael asked, "Can I wear your hat over there?"

Kate started to protest, but Slade slapped a gentle hand on his shoulder. "Sure. As long as I get it back while you eat your ice cream."

Michael agreed cheerfully and scrambled down the step to the grass, one hand holding the hat tilted back from his eyes.

"Be careful, honey. Don't get too far ahead," Kate called out as Michael bounded forward. He slowed his pace and Kate kept her gaze on him, her mind working out how she was going to approach Slade on the subject of her ad campaign.

She'd come this far; she'd be crazy not to carry it through now. As long as she kept her emotions under control, she assured herself, she could handle it—for Michael's sake.

Acutely aware of the man striding at her side, she hoped she was doing the right thing. She knew the futility of nursing false hopes. Even if Slade wanted to renew their relationship, for the sake of his son, it would be impossible for him to do so.

There was something in him, some hidden dark place that she'd never been able to reach, that prevented him from giving himself to anyone, no matter how much he might want it.

Whatever defenses she might have built up, one thing had become abundantly clear. Slade Montana had lost none of his potent sensuality over the years. In fact, time had added a devastating maturity that made him all the more appealing. She would have her work cut out to ignore all that animal magnetism, she silently admitted. Particularly since she would have to bring it out in the shots.

She could only pray that her self-control, and her common sense, would be enough to stand up against the lethal combination of an attractive, sexy man, and the memory of the fiery passion she'd once found in his arms.

Chapter 3

"Do you live in that trailer all the time?" Kate asked as they crossed the field with Michael striding ahead of them.

"Yep. It's convenient, cheap and reliable."

She heard his note of defensiveness and frowned. "Wouldn't a motel be more comfortable?"

"You think the way I live is inferior?"

She couldn't mistake the edge to his voice now. "I didn't say that," she said quickly.

"You didn't have to. Your tone implied it."

Her anger rose swiftly. "I was simply wondering if you ever felt like doing something different, after all these years."

"Like what? Parading around in obscene cowboy boots for a living?"

She flushed. "There are worse things."

He didn't answer and she risked a glance at his face. He was staring straight ahead, his eyes on Michael's slender figure.

She followed his gaze, and felt a tug of tenderness. The hat swamped Michael, accentuating his thin body. His skinny legs looked like sticks in the khaki shorts.

Nervous energy, the doctor had said when she'd complained about his lack of weight. Some kids were like that; no matter what they ate, they always remained slim.

She hadn't needed the doctor to remind her about Michael's nerves. Even after all this time... She automatically shut her thoughts down on the past. It was over and done with. One day she would succeed in erasing the horror from both her and Michael's minds completely. One day.

She turned her mind back to the present. Her time was running out; she had to think of some way to persuade Slade to agree to her proposal.

The quiver in her stomach reminded her just how difficult working with him was likely to be. His voice, breaking into her thoughts just then, unsettled her even more.

"Do you take the pictures?" he said, his tone casual.

"No." She glanced up at him, conscious of the strong flutter of hope. "I supervise. Kind of like a director. I tell the model how to pose, how to look, what kind of mood I want, that sort of thing. The photographer does the rest."

"Sounds kinky."

She gave him a sharp look, but he was still watching Michael. "I can assure you, it's all perfectly respectable. Our company has one of the best reputations in the northwest. I would not consider working for anyone who was in the least bit 'kinky,' as you call it."

"Glad to hear it. You work at home?"

"No," she said warily, wondering where this was leading to. "I work at the office and at the studio. I do a lot more than supervise shootings."

"Like what?"

Kate couldn't be sure if he was actually interested or was just making conversation. "Like sketching out ideas, scouting locations for outside shots, hiring models, composing layouts and all the tedious paperwork that goes along with all those jobs.''

''Who takes care of Michael while you're doing all this?''

This time she fought her irritation. ''He goes to a sitter.''

''It must be hard for you to have to worry about him while you're at work.''

''We manage.'' She couldn't quite keep the annoyance out of her voice. She felt him glance at her.

''Why won't you let him ride a horse?'' he asked quietly.

''He's not big enough yet.'' She hunched her shoulders. ''Michael tends to get excited, and it makes him careless. I don't want him falling off and breaking his arm or something.''

She had no need to explain anything to him, she reminded herself. And he had no right to be asking these questions. She wondered just how much right he did have as far as his son was concerned. It was a question that hadn't occurred to her until now.

''You know I wouldn't let him fall off,'' Slade said evenly. '' I think you can trust me on that.''

She sent him a quick glance. His expression was as unreadable as ever. She wanted him to spend time with Michael, she reminded herself. She just wished it didn't have to involve risks.

She heard Michael's voice some distance ahead of her. He stood by the entrance to the arena, waving impatiently. ''We'll see,'' she murmured. It was her stock answer; an evasion to gain more time. Judging from Slade's look, he didn't like it any more than Michael did.

She accepted her ice cream from Slade without meeting his eyes, and warned Michael not to wave his cone around when he talked, or he'd lose the contents.

Michael assured her he'd be careful, then gave himself up to the bliss of his favorite food and the attention of his newfound friend.

Watching them out of the corner of her eye while pretending to be engrossed in the preparations for the final parade, Kate could hardly believe that the man exchanging jokes and comments with her son was the same person who had confronted her a short while ago. He seemed so much younger, and infinitely more at ease. More like he used to be, she thought, and suffocated the memory before it could surface.

He and Michael certainly appeared to have achieved a swift and warm rapport with each other. As much as Michael wanted a father, he had a built-in skepticism when meeting strange men. She had never seen him relax so freely in such a short time, Kate thought, a warm glow beginning to spread throughout her body. His infectious laugh rang out again and again as Slade told him about some of the things that happened in a rodeo.

She wished she'd thought to bring her camera. She would have loved a picture of them together. At least Michael would have some happy memories after Slade left. She immediately sobered at the thought.

She was unprepared when Slade announced, "I have to go ride in the parade now, but if it's all right with you, I'd like to give Michael a short ride on my horse when I come back."

Aware of the small face watching her anxiously, Kate stifled her objections. "I guess it'll be all right," she murmured.

Michael's "All right!" echoed around the arena.

They watched the parade from the vantage point of the empty chutes, where Michael had been allowed to perch on the fence, held securely by a nervous Kate.

She knew she was probably overreacting, but Michael's recovery had been slow, and there were still times when his nerves got the better of him. She dreaded the thought of something happening to trigger one of his upsets.

She forced her mind off her worry as the parade ended amid rousing cheers, Michael's included. Flushed with excitement, he climbed down from the fence and waited impatiently for Slade to return.

Kate saw Slade's black hat before Michael did, and tried to restrain the shiver of awareness as his eyes met hers. Annoyed with herself she switched her gaze to Michael's glowing face.

"You will be careful, honey, won't you? And do everything Slade tells you. Don't try and do things on your own."

"I won't." Michael said impatiently, and she knew he hadn't heard a word she'd said.

"You worry too much," Slade muttered, and offered his hand to Michael. "Ready?"

"Slade—" Kate began, but he silenced her with a warning look.

"I'm not going to let go of him for a moment. He'll be perfectly safe, so just relax."

Kate followed behind the two of them as Slade led the way to where the horses were corralled.

"It will have to be a quick one," he told Michael as he lifted him into the saddle. "They're starting to load the horses into the trailers already."

Kate watched him walk the horse around the corral, beginning to relax as he showed Michael how to hold the reins, and how to tug on them when he wanted to turn the horse's head.

She couldn't help being aware of the stark contrast between Michael's fair skin and blond head, once more hidden beneath the champion's hat, and Slade's dark coloring. They looked so different, it was difficult to believe they were father and son. A stab of tenderness shook her, and she looked away, unwilling to examine the sensation.

When Slade finally returned with a reluctant but happy Michael, Kate was genuine with her thanks. "I don't know if you realize what this day has meant to Michael," she said.

"He doesn't get many treats like this. I'm sure it will be a day he'll never forget."

"It was my pleasure," Slade said gruffly. "I don't usually get such an appreciative audience."

He led them to the exit used by the rodeo personnel. Outside, men shouted as they urged the unwilling horses up the ramps of the trailers. One horse appeared to be determined not to enter the narrow container and his handler lost patience.

Kate flinched as the burly man began whipping the flanks of the horse with a long stick. She heard Michael's cry of dismay as the horse whinnied, its eyes rolling back in fear. Slade cursed, and in a few strides reached the man and caught his upraised arm. With one savage movement he jerked the stick from the man's grasp and snapped it over his knee.

Kate gasped as the handler drew back his fist in an aggressive gesture. Slade gabbed the man's wrist and twisted it behind his back. Even above the noise Kate heard the handler yell as he let go the horse's reins. She saw Slade mutter something at the man and shove him forward, letting him go. The horse backed off but Slade easily caught the dangling strap, and stood stroking the horse's nose, murmuring to it until it quieted down.

Then with a few more muttered words Kate couldn't hear, he handed the reins back to the sullen handler, who led the now obedient horse up the ramp and into the trailer.

Michael, who had been quiet through the whole incident, let out a huge sigh. "That was awesome," he said in a quiet voice he reserved for such observations.

Slade was breathing hard when he returned to them. "Sorry about that," he said, his voice still harsh with suppressed fury. "Some of those idiots shouldn't be allowed near a horse."

He looked down at Michael and winked. "I guess it's time I took my hat back," he said, his tone losing its rough edge.

Michael pulled off the hat, handing it over with an expression Kate knew well.

"You must thank Slade for a lovely day," she said quickly, "and then we have to go."

"I had a great time," Michael said, holding out his hand the way Kate had taught him. "Thank you, Slade."

Slade nodded. "Are you too grown-up for a hug?" he asked, his voice gruff.

Michael's smile lit up his face, and he held out his hands. Kate felt a sharp tug at her heart and closed her eyes when Slade crouched on his heels to take the small boy in his arms.

Straightening, he touched the brim of his hat as he looked at her. "Take care," he said, his voice still not quite even.

She took the plunge. "Would you at least consider my proposition? Come down to the studio and talk to the photographer. You'll find it's nothing like you're imagining it to be. It would take only a few days. You have to admit, that's pretty good money for a few days' work."

He shook his head. "I told you, I'm spending the next two weeks in the mountains."

"I know. Until the next rodeo in Nevada." Hating herself for the persistent hope, she rummaged in her purse and found her business cards. Her throat tight, she handed one to him. "The offer will be open if you change your mind."

She managed a smile. "At least for the next few days." That was about as long as they would give her, she thought ruefully, before they gave the contract to someone else.

He took the card and looked at it, then tucked it in his shirt pocket. "See you around," he said quietly. He laid a hand on Michael's head in a brief caress. "Keep smiling, friend."

Michael's eyes reflected her disappointment as they watched him walk away.

Michael was unnaturally quiet all the way home, and Kate had the uneasy feeling that she was in for some awkward questions later.

Her fears were confirmed at his bedtime. He was curled up in front of the television when she went into the living room. "You have to get to bed early tonight," she reminded him gently. "You've had a long day, and if you're going to do well at the swim meet tomorrow you need lots of rest."

He turned sleepy eyes up to her. "It was the best day of my life," he announced with an expansive grin.

"I know." She lowered herself to the floor beside him, and curled her arms around her knees. "I guess you really liked Slade Montana," she said softly.

He nodded with enthusiasm. "He's so cool. He got hurt and everything, but he didn't let it show. And he was so mad at that man who was hitting the horse." His face creased in a frown. "I would have pounded that man with his stick."

"Well, I think it was better the way Slade handled things. Don't you?"

"Yeah, I guess so." His expression changed, and he studied the toe of his sneaker, watching it move back and forth as he wriggled his foot. "How come you don't like him?" he asked casually.

Astonished at his perception of the tension between her and Slade, she evaded the question. "When did I say I didn't like him?"

He sent her a troubled glance, then looked back at his shoes. "I think he knows you don't like him. That's why he didn't want to work with you."

She couldn't mistake the note of accusation in his voice. She frowned, realizing that Michael blamed her for losing his new friend. She sought for the right words. "Slade Montana is a busy man," she said carefully. "He has to travel around to all the rodeos and ride the bulls, or he'll lose his championship. That's why he couldn't work for me. You wouldn't want him to lose everything he's worked so hard for, would you?"

Michael tugged at the lace of his sneaker until it came undone. "No," he muttered. He looked up as a thought hit him. "But he doesn't have another rodeo for two weeks. You said so. It's in Nevada."

Kate sighed. She was always forgetting how smart her son had become. "I know. But he has to rest in between. He's got a nasty cut on his head and that takes time to heal."

She reached for Michael's hand. "I do like him. Very much." It was true, she thought ruefully. In spite of all the hurt, he could still turn her insides to jelly with one of his burning looks.

"Sometimes," she hurried on, "no matter how much we like someone, we have to let them go. Slade likes you very much, too, I can tell. But he has his life to live, and it's a different life from ours. He can't stay in one place like we can. He has to go where the rodeos are."

Michael remained silent and she squeezed his hand. "Do you understand?" she asked gently.

His face was serious as he nodded. "I just wish he could have stayed around a little while longer," he said wistfully.

"So do I." It bothered her to realize just how much she meant that.

Michael scrambled to his feet and threw his arms around her neck. "I'm glad you like him."

She hugged his wiry body close to her and closed her eyes. "I like you, too," she whispered. "You know that I'll always love you very much, don't you?"

He drew back, embarrassed. "Of course. All mothers love their children."

She laughed. "And all children love their mothers, so they do what they're told. It's time for bed. I'll run your bath while you undress."

"Okay." He stumped off, trailing one end of his shoe-lace behind him.

Kate's smile faded. He'd sounded so matter-of-fact. *All mothers love their children.* She got up from the floor, lost in thought. He hadn't mentioned fathers. How much did he remember? she wondered.

She hoped none of it now. Perhaps he was more fortunate than she was, and had erased it all from his mind. Maybe as far as he was concerned, he'd never had a father.

She hoped that was the case. He certainly seemed to be losing his mistrust of men, if today was anything to go by. She smiled to herself as she went into the bathroom and turned the faucets on in the tub.

Memories of Michael's laughter that afternoon still rang in her ears. Slade Montana was quite an enigma, she thought, picturing the magnetic champion as he'd been that day with her son.

He was like Jekyll and Hyde, with Michael receiving the pleasant half, she thought ruefully. She sat back on her heels and tested the water with her elbow.

Slade had always been something of a mystery. He had never talked about his past life, never revealed his true self under that cloak of indifference he always wore. Even in his arms, she'd been aware that he kept part of himself shut away from her. She'd loved him but she'd never really known him.

She knew him even less now, she reflected with a sigh. He might just as well be a stranger. And now he would probably always remain one.

She turned off the faucets and heard the strident ringing of the phone from the living room. Straightening, she called out to Michael that his bath was ready and hurried to answer it. She recognized the voice of her lawyer right away.

"Ross! How are you doing? It's been a while, how's Eve and the baby?"

"Kate, this isn't a social call. I tried to get you earlier but you were out."

Something in his voice chilled her. "What is it, Ross?" she asked quietly. She closed her eyes as he confirmed her worst fears.

"I thought you'd want to know right away," he said. "Vic was released this morning."

"Released?"

"Are you all right?" Ross said sharply. Her terror must have sounded in her voice.

Kate shook her head to clear it. "It's…just a shock, that's all. Do you know where he is?"

"No." The lawyer hesitated. "They said he was rehabilitated. Cured. It's probably going to be all right."

"No," Kate said numbly. "It's not going to be all right." Her voice broke. "How could they let him go, after what he did? Don't they understand how dangerous he is?"

"Kate," Ross said in his soothing voice. "The doctors examined him. They had rigorous tests to ascertain the level of mental competence. They would not have released your ex-husband if he hadn't passed all those tests."

"You don't know Vic the way I do," Kate said, trying to control the trembling in her limbs. "He's clever. He could fool them all. You've said yourself there's a lot wrong with the system, too many loopholes. Vic should have gone to prison for what he did, not a mental hospital."

"He would have if I'd been prosecuting," Ross said grimly. "I'm sorry, Kate, I know how you feel. I still say they wouldn't have let him out if they hadn't proved him stable. He doesn't know where you live, and I doubt if he'll try and contact you, anyway. He knows what to expect if he does. The restraining order against him was for life."

"Do you honestly believe that's going to stop him?" Kate knew she was being unreasonable but the shock of what she'd heard had sent her reeling. She made an effort to pull herself together.

"I'm sorry, Ross, you're right. I'm worrying about nothing. I'm sure Vic won't want to see us. He certainly won't want to see Michael and he knows how I feel about him now." She really wished she felt as convinced as she sounded.

"That's my girl. I wish I hadn't had to tell you, but I wanted you to be prepared in case there are any legal ramifications."

Again her heart missed a beat. "Legal? Like what?"

"Oh, you never know," Ross said airily. "I wouldn't worry about it. I can take care of anything that might come up. Just put it all out of your mind. Promise?"

She promised and hung up. Put it out of her mind. How could she do that? she thought in despair. She hadn't been able to get it all out of her mind in nearly three years. The news that Vic was free to roam the streets, to call her, to try and see her, brought it all back in vivid detail.

She heard Michael call from the bathroom and struggled for composure. He was sharp; he'd know that something was wrong unless she was careful.

She found him dressed in his pajamas, brushing his teeth at the sink. "Who was that on the phone?" he asked through a mouthful of foam. "Was it Slade?"

Kate managed a shaky laugh. "Oh, no, honey, I doubt if Slade has a phone in that trailer of his. He's probably fast asleep by now, anyway, which is what you should be."

Michael rinsed his mouth and placed his toothbrush in the mug. "I wish we had a toilet like his," he said wistfully. "It's real cool."

"Well, pal, you'll just have to manage with the one we've got." She wrinkled her brow at him. "Just think yourself lucky you have a bathtub to practice your underwater exercises. Slade doesn't even have a shower."

Michael considered that. "He must use rivers to bath in." He grinned at Kate. "That's even more cool."

Kate sighed. "That's enough about Slade. If you don't get to sleep you'll be too tired to swim in your events tomorrow." To her relief the warning worked and Michael raced for the bedroom.

If there was one thing guaranteed to make her forget her problems, Kate thought as she picked up the wet towels, it was the vision of a naked Slade Montana emerging from a river.

Even so, the niggling feeling of uneasiness still bothered her when she awoke the next morning. She got out of bed with the grim determination to shake all thoughts of Vic out of her mind. The swim meet was very important to Michael, and nothing was going to spoil this day for her son.

She had just cleared away the breakfast dishes when she heard the chime of the doorbell. She stood for several seconds, her hands ice cold and her stomach churning. It couldn't be Vic, she told herself. He couldn't have found them this soon.

Heart thumping, she crossed the living room to the door, and had to force herself to open it. To her utter astonishment, Slade stood leaning against the doorjamb.

He was wearing jeans, and the sleeves of his light blue shirt were rolled back to his elbows. He straightened when he saw her, and held up a package wrapped in colorful paper. "I just wanted to drop this off for Michael," he said, not quite meeting her eyes.

It seemed like minutes before she found her voice. "Come in," she said when she'd regained her breath. "He'll be pleased to see you."

Still stunned, and disturbed by the intensity of her pleasure at seeing him, she stepped back to let him in. Her home address had been on the card she'd given him. It hadn't occurred to her he would simply turn up at her door.

She couldn't believe he was actually standing in her living room. He looked tired, she thought as he passed her, and his shoulder seemed hunched, as if he were tense.

"Hi, Slade!" Michael's delighted voice said from behind her. "How come you didn't go to the mountains?" There was a short pause. "Where's your hat?"

Slade sidestepped her and hunkered down in front of the boy. "I don't wear it all the time," he said. "But I know how much you like it so I brought you a present." He presented the package he'd been holding behind his back to Michael, who took it, his eyes wide with excitement.

"What is it?"

"Why don't you open it and see?" Kate suggested, still trying to calm her rapid pulse.

Michael tore the paper apart and gave a yelp of delight. He held up a scaled-down version of Slade's black hat. Sticking it on his head at a jaunty angle he rushed for his bedroom to inspect himself in a mirror.

"That was very nice of you," Kate said unsteadily.

Slade sent her a speculative look. "I wasn't sure you would approve."

"Why not?"

He slid his gaze away from her and took a slow inspection of the room. "You don't approve of a lot of things I do."

She flushed, annoyed that he could put her on the defensive so easily. "I've never said that."

His gaze returned to her face, unsettling her even more. "I know."

Michael returned at that moment, his face brimming with excited hope.

Kate's heart sank, guessing what was on his mind.

"Mom, can I wear it to the swim meet?" Michael asked, tilting his hat to look up at her.

"What's this about a swim meet?" Slade said.

Michael explained. "All the kids' parents are invited," he added after giving Slade a rundown on the events. "Mom's going to be by herself. Do you want to come?"

"Michael." Kate put authority into her voice. "Remember what I told you last night? Slade has to leave. He can't come to the swim meet. Now thank him for the hat and then we must get going."

Disappointment swamped Michael's face, and he looked down at the floor. "Thank you for the hat, Slade," he mumbled. Then, as if remembering his manners, he looked up again and attempted a wobbly smile.

"I guess I'd better come and hold it while you swim all those races."

Michael's eyes shone with excitement as Kate's pulse leaped. He looked up at her, his pleading expression catching at her heart.

"You'd better get ready," she said, smiling. "We don't want to be late."

With a whoop of sheer joy Michael dashed from the room. Kate sent Slade a warm glance. "It will mean a lot to him."

He shrugged and lowered himself into an armchair. Kate saw him wince and guessed his shoulder was bothering him. "I'm not leaving until this evening," he said, stretching his feet out in front of him. "I don't have any other plans for the day."

The reminder that soon he would be gone touched a nerve. Before she could control it she heard herself say, "Michael will miss you when you've gone." She was immediately furious with herself. It was the one thing she'd been determined not to do. No pressure.

He gave her a brooding look that seemed to find its way right to her soul. "He'll soon forget me."

Like I tried to? She turned away before she could say the words out loud. To her relief Michael came back into the room, carrying his blue sports bag.

His small face was drawn with tension, and the smile he gave her was a faint semblance of his usual grin.

"What's up?" Slade asked in concern.

"He's all right," Kate said, patting his shoulder. "He's just a little nervous, that's all. These competitions can be scary to a little guy."

Slade got to his feet slowly, and once more she saw the flicker of pain cross his face. "You're not scared, friend, you're just a little anxious, that's all." He gave Michael a gentle slap on the shoulder. "Let's go show them what you can do."

Michael's smile returned promptly and he dashed out of the door, followed by Slade. Kate closed the door behind her and locked it.

Refusing Slade's offer to drive, she ushered them both into the back seat of the car, then drove to the swim center painfully aware of his presence behind her.

In spite of Slade's attempts at conversation, Michael answered in monosyllables and Kate sent him an anxious glance in the rearview mirror.

These were the times that tested him the most, when he had to assume responsibility for himself. Her heart ached, knowing how difficult it was for him—and for her. It was a necessary part of his recovery, but at times she found it impossible to stick to the guidelines she'd been given by the child psychologist.

She'd been terrified when the doctor who had treated Michael insisted on sending them to the kind, bespectacled specialist. She'd cried in the office when he'd told her that Michael's disorder was simply a reaction to the ordeal her son had gone through. Normal, he'd gently informed her, under the circumstances. Treated with care, Michael would eventually return to his usual, secure self and would no longer become hysterical with terror any time she was out of his sight.

He'd come a long way, she admitted to herself as she turned into the parking lot in front of the swim center. It was only times like these, when he was under pressure to do something by himself, that he lost his confidence.

She felt his hand creep into hers as their footsteps echoed down the long hall that led to the pool. Children jostled and skipped alongside them, raising their voices in excitement. Kate tightened her grip on the small fingers. Lately he had avoided holding her hand, a sign that he was gaining his independence. The fact that he needed the security now was an indication of his uncertainty.

Slade walked beside them, saying nothing, though Kate caught the contemplative glances he sent Michael. This is how it could have been, she thought, piercingly aware of the man and boy on either side of her, then banished the treacherous notion from her mind.

The smell of chlorine greeted them as they reached poolside. Kate put her arms around Michael and gave him a hug.

"Okay, honey, this is it. Just be sure to come up if you run out of breath. I don't want you taking risks just to win a competition." She bent down and gave him a quick kiss on the cheek. "Maybe I should come with you into the changing rooms," she added, catching the brief apprehension that crossed his face.

"No." Michael pulled out of her arms. "Mothers aren't allowed." He took off his hat and handed it to Slade. "I'll see you later," he said solemnly.

"You bet. Good luck." Slade winked at him, then kept his gaze on the small figure as he walked slowly away from them to join the boisterous group of children filing into the changing rooms.

Feeling awkward now that she was alone with Slade, Kate looked up at the balcony. "There seems to be seats up there," she said, gesturing with her hand.

"I like it better over there," Slade said, nodding his head to the opposite side of the pool. He started to walk away from her and she followed him, reflecting that with all the screams and yells bouncing off the high walls, she wouldn't have to try and make conversation. He'd never hear her.

"How come they don't use an outside pool?" Slade said as he lowered himself carefully on a seat and leaned forward.

The seats were set much too close together in Kate's opinion. Wondering why she hadn't noticed that before, she sat down next to him. Raising her voice she explained, "This one belongs to the school. This is Michael's summer school program.''

''Does he like going to school in the summer?''

In spite of her good intentions, his question irritated her. She took a long, slow breath. ''Yes, he does. He enjoys it, and he's learning new experiences that will be a great help to him later on.''

''Why are you so sensitive? I was just being curious.''

His look unnerved her and her control slipped. ''Were you? I had the feeling you were being critical.'' She was immediately ashamed. Michael was his son; it was natural he'd want to know everything about him. So why did it bother her?

Because he'd left it so long, her mind screamed back. Where was he all those years when she'd needed him? Shocked at the intensity of her resentment she forced her mind back to the present.

''Michael is in three races,'' she said, her voice a shade too high. ''He does better swimming underwater for some reason; it's amazing how long that boy can hold his breath.''

Slade merely nodded and Kate gave up her attempt at conversation. She settled back on her seat and waited for the events to begin.

Michael started off well in the first race, which was the breaststroke across the width of the pool. His thin arms flailed the water, but two of his opponents surged ahead of him and he struggled in third.

Slade joined in the applause as Michael hauled himself out of the pool. ''Not bad,'' he said, his words ending on a grunt as he leaned back in his seat.

Kate glanced at him, catching her breath in concern when she saw him wince in pain. ''Your shoulder,'' she said, frowning at him. ''Is it bothering you?''

''Only when I lean against something.'' Slade shrugged and winced again.

"You'd better have someone take a look at it," Kate said, ignoring his look of exasperation. "It could be dislocated or something."

"It's fine." Slade waved a hand at the pool. "The next race is starting."

Their conversation was minimal throughout the next two races, then it was Michael's turn again. Kate leaned forward, her hands gripped together. "He doesn't do too well with the crawl. He wears himself out too soon."

"He's trying too hard," Slade commented.

She looked at him, wondering if this was another criticism, but his gaze was concentrated on the boys lined up at the edge of the pool.

The coach blew the whistle, and the shrill sound seemed to repeat around the walls before being drowned out by the cheers of the spectators.

This time Michael finished next to last, and Kate could see his dejection in the slump of his shoulders.

She wanted to go down to him, and give him some words of encouragement, but she made herself stay in her seat through the next five events, until Michael was once more lined up at the edge of the pool.

Beside her Slade shifted his weight, as if finding his seat uncomfortable, but Kate's attention was on her son now. She leaned forward as silence settled over the area. Her fingers curled into her palms and she muttered, "Come on, Michael, just one more and it's over."

"You make it sound like he's going into battle," Slade said at her side.

His voiced sounded odd to Kate, but she refused to look at him, afraid of being drawn into an argument. "In a way, he is," she said in a voice too low for Slade to hear.

This time the race was freestyle, and she knew it was Michael's best chance. Even so, Kate felt her entire body tense when she heard the shrill sound of the whistle. Michael hit the water cleanly and glided for what seemed an eternity.

She let out a shuddering breath when he surfaced, way ahead of the rest of the field.

They began catching up to him as they all splashed furiously toward the edge of the pool, but Michael, with a desperate lunge, touched the wall first.

Kate cheered at the top of her voice, only half aware of Slade coming to his feet more slowly, applauding loudly with the rest of the audience.

When Michael had taken his victory wave and disappeared into the changing rooms, she turned to Slade. Shock sliced through her when she saw his face.

He looked as if his teeth were clenched, and his eyes were half closed. Bright spots of color burned in his cheeks, and as she watched him he swayed slightly toward her.

"Slade!" Automatically she reached up and laid a hand on his forehead. His skin felt hot and dry beneath her fingers. Full of concern now she stared anxiously into his face. Unless she was very much mistaken, he was burning up with fever.

Chapter 4

Slade's eyes snapped open at her touch and he jerked his head back. His grunt of pain confirmed her suspicions.

"You," she said firmly, "are going straight to the emergency ward of the hospital when we get out of here."

"No way." The odd note in his voice, she now realized, had been an indication of how much he was hurting.

"We'll talk about it later," she said as the murmur of conversation around her died down.

Michael's grin spread from ear to ear as he received his two prizes for first and third. Kate felt the prickle of tears and blinked them back. No one would be more horrified than her son if she got "mushy," she thought ruefully.

She had to restrain Michael from throwing himself at Slade when they went down to collect him. "His shoulder is sore," she explained, ignoring Slade's muttered denial.

Michael was full of his victory and Kate didn't notice the photographer until the brilliant flash of light temporarily blinded her.

She'd seen him taking pictures of Michael and the other winners earlier, but now she stared at him in confusion, wondering why he should want a picture of her. His motive became clear when he stepped past her and grabbed Slade's hand, pumping it up and down while he sympathized with the champion about his near miss with the bull the day before.

Kate uttered a murmur of protest when she saw Slade's jaw clench in agony, but his swift glance at her warned her to keep quiet. He assured the photographer he'd suffered no ill effects with such conviction she would have believed him herself if she hadn't known better.

It was Michael's impatient voice asking when they could leave that finally discouraged the newsman from asking any more questions.

Slade took a long time to settle himself in the car, and Kate warned Michael to sit still as she started the engine. She caught a glimpse of Slade's face in the rearview mirror and made up her mind.

That fever meant an infection, she decided. Probably the cut in his head. There was no point in arguing with the man; she'd have to take matters into her own hands. Putting her foot down, she drove straight to the hospital.

The expected explosion erupted as soon as Slade realized where they were. Carefully omitting the curses she knew were hovering on his lips, he informed her that he had no intention of getting out of the car.

Throwing caution to the wind, Kate remarked in a scathing tone, "Are you trying to tell us you're *afraid* to go in there?"

Michael giggled and Slade sent her a long look of exasperation. "If it's going to make you feel better," he said, his voice resigned, "I'll go in there and waste their precious time."

"All I'm asking you to do," Kate answered patiently, "Is to let them look at your shoulder. And the cut on your head while they're about it. That's not going to hurt you, is it? We'll hold your hands, won't we, Michael?''

Michael nodded with enthusiasm and Slade lifted his hands in defeat. Muttering something under his breath, he eased himself out of the car and stood.

Kate hid her concern under a smile as she took hold of his arm. "Okay. Let's take it easy."

To her surprise Slade let her lead him to the door and open it for him, a fact that worried her far more than his rebuff would have done.

He did, however, insist that she take Michael for an ice cream while he waited his turn to see the doctor, and she agreed. Waiting rooms of emergency wards were not the most pleasant places in which to pass time, she acknowledged.

Extracting a promise from Slade that he would not leave without them, she went back to the car, trying to reassure a worried Michael.

Slade watched them leave and eased himself down on the nearest vacant chair. Now that he was here he had to admit he felt relieved. His shoulder burned like hell and the fuzzy feeling in his head didn't help matters any. The sooner they gave him something to put him back in shape the better. Then maybe he could think straight.

He still didn't know quite how he'd ended up in this situation. He'd fought long and hard over the decision to come this close to Portland for the rodeo. He wouldn't have done if it hadn't been a necessary point on the circuit.

Other years he'd managed to skip this one, having chalked up enough points to make the championship without it. But this year had been different. He'd taken more falls, lost more time, and without this competition he wouldn't have stood a chance at the championship. The minute he'd seen Kate walk into the compound he knew he'd made a mistake.

He shifted to ease the pain in his shoulder. She stirred memories that he'd sooner not think about. Memories of her eager body, the touch of her lips, the sweet smell of her hair and the soft little moans that fired his blood—

He halted the train of thought, determined not to dwell on the past. The present was hard enough to deal with. All these years of self-torment, wondering what his son looked like, what kind of boy he'd grown into. How many times had he caught himself watching somebody else's son and thought about his own?

Too many, he answered himself. He'd hoped the inevitable wouldn't happen, that he wouldn't have to face his son. Now that the ghost had become a reality, the past would haunt him all the more.

He'd fully intended to get out of town as soon as possible. He'd been crazy to take the present that morning, he told himself wearily. He'd seen the hat in the gift shop and hadn't been able to resist leaving some small memento of himself behind. Then he'd looked into that boy's eyes and hadn't been able to refuse his invitation.

He should get out of their lives right now. It was the best thing he could do for them. He'd only end up hurting them, and they'd been hurt enough. He'd been hurt enough.

He lifted his head when he heard his name called and stood unsteadily. The pretty nurse who took his arm talked in bright, efficient tones as she led him to a large room divided into cubicles, but he couldn't absorb what she was saying. She sat him on the edge of a high bed, pulled the drapes around him with a clatter of curtain rings and left.

Alone in the confined space, Slade waited with growing irritation. He hated the smell of hospitals. That aroma of chemicals and disinfectant reminded him of a part of his life he was constantly trying to forget.

The curtains parted and he looked into the face of a thin-faced man with sparse gray hair and a stethoscope dangling from his neck. "Mr. . . . Montana?" the doctor said, studying the clipboard in his hand.

Slade nodded.

"Is that your real name?"

"Does it matter?"

The doctor shrugged. "It depends, I guess, on how you want to pay for this."

Slade shifted his position, grimacing as pain stabbed through his shoulder. "I told them at the desk," he said shortly. "I'm insured. It's all legal."

"Fine." The doctor laid his clipboard down. "Let's take a look, then," he said, and helped Slade out of his shirt.

The brief examination was relatively painless until the doctor muttered something and wrenched Slade's shoulder, nearly sending him through the roof.

"Dislocated," the doctor explained as he sat down next to Slade on the bed and reached for his clipboard. "It should feel better soon. We'll put your arm in a sling. Wear it for at least a week."

He scribbled something on a sheet of paper, then looked up. "Well, Mr. Montana, I imagine you know that the cut on your head is infected. You have a slight fever. I'll give you a shot of penicillin and prescribe some medication. Please make sure you take all of it."

Slade nodded. "First time that's happened," he said, reaching for his shirt. "I've been cut lots of times. A lot worse than that."

"And broken some bones by the look of it." The doctor ran his finger down the scar above Slade's elbow. The expression in the other man's eyes worried Slade.

"How many years have you been riding in rodeos?" the doctor said, putting his pen back in his pocket.

Slade shrugged. "Twenty years, more or less."

The doctor nodded. "Ever think of retiring?"

Slade shifted uncomfortably. "I figure a couple more years before I think about that."

The doctor frowned. "I'd think about it a lot sooner," he said. "Your body has taken some beatings over the years, and sooner or later it's going to rebel. I'd say, judging by the state of you, it's already beginning to do so. I would recommend taking several weeks' rest before riding again."

Slade stared at him. "Come on, Doc. It's can't be that bad. I just feel a little light-headed, that's all."

He watched the doctor shake his head, and felt a growing uneasiness in the pit of his stomach.

"Your resistance has reached an extremely low level. The infection is a sign of that. You can't go on abusing your body this way without accepting the consequences."

The doctor stood and held out his hand. "If I were you, Mr. Montana," he said quietly, "I would think very seriously about retiring from the circuit."

Stunned, Slade watched the curtain swing together behind the doctor. He couldn't give up the circuit. Not yet. He still had two more years at least before he had enough to buy the ranch, maybe more if he didn't do too well.

He pressed his thumb and forefinger against his eyes. He'd found it was getting harder to stay on a bull, but hell, he was still champion. Even if he lost that, which was beginning to look more likely as the season wore on, he could still make money with a few less wins.

But leave? He dropped his hand and looked up at the white ceiling in despair. Not now. Not yet. All he needed was a rest. Just long enough to get the stamina back to see him through the next two years.

He shook his head. It looked as if he had some tough decisions to make. He was deep in thought when the curtains parted again and a well-padded nurse with arms like a wrestler's appeared.

She advanced on him brandishing a needle. "Drop your pants," she ordered.

He decided not to argue.

Outside, Kate waited anxiously in the corridor. She'd left Michael locked inside the car with the excuse that he wouldn't be allowed to take his ice cream inside the hospital.

She hoped Slade wouldn't be too long. She didn't want Michael to get bored and come wandering in to look for her. She had an idea Slade wouldn't be in too good a humor by the time he came out.

She knew she was right when he walked around the corner, his arm in a sling, looking pale in spite of his bronzed skin. She took one look at his face and guessed what had taken place.

Deciding that attack was the better way to deal with him she joined him as he strode unsteadily down the hallway. "I was right," she said, looking up at him. "Your shoulder was dislocated."

His scowl confirmed it.

"And the cut in your head is infected, right?"

When he still didn't answer she added, "And they gave you a shot." In spite of herself she could feel the smile nudging at her mouth.

He gave her a look of outrage that only increased the urge to laugh. "It's the first time," he said in a tight voice, "that I've ever dropped my pants for a woman and didn't get any pleasure out of it."

She felt the giggle form in her throat and pressed her lips together in an effort to control it.

Slade stopped short and looked down at her. "Are you laughing at me?" he demanded.

"No," she said weakly, and choked. The laugh bubbled up and, before she could stop it, escaped in a helpless gurgle. She stole a look at him, and saw a reluctant grin tug at his mouth.

"You looked so indignant," she spluttered, then dissolved into laughter. His soft chuckle answered her as they went through the door together.

Once outside, Kate braced herself as they approached the car. She might as well make the most of his good humor, she decided. "Well," she said, traces of laughter still clinging to her voice, "you won't feel like riding any bulls for a while. Why don't you take a break and pose for me? You can earn money just sitting around until your shoulder heals."

Dismayed, she watched the scowl appear on his face. "There's nothing says I can't get on a bull tomorrow if I want to," he said.

There was no answer to that and, saying nothing, she waited for him to climb into the car.

Michael bombarded him with questions and he fielded them with expert ease, but Kate could hear the tension in his voice. She had the uneasy feeling that Slade had not liked what he'd been told in the hospital.

They arrived back at the apartment building, and Michael insisted that Slade come inside with him. This time he refused, and didn't interfere when Kate explained that he had to rest his shoulder.

Michael took it well, and was careful where he put his arms when he gave Slade a final hug. "I'll come and see you at the next rodeo," he promised.

Kate looked up at Slade, her throat tight. "You take care of that shoulder," she said, "and if you should need anything, you know where I am. You can get me at the office on weekdays."

He gave her a brief nod. "Thanks for taking me to the hospital." He gave her a long look, then glanced down at Michael and ruffled his hair. "Take care of your mom, friend," he said, his voice husky. "And don't lose your hat."

"I won't." said Michael solemnly.

Kate felt his hand reach for hers as they watched Slade climb with difficulty into his car. "You're going to be all right?" she called out before she could stop herself.

He leaned out of the window and lifted his hand in a salute. "I'm going to be fine." He gave her a slow smile, winked at Michael and withdrew his head.

Michael's hand tightened on hers as they watched the station wagon until it disappeared behind the building.

"You never did tell me what your prizes were," Kate said, worried about the crestfallen look on Michael's face. "Did you leave them in the car?"

He nodded without enthusiasm. "I'll get them," he said listlessly, and opened the back door of the car.

Kate's heart ached as she followed the small boy into the apartment. She knew how he felt. No matter how much she'd told herself she was chasing rainbows, she'd hung on to the hope that Slade would care enough to spend at least a little time with his son.

It was after Michael was in bed, and she was alone, when she admitted the rest of it. She'd hoped Slade had cared enough to spend time with her, too.

It was just as well he hadn't accepted her proposal, she assured herself as she viciously plumped up the cushions on the sofa. It was painful being around him. Working with him would have been pure torture.

She awoke late the next morning, and had to rush an unusually quiet Michael in order to get him to school on time. She gave him an extralong hug when she dropped him off in front of the brick building.

"Everybody's going to be so proud of you winning two prizes," she told him. "Almost as proud as I am."

She watched with a heavy heart as he walked into the school, and she still had him on her mind when the phone rang at her desk later that morning.

The surge of surprised pleasure she felt when she heard Slade's deep voice warned her just how vulnerable she was. She made her voice deliberately casual.

"I didn't expect to hear from you again," she said, then felt a rush of concern. "Is something wrong? Do you need help?" She waited anxiously through the long pause.

"Yes," Slade said at last. "I guess I do. I've decided to accept your offer. I'll do your damn ads for the pimp boots, but I warn you, I'm not going to like it."

She didn't know if the sensations exploding throughout her body were caused by relief that her contract was secure, excitement because she hadn't seen the last of him, or fear that she was making a bad mistake in letting him back into her life, even if it was for professional reasons.

Whatever she felt about Slade Montana, she acknowledged with more than a twinge of anxiety, it certainly wasn't professional. And no matter what, she couldn't afford to let those feelings surface. Not if she wanted to avoid the kind of pain she still couldn't forget.

With a strong suspicion that she was messing with Pandora's box, she said calmly, "I'm sure you'll find it an interesting experience. And profitable." She wondered what had changed his mind, and asked him.

It was a while before he answered her question. "I've got some time on my hands," he said finally. "You were right about the shoulder, and I'm not one to sit around. If I'm going to miss the next competition I figured I might as well make some money while I'm recuperating."

She was annoyed at her momentary twinge of regret. Nothing personal, strictly business—she would have to adhere to that if this was going to work. "Fine. When can we get started? Is your shoulder better?"

"Getting there. Give me a week. I'll be there next Monday. How long is this going to take?"

"That depends on you. Everyone is different." She paused. "It could take a couple of days," she said carefully. "Then again, it might take a week or more."

His pause went on a shade too long. "Just to take a few pictures?"

She made an effort to keep the professional tone. "We take more than a few. We try several different poses in different locations. Then select the best of the bunch. Obviously the more shots we have, the better choice we have."

She waited, heart thumping, praying he wouldn't change his mind. She was certain he heard her sigh of relief when he said abruptly, "All right, deal me in. I'll be there Monday. What time?"

She told him, and asked his size in clothes and shoes. He sounded edgy when she told him that his wardrobe would be taken care of, and she grimaced at the phone after she'd hung up. He was probably going to show his disapproval through the whole thing. She would have her work cut out for her to get the shots she needed.

In spite of her misgivings, she couldn't resist a little stab in the air with her fist to express her elation. With a triumphant smile, she picked up the phone to inform her boss that the assignment was on.

The week dragged on while Kate agonized over the right moment to tell Michael that Slade would be working with her. He hadn't mentioned Michael when he'd talked to her, and had given no indication he wanted to see his son again.

She couldn't bring herself to believe he would avoid Michael, but she hated to get the boy's hopes up, only to have them dashed. If only the man wasn't so damned unpredictable, she fumed as the days slipped by without hearing from him.

He called that weekend. Kate's treacherous heart bounded when she heard his deep voice in her ear. He asked if he could take Michael to a ball game and, delighted, she readily agreed. She spent the rest of the day wishing she could have been with them.

Michael, who had been ecstatic to discover that Slade hadn't left town after all, arrived home full of his day, and didn't even complain when Slade refused Kate's invitation to stay to dinner. Kate had a tough time covering up her own disappointment, after having built up enough nerve to issue the invitation.

That night a sleepy Michael announced how happy he was that Slade was going to do the pictures, and Kate had to resign herself to the fact that for the next few days at least, Slade Montana was going to be the hot topic of conversation.

By Monday morning every nerve in Kate's body felt like a stretched rubber band. The hem had come unraveled on the dress she'd planned to wear and she had to settle for a pink cotton skirt and striped blouse. She spilled coffee on the counter and burned the toast. When the car wouldn't start she twisted the ignition key so hard she broke a fingernail and if Michael hadn't been sitting next to her, she would have filled the air with potent curses.

She managed a bright smile and a hug for him when she dropped him off, but by the time she pulled into the studio's parking lot, her heart hammered against her ribs and her lungs felt as if they were clamped in a vise.

She busied herself in the studio helping the photographer set up for the first series of shots. They were using a backdrop of ranch lands and distant mountains, and Slade would be posed sitting on a fence in front of it.

She was in the middle of a discussion on lighting when the gravelly drawl behind her sent her pulse soaring.

"Is that supposed to look real?"

Kate spun around and found him gazing at the backdrop as if it were a piece of moldy cheese. "It'll look real in the pictures," she assured him.

He looked better, she saw with relief. The drawn look had disappeared, and his color had improved. She was still studying him when he switched his gaze to her face, and she turned away, embarrassed to be caught staring.

She quickly introduced Bob Thornton, the photographer, and waited while the men shook hands. "The dressing room is over there," she told Slade when he turned to her. "The outfits are all numbered in the order you'll wear them. I'll send the makeup girl in to you."

"Makeup?"

She recognized the tone and hurried to explain. "Don't worry, just a dash of color on your cheeks and a dab of powder to prevent a shine." She felt a nervous tug when she saw the grim look on his face and steeled herself. This was her job, and she was good at it. He would have to trust her judgment and abide by it.

The idea of Slade Montana doing what anyone told him, let alone her, was as remote as Mars, she thought as she watched him stride to the dressing room. Nevertheless he would have to get used to it. She waited several nerve-racking minutes for him to reappear, and when he did her lips tightened in anticipation. He was carrying the boots.

She let her meaningful glance speak for her, and heard his answering sigh. "I guess I have to wear them?"

She gave him a dazzling smile. "That's what you're here for."

She got up from her chair and gestured at it. "You can sit here and put them on."

She almost felt sorry for him when he tugged the garish boots over his calves. They were pale gray, adorned with brilliant yellow and turquoise sailboats.

Up until that moment she hadn't realized how incongruous they looked. She straightened her mouth before he could see her grin. She waited for him to stand, then ran a professional eye over him.

At least it was supposed to be professional. Once she got past the boots she forgot about the photos. Slade's black jeans were skintight, and outlined every curve and muscle of his lower body. The dark red shirt fitted his torso like a glove, accentuating his deep tan and dark hair. Butterflies performed a ballet in her stomach by the time she reached his face.

Her expression must have betrayed her reaction to him. His dark eyes met hers, sending a spark sizzling between them on a potent current of awareness. With an effort Kate dragged her attention back to the photo session.

"Go and stand by the fence," she said, trying for an authoritative note and failing miserably. She watched him settle the Stetson on his head, then stood back to look at him, concentrating on the pose.

"Good," she murmured. "What do you think, Bob? Tilted back a bit more?"

Bob ran a hand over his short black beard. "Maybe if we lift the chin a little, and leave the hat where it is?"

Kate nodded. "Yes, good. Now, Slade, I want you to imagine it's early morning. You're feeling good, you know it's going to be a good day. You want to share that feeling with everyone. Smile, and put your heart in it."

She watched the stiff smile appear on his face and sighed. "No, Slade, smile as if you mean it. Pretend you've just seen someone you really like walking toward you."

His eyes met hers, and she felt the breath catch in her throat. His smile began slowly, and widened to a grin, completely destroying her composure.

She thrust her hands into the pockets of her skirt and mentally scolded herself. She couldn't fall apart every time he looked at her; she'd be a basket case by the time it was over.

Calling on all her concentration, she suggested, ordered, demanded, encouraged and praised until Slade was following her directions with a relaxed ease that delighted her.

All through the quick lunch he joked with her and Bob, and at times she could almost forget there had ever been any animosity between them.

Slade actually seemed anxious to get on with the shoot that afternoon. He was a natural, Kate thought, watching him twirl a lasso expertly around his head while Bob swooped and swayed around him with the camera clicking constantly.

Halfway through the afternoon, she decided it was time to change the mood. They had been concentrating on the fresh and open outdoors look; now she wanted something different.

Aware that the next step would be difficult to explain, she'd put it off until the last possible moment. She'd expected this part of the session to take all day at least, but Slade had been so cooperative they already had more than they needed.

She signaled to Bob that she needed another wardrobe change and he nodded. Together they changed the set while Slade changed out of the denim shirt and jeans he'd been wearing.

This time the backdrop portrayed the night, with a leaping bonfire in the background for effect. The black velvet sky glittered with stars and a huge harvest moon hung in the center. They were using the fence again, and Kate was spreading straw along it when Slade returned.

She looked up and felt excitement shiver up her spine. He looked magnificent. Wearing the tight black jeans again and a black shirt with white edging, he looked virile, handsome and dangerous. The black hat added to the image, and even the boots were halfway presentable, their shiny black leather accented by a golden snake writhing up the sides.

His mouth curved in a half smile as he waited for her verdict and she knew in that instant that half the women in America would be in love with him by the time the campaign was over.

"You look . . . great," she said, her voice sounding strangled.

He nodded his acceptance of her approval, his gaze resting on her face. She felt a pulse fluttering in her neck like an imprisoned bird.

She waved a hand at the fence. "Over there." It was all she had breath for.

He nodded and stepped over to the fence. Leaning his back against it he propped himself on his elbows. "Like this?"

Forcing her mind back to a professional level, she studied him. "We're going for a different mood," she said, moving toward him. "Let's undo a couple of buttons."

He raised both eyebrows. "What kind of mood are we going for?"

"The sexy look," Bob said cheerfully. "Nothing sells a product better than sex."

Kate sent him a furious look over her shoulder, but he appeared not to notice. "You go ahead," he said to Kate. "I'm out of film. We're doing better than I expected." He raised a hand as he hurried across the floor. "Be back in a few minutes."

Kate drew a shaky breath and looked back at Slade. He was watching her, anticipation gleaming in his eyes.

"The buttons," she said unsteadily. "Two should be enough."

Without taking his eyes from her face he slowly undid the buttons.

She wished he'd say something. She almost preferred his belligerence; she could deal with that.

"When Bob comes back," she said, trying to ignore the smug expression on Slade's face, "I'm going to ask you to treat the camera like an attractive, desirable woman."

It was a technique she used all the time to get the expression she wanted, and she concentrated on the routine.

"I want you to think about that woman in your arms, feel her body, smell her perfume. Imagine you are about to make love to the camera."

The words were usually automatic, as unconscious as her actions. This time they sounded to her like a sensuous invitation.

Slade smiled. "I'd rather imagine making love to a woman," he said softly. The expression she wanted was there, all right—burning in his hooded eyes, smoldering on his parted lips.

She made a helpless sound in her throat as he stepped forward and closed his arms around her. "It's been a long time. I need a practice run," he murmured.

In the seconds before his mouth covered hers Kate thought about resisting. The moment their lips touched she knew it was a lost cause. In spite of all her convictions and resolutions, she knew deep down that she'd wanted this from the moment she'd first walked up to him at the rodeo.

She gave herself up to the kiss, parting her lips to give him access as his tongue probed in insistent demand. It was a hard kiss, with none of the gentleness she remembered. She welcomed his ruthlessness as he pulled her closer. His hand closed over the back of her head, while his mouth increased the fierce claim on her senses.

She could feel his heart beat against her breast, the hard lines of his body's searing imprint against hers. She clung to him, her fingers digging into the solid muscles of his back, her tongue searching for his, and felt him shudder beneath her hands. She was shaking when he lifted his head.

She heard his harsh breathing as he gazed down at her, his arms still trapping her against him. "That wasn't supposed to have happened," he said, his voice a husky whisper.

"It's all right." She managed a weak smile. "I guess we got carried away. I just hope you can hold that look."

"Is that all it was to you, a way to get your perfect pose?"

He was half-serious, and she lowered her gaze to his mouth. The sweet, sharp tug deep in her belly warned her. She moved back, out of his arms.

It took all her willpower to lie and say, "I'm not above taking advantage of a situation, when the need arises. If I can capture that look on camera you'll have every woman over the age of consent panting after you."

He had closed off all expression again, and she felt a sharp tug of regret. "I thought they were supposed to be panting after the boots," he said evenly.

"They will be." She forced a smile. "If they can't have you, they'll have the next best thing. They'll be rushing out to buy the boots for their men, just like they bought Hawaiian shirts for them when Tom Selleck first climbed into his red Ferrari."

"And we all know what that did for Tom," Bob said behind her.

Kate whirled around in embarrassment, wondering how much the photographer had seen. He made no further comment and she made herself concentrate on the shoot again, though she couldn't quite dismiss the tiny shivers every time she met Slade's eyes.

By the time the day's shoot was over she felt exhausted. Slade had been all she could ask for and more in a model. She knew that his naturally brooding expression would translate into a sensuous, magnetic look on film. She'd even managed to coax a spark of heated interest in his eyes once or twice, which she hoped Bob had caught with his camera.

Now they were through for the day, and she waited for Slade to finish changing into his own clothes before closing up the studio.

One more day inside, she decided, looking at her notes, then they could do the outside shoot. A lot would depend on how well Slade's shoulder had healed. She would have liked some shots on a bull, but that was out of the question now. She would just have to settle for a horse, and a tame one at that, she thought ruefully. She made several notations and closed her notebook, then glanced at her watch.

She would have to hurry if she was going to pick up Michael from school. She looked up and saw Slade walking toward her and her heart turned over. For the past hour she'd made herself forget the kiss. She was afraid to dwell on it, afraid she would read too much into it.

Now alone with him in the quiet studio, the memory of it hovered like a dense, provocative cloud between them.

"Same time tomorrow?" Slade asked. His voice was casual enough, but the telltale muscle twitched in his cheek, betraying his tension.

"Yes." She made her smile superficial. "We should be finished with the studio tomorrow, then we can concentrate on the location shots. You've done very well, considering your lack of experience."

He nodded. "I forgot to mention, I have an appointment at the hospital tomorrow afternoon. They want to check my shoulder. I made it as late as possible but I have to be there by five."

"No problem. We should be through by then." She picked up her purse, avoiding his gaze. They were talking like two strangers, she thought miserably. It was obvious he regretted the impulse that had prompted that kiss. Well, he wasn't the only one. She was a fool to have let it happen.

She made a pretense of looking at her watch. "I must run," she said, taking care not to look at him. "Michael's school is out at five-thirty and I have to pick him up."

"Mind if I come along?"

She looked up then, but his face remained as impassive as ever. "Not at all," she said, and turned away from him. "Michael will be happy to see you."

"Good. I'd like to take him out for a hamburger, if that's all right with you?"

"No, that's fine." She walked rapidly toward the door, trying not to mind that the invitation hadn't included her.

He caught up with her when she stepped outside into the bright sunlight. "I'll follow you in my car," he said, "so don't drive too fast."

"I never do." She managed to give him a faint smile. "It's only a few blocks away, you won't get lost."

He nodded, started to move away, then hesitated. "Would you like to join us?"

Piqued at the afterthought, Kate shook her head. "Can't. I've got some things to take care of."

He looked at her a moment longer, his eyes empty of emotion, then shrugged and turned away. She watched him walk toward his car, angry with him for creating the depression settling in her stomach, and furious with herself for caring so much.

When would she ever learn? she stormed inwardly as she nosed her car into the rush-hour traffic. Slade Montana was a loner, a charming drifter who was incapable of deep feelings or lasting emotions.

She would see that Michael got the best out of the time he had left with his father, but she was damned if she was going to raise any hopes that Slade might stick around. As soon as the shoot was over, he'd be off again. She knew it and he knew it. That's why he regretted kissing her.

That wasn't supposed to have happened, he'd said. He was damn right it shouldn't have happened, and she should have prevented it.

She stomped on the brake when she reached the corner and turned. She was going to make darn good and sure that it didn't happen again, she vowed as she entered the school parking lot. The sooner Slade Montana was out of her life again, the better.

Michael was waiting for her, and let out a yelp of excitement when told he was going to eat dinner with Slade. He seemed momentarily perturbed when she told him she wasn't going with them, but soon recovered when Slade promised him they'd bring home a treat for Mom.

Kate hugged the thin body and watched him climb into Slade's car, holding her smile until she waved them out of sight. She knew now that offering Slade Montana the modeling assignment was the second biggest mistake of her life.

It didn't help to acknowledge that, while she might have resigned herself to spending her life without him, she was every bit as much in love with him now as she'd ever been.

And being around him was not going to help her deal with it.

She drove home slowly, aware that this time the pain of losing him was going to be far more potent, and infinitely more long lasting, than it had been the first time around. It was a heavy price to pay. She could only hope that one day Michael would fully appreciate what she had done for him.

Chapter 5

Too restless to read or watch television, Kate was cleaning out the refrigerator when Slade and Michael returned. Michael talked incessantly, describing his meal in minute detail.

"We brought you a present," he announced when the three of them were seated in the living room. "Slade has it in his pocket."

Kate glanced across to where Slade sprawled in her armchair. His legs seemed too long to fit comfortably. He wore a cream shirt with his jeans, and looked a lot cooler than she felt.

He raised his hips to reach into his pocket and Kate looked away as the tug in her stomach teased her again.

"We both picked it out," Michael said, his eyes shining with excitement.

Slade leaned forward and gave the small, flat package to Michael. "You can do the honors," he said, giving him a wink.

Michael took it and looked solemnly at Kate. "We wanted you to know we missed you," he said, holding out the gift.

Kate smiled. She took the package and leaned forward to plant a kiss on his cheek. "Thank you, honey," she said softly. "I missed you, too."

She wasn't going to put any emphasis on that "we," she thought as she unfolded the square of tissue. She caught her breath in delight as she stared down at the little silver horse in her palm. A tiny turquoise bead formed its eye, and a delicate silver chain served as reins.

She looked up, and found Slade watching her, his expression unreadable. "It's exquisite," she said warmly. "I love it. Thank you."

For an instant an answering warmth flickered in his dark eyes, then Michael said, "See? I told you she'd love it!"

Kate turned and hugged him. "You bet I love it. I'll treasure it forever and ever." Over his head her eyes met Slade's.

The warmth was still there. The memory returned, sharp and clear, of his mouth on hers, demanding and relentless. She couldn't contain the leap of awareness that seemed to flow in a river of communication, joining them, pulsing between them like a living thing.

She saw his eyes darken, his mouth soften, and knew he felt it, too. The Michael wriggled out of her arms. "Can I show Slade how to play Chutes and Ladders?" he asked eagerly.

Kate looked at her watch. "One quick game, if Slade has time?"

"I have time." His gaze lingered on her face for a second longer.

"All right!" Michael bounded off the couch and dashed for his room.

He returned with the game and she left them to it while she finished cleaning the refrigerator. Unashamedly listening to their conversation, she tried to ignore the warm, tingling sensations that washed over her when she heard their voices arguing, teasing, explaining, laughing—all the sounds of a father and son being where they should be. Together.

Michael had never had that with Vic. He'd never known a father's love, the caring and understanding. He'd known only neglect, terror and pain from Vic.

Her face twisted at the agony of remembering. It had taken all her courage to break free, and when she had, she had nearly lost the one thing that mattered to her—her son.

She sank back on her heels and pushed wisps of hair back from her forehead. Not tonight. She would not let the nightmares spoil tonight. She stood and went through the door into the living room.

Michael sat cross-legged on the carpet, while Slade lay full-length on his stomach, his chin propped on his hands. The board, scattered with game pieces, lay between them.

Kate suppressed the sweet ache of tenderness and smiled at Michael. "Okay, your time's up. I'll run your bath while you pick up."

Michael looked as if he would protest, but one look at her face and he changed his mind. "Okay," he said, his voice heavy with reluctance.

Slade rolled over and sat up. "You go ahead, Mike, I'll clean this up."

"Thanks." Michael got slowly to his feet. "Will you come and say good-night?"

"Sure." He grinned. "If you promise to tell me a story."

Michael looked surprised, then delighted. "Okay!" He rushed from the room and Kate laughed.

"That's the first time he's been excited about going to bed."

Slade was on his knees, gathering up the pieces of the game. Without looking up he said casually, "Does he have nightmares?"

She felt a faint chill touch her spine. "Why do you ask?"

"I just wondered."

She stared down at him, feeling the chill spread across her back. "Has he said anything?"

This time he looked up at her, and she saw the wariness in his eyes. "About what?"

"About nightmares."

Slade looked down at the counters in his hands. "What's been going on, Kate?"

She swallowed. In the back of her mind she knew the questions would eventually come. She wasn't ready for them yet. She didn't know if she would ever be ready for them.

She was saved from answering when Michael called from the bedroom, "Mom? You've gotta run my bath."

"I'll be just a few minutes," she said, and hurried from the room, thankful for the reprieve.

Slade stared down at the colored counters without seeing them. It wasn't so much what Michael had said while they were eating hamburgers at the restaurant. It was more in the evasions and the look in his eyes when Slade had mentioned Vic. No seven-year-old boy should have that look in his eyes. It was uncomfortably close to his own memories, and he couldn't bear to think about the possibilities that look aroused.

He'd brought up the subject of Vic more or less by accident when questioning Michael about his interests. He'd been shocked by the boy's reaction. It had taken him some time to coax Michael back to his carefree mood again.

Slade folded the board and placed it in the box. He had to know, he decided with a fierce determination. Maybe it was none of his business, but he had to know. He couldn't leave with this suspicion gnawing at him. He would wonder about it for the rest of his life.

He tipped the counters on top of the board and replaced the lid. He had to be mistaken. He couldn't let himself think otherwise. He just wanted to know that he'd misunderstood Michael's reaction, and could leave with a peace of mind.

After all, he assured himself, Michael was his flesh and blood. He may not have the right to probe into their personal business, but it didn't change the way he felt. If he was to have any peace, *he had to know*.

He looked up with a start as Kate came back in the room. The loose blue top she wore with her jeans matched her eyes. For just a moment he saw the woman that had once clung to him, filling his night with stormy desire and a fierce, untempered passion.

He fought the urge to take her in his arms. He'd made that mistake earlier that afternoon. He couldn't afford to make another one. That kiss had taught him one thing. All the control he'd built up over the years, all the discipline he'd forced on his body, crumpled like dust when he held her in his arms.

He dared not get that close again. He would not leave himself open to that kind of pain ever again. With an effort he dragged the protective layer back in place. It had served him well over the years; it would protect him now.

Kate made an effort to smile as she met Slade's brooding stare. She would have given her right arm to know what he was thinking, but she knew the futility of asking. "Michael's waiting to tell you a story," she said lightly. "Try not to get him too excited. He has enough trouble going to sleep as it is."

Slade lifted his hand in a mock salute. "Yes, ma'am."

She watched him leave the room, a slight frown creasing her brow. She felt uneasy, sensing a purpose behind his casual smile.

She sank onto the couch, not really surprised to find her hands trembling. How much should she tell him if he asked? How much did he have a right to know?

She was still trying to make up her mind when Slade walked back into the room. "That kid has one hell of an imagination," he said, chuckling.

"I know." She looked up at him, her mind a chaos of warring emotions. It was too late now to worry about the consequences of her foolishness in contacting him again. She could only hope that both she and Michael would have the resilience to survive losing him.

"Would you like a drink?" she offered. "I have beer in the fridge, or wine?"

"A beer sounds good. I'll get it." He disappeared into the kitchen. "What are you having?"

"Wine, please. You'll find glasses in the cupboard." She slipped her sandals off and pulled her feet up under her in her favorite position for relaxing.

It sounded so good to hear him rattling glasses in the kitchen. A warm, domestic sound, comforting and secure. She caught herself, cursing her lack of restraint. It would be all too easy to slip into an acceptance of his presence. It would make it all the more painful when he left.

She looked up when he returned with the drinks and took her glass from him with what she hoped was a casual smile. "Thanks." She sipped the wine and set the glass down on the table.

"Kate." The way he said her name warned her, and she tensed.

"I want to know what happened," Slade said quietly, and lowered himself into the armchair.

She didn't pretend not to understand him. It would have been a waste of time. She concentrated on relaxing her shoulders, and picked up a cushion. Hugging it she said, "I don't think I can talk about it."

"I need to know, Kate."

She looked at him then, unsettled by the urgency in his voice. "Why? Is it that important to you?"

"He's my son. I have a right to know."

She would have argued that point, if it hadn't been for her own guilt. Hugging the cushion tighter, she stared at the floor. "I thought I knew Vic," she said slowly. "He'd been part of our family for so long. After my family . . . after the fire, he was all I had left of the memories.''

''I know. I knew you were close to him, but I never thought you felt that way about him.''

''I didn't.'' She kept her eyes on the floor, afraid of looking at him now. ''When we . . . when I realized that you were so unhappy, that whatever you were trying to be just wasn't working, I knew we could never have a life together. You were like a caged bird, always looking out through the bars, longing for your freedom.''

''I would have stayed, if you hadn't told me to go.''

''For how long? Until we'd buried whatever we had together under a mountain of regrets, disappointments and lost dreams?''

She stirred restlessly, and pulled her feet out to stretch them in front of her. ''You didn't love me, Slade. Not in the way I needed you to love me. You gave me everything except yourself, and I couldn't live with that. I couldn't go on watching you trying to make me happy when you didn't even understand what it was I wanted.''

He didn't answer, and she made herself go on. ''When I found out I was pregnant, I didn't know what to do. Vic was the only person I could talk to. He was so kind, so understanding. He said he'd always loved me. He hadn't said anything before because he felt that fifteen years made too big an age gap. And by the time I was old enough for it not to matter, I'd met you.''

She glanced at Slade, but the intensity of his gaze disturbed her, and she looked away. ''Anyway, I told Vic I didn't love him, but he said it didn't matter. He just wanted to take care of me and the baby. He would ask for nothing more.''

She lifted her hand in a helpless gesture and let it drop. ''I was determined to have the baby. Marrying Vic seemed the only way out. I even thought I might come to love him in time. He was comfortable to be with, and he wanted the same things I wanted—a home and a family.''

"So what went wrong?"

She heard a note of impatience in his voice and curbed her resentment. Hearing all this must be as difficult for him as it was for her to tell it.

"Everything was fine until after Michael was born. Then Vic seemed to change. He was jealous of Michael, of the attention I was giving him. He started making snide remarks and ordering me around. He became domineering, insisting I was spoiling Michael."

She shuddered and clasped the cushion to her chest, as if to protect herself from the memories. "We argued, always about Michael. When Michael started having nightmares, Vic wouldn't let me go to him. Michael became afraid of the dark; he'd cry for me, and I'd have to lie there and listen to him.''

She jumped when Slade swore. "Why did you put with it?" he demanded harshly.

She looked at him, tears prickling at her eyelids. "Because he threatened to beat Michael. He said it would make a man of him.''

A tear fell to her cheek and she brushed at it angrily with her hand. "Michael was only three years old. I was terrified Vic would hurt him if I didn't do what he said. There were times when Vic would behave irrationally, throwing things and swearing, accusing me of all kinds of crazy things. I knew I'd made a mistake, but I was afraid to leave him. I was afraid he would take it out on Michael.''

She took a shuddering breath and went on. "One day I came home from the grocery store. Michael had a cold and Vic was taking care of him. Michael was crying when I got home, and Vic said he'd fallen down the back steps. When I looked at him I saw he was covered with bruises.''

She gulped in air. Even now nausea gripped her when she thought about it. She waited for it to subside, conscious of

Slade's silence. "I questioned Michael, but he wouldn't say anything. I knew those bruises hadn't been caused by a fall. I knew then I had to do something.

"I called a lawyer, Ross Madigan. He told me to get out of there right away. He took me into his own home until he found us a place to stay, and I filed for divorce." She paused, finding it too painful to go on.

Across the room Slade moved, shifting his weight to lean forward. "So where is Vic now? Has he tried to see Michael?"

She began to cry quietly, in a helpless way that sliced into his heart like a thousand knives. The depth of her emotion scared him. He wanted to take her in his arms, to comfort her, yet something held him back.

She'd been right about the cage, he thought helplessly. Except he hadn't been on the inside looking out; he'd been on the outside looking in. Everything he longed to be part of had been shut away from him. He'd had to learn that some things were locked away, forever beyond his reach.

He couldn't deal with this kind of emotion; he'd spent his life trying to avoid it. He wanted to explain, but how could he expect her to understand? How could he tell her that the freedom she thought he was looking for was the deserted island he'd been forced to roam, exiled and alone?

Through her tears she began to talk again, and he was horrified to hear the words she was saying. "The day the divorce became final," she said, her voice breaking, "I left Michael with a sitter while I went for a job interview. When I came back I found the sitter locked in the bathroom, and Michael unconscious on the floor."

Her voice dropped to a near whisper. "The sitter was hysterical, but she managed to tell me that Vic had forced his way in and threatened her. She'd run for the bathroom and had heard Michael's screams. She knew Vic was beating him, but was too afraid to try and help..."

Kate's voice trailed off and she reached for a tissue in her pocket. Dabbing at her cheeks she smothered a sob. It was the first time she'd talked about it since the court case. It had been painful, but in some strange way therapeutic, too.

She found she could look at Slade and was shocked by the agony on his face. "I called the police," she said, rushing to reassure him. "They took Michael to the hospital and arrested Vic. The jury found him mentally unbalanced and he was sentenced to a mental hospital."

Slade still had that haunted look in his eyes and she struggled on, striving to erase the horror. "Michael spent four weeks in the hospital. He had some problems when he came out, mostly nerves. He'd doing a lot better now. Every day is a step farther from the past. We've managed to put it behind us."

Slade blinked, as if he were coming out of the darkness into the light. "You might have put it behind you." He reached for his beer. "That boy hasn't. The fear is still there. It's in his eyes, in his voice; it still haunts him. For God's sake, how could you have picked a man like that to be his father?"

Shaken by his hostility and his lack of understanding, Kate stared at him. "Don't you think I've asked myself that a thousand times? Isn't it a little late for all this concern? Where were you when it was all happening? When we needed you?"

She stared at his face in horror. Had she really said the words out loud? She knew she had when she saw the despair in his eyes.

"You didn't want me in your lives, remember? I thought you knew what you were doing. I thought Vic would make a better father than I ever could. I could almost forgive you for what you did because I figured the boy would have a better life with someone he could rely on."

"And now you can't forgive me." She swallowed past the lump in her throat. "You've found out I made a mess of things, and you're blaming me for what happened."

He put his glass down on the table and stood. "I blame us both, Kate. Between us we managed to put a little boy through hell. That's going to take some living with. I'm not sure how I'm going to deal with that."

She made no effort to move as he walked to the door and opened it. She sensed him looking at her, but refused to meet his gaze. The door closed quietly behind him, and she let the tears fall, too drained to check them. It was sometime later before she realized she hadn't told him that Vic had been released.

Even Michael noticed her depression the next morning, though she did her best to hide it. He gave her a fierce hug when she dropped him off at the school. "Don't you feel good, Mom?" he asked anxiously.

Smiling, she reassured him and, with her heart brimming with love, watched the small figure in the yellow shirt until he disappeared around the corner of the building.

She waited with some trepidation for Slade to arrive at the studio. When he walked in, five minutes late, she knew by her rush of relief that she had half expected him not to turn up.

He was as cooperative as ever, exchanging light comments with Bob, but coolly polite toward her. Once more he had become a stranger, and she was very much afraid that this time he'd withdrawn from her for good.

She was relieved when it came time for him to keep his appointment at the hospital. "Don't forget," she told him on his way out. "We'll be doing location shots tomorrow. It would help if you could get here a half hour earlier?"

He nodded without giving her more than a brief glance. "See you in the morning, then," he said, and left.

She walked back to her office, wondering if he would simply choose not to turn up in the morning. Depressed and indescribably weary, she was irritated when her boss called and asked her to finish up a report he needed that evening.

She glanced at her watch and grimaced. It would take at least an hour. She picked up the phone in her office, called Michael's school and asked that he be put on the bus. That done, she called Ellen, his sitter, and told her to expect him at his usual time. Then she resigned herself to a solid hour's work.

It took longer than an hour. Unable to concentrate she found herself staring at a blank page, and cursed her wayward thoughts. She could feel a headache threatening, and glared at the phone when it rang at her elbow.

Snatching up the receiver she muttered her name, becoming instantly alert when she heard Ellen's voice. "Kate? I'm sorry to bother you."

"What is it?" She'd spoken sharply, hearing the tension in Ellen's normally calm tones.

"Kate, I don't want to worry you, but did you change your mind about sending Michael here?"

She struggled with the sharp rise of panic. She'd learned to control her overreaction to the slightest provocation. Even so, something cold and evil crawled into her belly. "He's not with you?"

She knew, before Ellen answered, that the nightmare—the terrible, unbelievable nightmare she'd refused to consider—had finally happened.

"Kate, I'm sorry. When he didn't turn up I called Pamela. She's my neighbor's child. She said that Michael didn't get on the bus. I was going to call the school but I thought I'd better check with you first in case—"

"I've got to hang up," Kate said abruptly. "I have to call the school." She jammed her thumb down on the rest button and released it, stabbing out the numbers as soon as she heard the dial tone.

The phone rang several times, each purr adding another layer of icy fear. "Damn it, answer!" she shouted into the receiver and almost immediately the line clicked.

"Janitor."

She could have wept in frustration. "I need to talk to the secretary. It's an emergency."

"I'm sorry, ma'am, she's gone. They've all gone home."

Nausea, swift and potent, rose to her throat. Swallowing, she pleaded, "Isn't anyone there? A teacher, anyone?"

"I don't think so, ma'am, but if you'll hold on, I'll check."

She waited, drumming her fingers on the table, her nerves slowly tightening until the drumming seemed to reverberate throughout her entire body. She reached the end of her patience and slammed the phone down, snatching it up again immediately. Dialing Ellen's number, she waited.

"Hello?"

"This is Kate. I need to talk to Pamela."

"Oh, Kate, I was going to tell you, but you hung up so fast. Pamela said that Michael got into a car with a man, that's what worried me. Pamela said that Michael had been talking about his new friend—a rodeo rider? I wondered if it was a friend of yours, and that he'd picked up Michael for you."

"What did he look like?" Kate demanded, hanging on to a last slender thread of hope.

"What?"

"The man who picked up Michael. What did he look like?" Aware that she'd raised her voice, she muttered an apology.

"No, look, I'm sorry..." Ellen sounded frantic. "I'll go get Pam, you can talk to her, just hold on."

The silence at the end of the line stretched into cold, empty space. Kate reached for a pencil, something to hang on to, something to control her trembling fingers. The pencil snapped in two as Pamela's high voice came on the line.

"Hello?"

Kate took a deep breath. There was no point in frightening the child; she'd get nothing out of her that way.

"Hello, Pamela. This is Michael's mom. Ellen tells me you saw him get into a car this afternoon?"

"Yes. It was a real old car, not shiny like yours."

Slade had an old car. Kate closed her eyes and prayed. "Did you see the man? What did he look like? What was he wearing?" What *was* Slade wearing? She tried to think, her brain fuzzy.

"I don't remember what his clothes were like. He had dark hair."

For a brief moment she allowed herself to hope. "Was he a tall man, or short?"

The pause on the end of the line threatened to snap the last vestiges of her control. "Short," Pamela said in her clear voice. "Short and fat. He had a round, red face like my doctor, only my doctor's eyes are brown and Michael's friend's eyes are blue."

Kate's teeth sunk into her bottom lip as Pamela added, "He didn't look like a rodeo rider and Michael was acting real funny, like he was scared or something. He didn't look at me when I spoke to him, he just got in the car and—"

"Thank you, Pamela." Kate eased her fingers on the receiver, allowing the blood to flow back into them. "Let me talk to Ellen now."

"Kate? What do you want me to do?"

Grateful for her friend's composure Kate said unsteadily, "Pray. I'll let you know as soon as I know something."

She let the receiver fall back in place, and pressed both hands over her mouth. Not now. She couldn't fall apart now. She needed to think. Where would Vic take him?

Oh, God, Michael, hold on. I'll find you, just hold on. She forced the image of his terrified face out of her mind. She needed to think. She couldn't concentrate if she let herself think about Michael now.

A sudden sharp, intense longing for Slade sliced through her senses. Slade. He had to be told. He had a right to know. And she needed him now as she'd never needed him before.

He was still in the trailer behind the arena. He'd told her he'd asked for an extension, until he was ready to travel again. There was no phone in the trailer, Kate thought in silent desperation; she'd have to go out there.

It would take too long. There had to be something she could do. Impatient with herself she lifted the receiver and dialed the emergency number for the police.

The voice that answered her was polite, sympathetic and unbelievably apologetic. After listening to Kate's story, and her convictions that it was her ex-husband who had kidnapped her son, he informed her that since it was a custody case, his hands were tied.

"This is a civil matter," he told Kate gently. "The best thing you can do is call your lawyer."

"You don't understand," Kate said, her voice raw with desperation. "Vic Wheeler is dangerous. He'd just been released from a mental hospital. He hates Michael. He'll hurt him if we don't find him, I know he will."

"I'm sorry, Mrs. Wheeler. Legally he's the boy's father. He hasn't committed a crime, and we can't arrest him for taking his own son. That's something you'll have to fight out in court."

"And what if he hurts Michael, or kills him? Do I fight that in court?" Kate asked bitterly.

"Come now," the officer said soothingly. "It's very doubtful he'll hurt the boy. Fathers who snatch their children usually do so because they love them, they want to be with them."

"And do fathers usually end up in a mental hospital for abusing their children?" She could hear the hysteria in her voice and made an effort to control it.

The officer sighed loud enough for her to hear. "I'm sorry. I do understand what you're going through, Mrs. Wheeler. I wish I could help. I suggest you call your lawyer."

She slammed the receiver down in a fury of frustration and fear. "It's Templeton," she yelled at the offending instrument. "Not Mrs. Wheeler—Templeton. Miss Kate Templeton." The last word ended on a sob and she held her breath until it subsided. She had no time for the luxury of tears.

She reached for the phone again and dialed Ross Madigan's number. His answering service announced he'd left for the day and she called his home.

Eve, his wife, answered. Full of shocked sympathy to hear Kate's story she suggested Kate drive over to the house to wait for Ross, who was at a business meeting.

Kate declined. "I want to be at home," she explained, "in case—" Her voice broke and she struggled in silence for several seconds.

"I'll have him call as soon as he gets home," Eve said. "Do you want me to come over?"

"No," Kate said shakily. "No thanks, Eve. You have the baby to take care of. I'll be fine. Really."

She hung up before Eve could protest, and picked up her purse. She'd have to go home and wait for Ross's call. Maybe she'd be able to concentrate at home, she thought, letting herself out of the office. Ross would know what to do.

The emptiness of her apartment seemed to close around her, choking her with clammy fingers. Michael's slippers lay where he'd dropped them that morning, and she picked them up, pressing the soft fur against her face.

She felt cold inside, so very cold, yet she couldn't bring herself to make coffee. She opened the door to the refrigerator, then closed it again. The thought of food turned her stomach.

Again and again she looked at her watch as she wandered from room to room, unable to settle. She stood by the phone in the living room, willing it to ring, knowing that even when it did, she couldn't expect too much. If the police couldn't help, what could Ross do?

She wanted to go to Slade, but was afraid to leave the house. The need to see him, to tell him, became unbearable. She looked up the number of the rodeo arena in the phone book. Maybe someone was there who could bring him to the phone, she thought, without much hope.

She had her hand on the phone when it rang, startling her. She snatched up the receiver, unable to quell the hope that it would be Michael's voice on the line. The strength seeped from her legs when she heard Vic's asthmatic wheeze.

"Hello, Kate."

She sank onto the couch, the receiver jammed against her ear. "Where is he? If you've hurt him—"

"He's fine." Vic coughed. "He'll stay fine as long as you don't interfere."

Kate closed her eyes and prayed for the right words. "Vic, listen to me. He's only a little boy, he doesn't even understand what's going on. Why don't you come over here? We can talk and—"

"No way. You and that fancy lawyer of yours are not going to get me again. You put me in that snake pit, and it took me three years to make it out. There's no way I'm going back."

She recognized that tone. She'd heard it often enough when he was building up into one of his rages. She gripped the phone. "No one wants to send you back, Vic. Bring Michael back and—"

"I told you. No way. I've missed him; I want to spend some time with my son."

"Well, we can come to some arrangement." She struggled to put conviction in her voice. "He has to go to school in the week, but perhaps on the weekends—"

His laugh made her blood run cold. "You'll what? Let me take him out? What's his daddy gonna say to that?"

Her lips felt numb. She had to make them move, somehow. "You're his daddy," she whispered.

"Is that right? Then why is that rodeo drifter hanging around him? Does he know I'm Mikey's daddy, or is he figuring on staking his claim now that I'm out of the picture?"

How he'd found out Slade was in town she didn't know. She only knew that the situation was even more dangerous than she'd feared. "Slade is working for me," she said, striving to keep her voice calm. "It has nothing to do with Michael."

"Oh, no? Then perhaps you'd like to explain to me how come he was at Mikey's swim meet, all cozy and friendly?"

The news reporter's photo, Kate thought, her heart sinking. It had appeared in the local paper. A copy of it hung on the wall of Michael's bedroom. The three of them, with Michael gazing up at Slade with unmistakable adoration shining in his face—plus a full account of where Michael went to school.

"I gave that boy a home," Vic said fiercely. "I gave you both a home when that drifter took off and left you. We could've worked things out, you and I. But you always were strong willed. I spoiled you, that's the trouble."

He coughed again, and frightened tears ran down Kate's cheeks. "Vic, please, Michael will be scared, he doesn't understand. Bring him home and I swear—"

"You can swear all you like," Vic interrupted savagely. "If you think I'm gonna trust a lying bitch like you, you're out of your mind. I missed my boy, and I'm gonna catch up on some time. You stay out of it, and he'll be fine. You set the police after me, or especially that no-good bum you're hanging around with, and you'll never see Michael again. I'll see to that.''

"No!" Kate screamed as the line went dead. "Vic, for God's sake...." The tears came then, fast and furious. She couldn't seem to stop them. They seeped through her fingers and ran down her chin, while huge sobs racked her body.

It was the frantic ringing of the doorbell that finally quietened the storm. Her tears stilled by the sudden blazing hope, she stumbled across the room and dragged the door open. Her crushing disappointment when she saw Ross almost destroyed her.

"I'm sorry," he said as he stepped through the door. "Eve called me; I came straight over."

"Thank you," Kate whispered. "For a moment I thought it might have been Michael."

Ross groaned. "Oh, God, I'm sorry, Kate. You'd better sit down and tell me everything you know."

She did so, in a lifeless voice she hardly recognized as her own. Ross listened without interrupting until her words trailed off into silence.

"Listen to me, Kate," he said, leaning forward to take her cold hands in his. "Vic won't hurt Michael. You've got to believe that. Vic has been cured, he's no longer irrational. Maybe he does simply want to spend time with the boy. He didn't make any threats against him, did he?"

Kate shook her head. "Just that I wouldn't see him again if I sent anyone after him." She stared down at their joined hands, her face creased in despair. "He hates Michael. He took him to get back at me. He saw the photo in the paper, of Slade and me together with Michael. He's jealous, he's always been jealous of Slade."

She looked up to find Ross looking at her, his unusual golden eyes filled with curiosity. He didn't know, she realized suddenly. She hesitated, wondering if she should tell him, then decided it really didn't make any difference now.

"Michael isn't Vic's son," she said quietly. "He's Slade Montana's."

If Ross was shocked he gave no sign of it. "Does Vic know that?"

Kate nodded. "He's always known."

"I see." Ross stroked his chin with his long fingers. "That does put a different light on it."

Kate made a small whimpering noise in the back of her throat and he clasped her hands again. "I'm still convinced Vic doesn't want to hurt the boy. He'll probably keep him for a while, just long enough to drive you insane with worry, then he'll bring him back. He said himself he doesn't want to go back to the hospital. He's smart enough to know that's exactly what would happen if he hurt Michael."

"And I'm supposed to sit around and wait?" Kate pulled her hands from his grasp. "I can't do that, Ross. There must be something I can do."

He sighed, and got to his feet. "I wish I could say there was, Kate. I'll go to the police and make sure they file a report, but other than that, as they said, Vic hasn't committed a crime."

Kate sprang up, refusing to believe his calm acceptance. "He has a restraining order against him. Isn't that committing a crime?"

"A civil complaint. That's all we have. The police won't touch it. They simply don't have the time. They're up to their armpits in burglaries and assaults, not to mention rape and murder. A civil case is not on their list of priorities." He reached for her and gave her a gentle hug.

"I'll do what I can, Kate. I promise you. You want Eve to come over?"

Kate shook her head. "I have to find Slade, he has to be told."

"Of course." Ross turned toward the door, then looked back at her over his shoulder. "Don't do anything foolish, Kate. Promise me?"

She nodded absently, without attempting to look as if she meant it.

"Kate." Ross pulled the door open and fixed his pale gold eyes on her face. "Don't push Vic. Don't give him a reason to make a rash move. He's warned you about sending someone after him. Whatever you do, don't let Montana go looking for him."

Kate managed a shaky smile. "Thanks, Ross. I'll be careful."

He hesitated a moment longer, a worried frown drawing tiny lines on his brow. "I'll keep in touch," he said quietly, then stepped through the door and closed it behind him.

Kate stared at the door for a long moment, then went swiftly to the bedroom. She changed into jeans and a yellow sweatshirt, then dashed into the bathroom to splash her face with cold water and comb her hair.

Her car keys in one hand, her purse in the other, she let herself out of the apartment. No one wanted to help her, she thought in despair as she drove out to the freeway. Everyone she'd turned to had given her the same story. There was nothing she could do except wait.

There had to be something she could do; even if she had to do it alone. Slade would tell her what to do, how to start looking for Michael. She needed to see him, to make him understand. She was pinning all her hopes—her last hopes—on his ability and strength.

She roared up the ramp and into the flow of traffic, ignoring all the rules for safety. She had one objective on her mind—to find Slade and beg him to help her.

Please, she pleaded silently as she sped along the darkened highway. *Please, Slade, don't let me down now.*

Chapter 6

The field was in darkness as Kate drove slowly across the grass toward the trailer. Light gleamed in the tiny windows, raising her hopes. She stepped on the brake and cut the engine, then threw open the door and scrambled out.

Using both fists she pounded on the trailer door. Heart-stopping moments ticked by while her pounding went unheeded, then the door opened.

Slade stood silhouetted against the light, dressed only in a pair of jeans. He held a towel in his hand, and beads of water still clung to his dark chest hair. He stared at her in astonishment, saying nothing.

She opened her mouth to speak, but could manage no more than a weak croak. Holding her hands out toward him she took a faltering step, and her knees buckled. He reached for her, and drew her across the threshold. Kicking the door shut he drew her into his arms and she buried her face against his cool skin.

He wasn't going to do this again, Slade thought as the contact of her face against his bare flesh reminded him how potent his reaction had become to her touch. If she didn't look so stricken, so helpless... His stomach contracted when he felt the trembling that shook her from head to toe. He made himself hold on to her.

"What is it?" he muttered, cradling her closer in an attempt to stop the shivering. "For God's sake, Kate, what's happened?"

She drew a shaky breath and lifted her face. "Michael," she whispered. "Vic's taken him. I don't know where he is."

It took him a moment to take in what she'd said. Then disbelief and shock hit him in quick succession. "You said Vic was in a hospital."

"He was." She stirred, then pulled back. He let her go. "He was released just over a week ago."

Anger rose so swiftly it threatened to choke him. "How did he get hold of Michael?"

Kate's shoulders lifted in a helpless gesture. "He picked him up after school. I was delayed, so I left a message for Michael to go to his sitter's."

Her legs felt rubbery and she sat down quickly on the long, narrow seat. "Vic must have told the teacher he was Michael's father. Michael would have had to confirm that. He probably told Michael I'd sent him, I don't know—" Her voice broke and she pressed a trembling hand to her mouth.

Slade draped the towel around his neck and sat down next to her. "Take it easy. Are you sure it was Vic?"

Kate nodded, swallowed and tried again to control the awful dry sobs that tore at her throat. "He—called me," she said when she could speak again. "He said he just wanted to spend some time with Michael, and if I tried, if I sent the police or you—"

"He knows I'm here?" Slade's voice rose sharply.

Again Kate nodded. "The picture in the paper, he saw it. That's how he found Michael. That's probably why he did it. He's jealous. Oh, Slade."

She looked up, appalled by the stark despair in his dark eyes. "There has to be something I can do," she pleaded.

"What about the police?"

"I called them. They said it was a civil case, they can't do anything." She was beginning to feel calmer now. Just being close to him was enough for the moment. His solid presence was comforting, though the expression in his eyes worried her.

"I called Ross, too," she said. "He more or less told me the same thing. He said there's nothing we can do but wait."

Slade's vicious oath startled her. "The hell we can't." He stood, both hands tugging at the towel around his neck. "Do you know where Vic was living, where he went to after he left the hospital?"

"No," she said miserably, then a thought struck her. "The hospital! I don't know why I didn't think of it before. They'd know, wouldn't they?"

"There's one way to find out," Slade said grimly. "We'll call them. You're his ex-wife, they may tell you. Wait while I get a shirt."

She sat, twisting her hands in her lap, while Slade rummaged in the drawer beneath the opposite seat. He dragged out a soft denim shirt and pulled it on, buttoning it swiftly before tucking it in his jeans.

"We'll call from your place," he said, switching off lights before opening the door. "We'll take your car. It will take too long to unhitch mine."

They were halfway there before the significance of that remark dawned on her. He'd hitched up his trailer. He'd intended to leave, without finishing the assignment. Without telling her?

She was too drained to be angry. Her problems with Slade paled into insignificance compared to her worries about Michael.

The apartment seemed colder than ever, in spite of the warm summer night. She flicked on the lamps, seeing Michael's ghost in every corner. Just last night, he'd been sprawled on that floor, laughing and joking with Slade...

She shut the images out of her mind. If she was going to survive this, she had to hold on to every ounce of control. "Would you like some coffee?" she asked as Slade reached for the phone book. "Or something stronger?"

"Coffee." He looked up. "Do you want me to make it?"

"No." She shook her head. "I need to do something. You look up the number." She gave him the name of the hospital, and went into the kitchen to plug in the percolator.

Her hands still shook when she reached for the mugs, but her stomach had stopped cramping and her head felt clearer now. For the first time in all the dreadful hours since she'd first heard the news, she was beginning to feel her strength returning. And with it a fierce determination.

If she had to search every town in the country, she would find Michael. No matter what it cost, no matter what it took, she would find him.

Slade called out to her and she hurried back into the living room. He was holding out the receiver, his set expression unsettling her. "I've got some doctor on the line, but I don't think he's going to help."

Kate took the phone from him and pressed it to her ear. She spoke rapidly, telling the voice on the line who she was and what had happened. The doctor was apologetic, but adamant. He could not give that kind of information out over the phone. Now if the police called him...

Kate handed the receiver back to Slade, shaking her head at the question in his eyes. "No one wants to help," she said hopelessly.

"They want to help," Slade said, replacing the receiver. "It's the system that's the problem. They're too damned worried about people's rights."

"What about Michael's rights? Or mine?" Kate gave a helpless shake of her head and went back to the kitchen where the percolator was bubbling noisily. The aroma of freshly brewed coffee did little to revive her sagging spirits.

She carried the steaming mugs into the living room, almost dropping them when a new idea occurred to her. "Gladys," she said, her heart accelerating with hope.

Slade looked at her, his eyes bright with renewed interest. "Who's Gladys?"

"Vic's sister." Kate slapped the mugs on the table, heedless of the coffee slopping over the rims. "She's the only relative he's got. I bet he's taken Michael there, or at least she knows where he is."

She was leafing through her address book while she was talking, her fingers scrabbling feverishly through the pages. "Here!" She held up the book. "I knew I'd kept it. She lives in Nevada; I have her phone number here."

"Then call her," Slade said urgently.

Kate punched out some numbers, then hesitated. "What should I say? If he's there she's not likely to tell me. God knows what Vic has told her about me."

"Do you want me to talk to her?" Slade held out his hand.

Kate gave a violent shake of her head. "No. Vic warned me not to let you interfere. I'll do it."

She finished dialing the numbers, then waited, her heart pounding with hope. She flashed a look of triumph at Slade when she head the click of the line opening.

"Hello?" Gladys's voice sounded frail—and tense.

Kate took a firmer grip on the receiver. "Gladys? This is Kate. How are you?" A ludicrous question, she thought. She hadn't spoken to Gladys in four years, and had exchanged little more than a few conventional phrases with the woman.

The silence on the end of the line unnerved her. Afraid that Gladys might hang up, she said quickly, "Is Vic there? I'd really like to talk to him if he is."

"He's not here," Gladys said. "I ain't seen him."

"Has he called?" It took tremendous effort to hold the casual note in her voice. Her eyes met Slade's and he nodded in encouragement. "I have something important I want to tell him," she added desperately.

"I told you, he ain't here."

"But you know where he is," Kate said with quiet conviction.

"Leave them alone," Gladys said with a spurt of passion that surprised Kate. "Haven't you done enough?"

"Gladys—" The line went dead and she shook the phone in helpless frustration. "Damn."

She put the receiver back and looked at Slade. "She knows where they are," she said firmly. "I'm sure of it. I'm going to see her."

"Good idea. I'll come with you."

She met his gaze squarely. "No, just me. You can't come with me, Slade. You'll frighten Vic off for good."

Slade got up from the couch, his expression warning her of his resolve. "That's a chance we'll just have to take. I feel partly responsible for what happened. You're not going to do this alone."

"Yes, I am." She held up her hand as he started to speak. "Slade, we're talking about Michael's safety here. Vic made it clear what would happen if you tried to go after him."

She held out both hands in appeal. "You know as well as I do that he could take Michael out of the country, and they'd never be heard from again. It's happened time and time again, where children have disappeared off the face of the earth. I can't take the risk."

He stared at her, the muscle in his jaw working back and forth. "And what do you propose to do when you catch up with Vic? The police won't help you. Are you just going to walk up to him and demand he give Michael back? That's if you get close enough to ask anything."

"I can handle Vic," Kate stated with more confidence than she felt. "Once he sees me he'll listen to reason."

"And did he listen to reason when you talked to him this evening? Would he have listened to reason three years ago when he was beating Michael to a pulp?"

"Stop it!" she yelled, finally reaching the limits of how much she could take. "Do you think I want to go on my own? I just can't take the chance."

"And I won't take the chance of you blowing it." He didn't say "again," but she knew it hovered on his lips. "We go together, or not at all. I'm not letting you out of my sight until we get Michael back. And that's it, Kate. No deals."

She yielded under his grim persistence. Part of her had wanted to give in to him all along; she could no longer fight his iron will. She was too tired, she thought wearily, too empty to find the energy to oppose him.

Besides, most of what he said made sense. No matter what she did, she'd be taking a chance. Even if she did nothing, there was always the chance Vic would hurt Michael in some way. Together, she and Slade might have a better shot at getting him back.

"All right," she said, her voice flat with fatigue. "We'll go together."

"Good." He was already calling the airport even as she spoke.

She waited while he spoke rapidly into the phone, her anxiety mounting when it became apparent that there were no available flights that night.

Finally, his voice thick with exasperation, he booked two seats for an early morning flight to Reno. "I'm sorry," he said, replacing the phone. "It was the best I could do."

"I know." She felt a sudden rush of relief. Now that the decision was made she could admit her dread of facing the trip alone.

"You'd better get some sleep," Slade said. "It's likely to be a long day tomorrow."

"I don't think I can." Tired as she was, she couldn't imagine sleeping.

"Then you'll just have to try." He stood and gave her a searching look. "Go and soak in a warm bath. I'll warm up some milk and brandy, if you have any."

She looked up at him, surprised by his display of caring. "I have some whiskey, I think. In the cupboard over there."

He opened the cupboard and looked inside. "Scotch. This will do just fine. Now go run that bath."

She pulled herself to her feet and gave him a wan smile. "Slade?"

His eyes revealed nothing when he looked at her.

"Thanks," she said softly.

He nodded, then bent his head to examine the label of the bottle he held. She watched him for a moment longer, then turned and made her way to the bathroom.

He couldn't sleep. He really hadn't expected to. It wasn't just the inadequacy of the couch, though it was almost impossible to get comfortable when he surpassed the length of it by several inches. He was used to sleeping in cramped quarters and would have succeeded in doing so now if he could forget that Kate was just a few yards away in the next room.

Lying flat on his back in the dark only intensified the hunger that gnawed at him whenever he was near her. It galled him that his body could react this way when he should have more urgent things on his mind. But right then he couldn't do much about the crisis with Michael, and his needs were facing a crisis of their own.

He groaned quietly and shifted on his side to ease his discomfort. He should never have insisted on staying the night, but although Kate protested when he suggested it, she capitulated fast enough to convince him she was grateful for his presence. She didn't want to spend the night alone any more than he did.

Except right now he wanted a whole lot more than a skimpy couch in an empty room. He wanted to be in bed with her, holding her naked body to his burning flesh. He wanted to bury himself in her so deep he could erase all the hurt and misery of the past. He wanted to hear the low moans that used to set his blood racing and his heart pounding, and he wanted to feel the soft touch that always drove him out of his mind.

He brought his knees up to his chest as the agony of his need tortured his body. He had to stop thinking about it, he thought savagely. This wasn't the place or the time. And even if it was, she wasn't going to welcome him back in her bed with open arms.

He'd had his chance eight years ago and he'd blown it. And there wasn't a whole lot he could do about it. Cursing under his breath, he shifted his aching body again, and closed his eyes.

Kate had fallen into an exhausted sleep as soon as her head touched the pillow, but less than a hour later she was awake again, Michael's name on her lips. She slept fitfully after that, dozing off for moments at a time, only to come wide-awake with sweating palms and rapidly beating heart.

The thought of Slade sleeping on her couch in the living room kept her in her bed. She dared not get up and risk walking into him. She had never needed him quite as badly as she needed him now.

If only he could have been there, lying next to her, holding her in the warm security of his arms, some of the fear might be a little more bearable. She longed for the solid comfort of his body, and for the quiet reassurance of his voice, to hear his heart beating in the night and know he was there for her.

She stirred restlessly, staring into the darkness. It was impossible, of course. He'd misinterpret her motive if she told him what she wanted. He'd think she wanted him to make love to her.

Isn't that what you want? her mind demanded. She flung an arm across her face. God help her, it was, she thought hopelessly. Only in his arms could she erase the horror of what was happening. If only for a little while, she wanted to lose herself in the mindless heat of passion that only he could arouse in her.

Why? she asked the lonely night. Why couldn't he learn to love her? Why couldn't she reach that dark corner of his mind he escaped to whenever his emotions threatened to emerge?

If she knew that, she told herself ruefully, maybe then she could begin to understand him.

By the time her clock read 4:00 a.m., she had lost all desire to sleep and lay willing the next hour to pass quickly. She waited until five-thirty before she finally slipped out of bed.

They shared a light breakfast of cereal and coffee, which was all Kate could handle. Slade showered, then returned to the trailer to pack a bag, and she used the time alone to call her boss before doing her own packing.

She told him the whole story, explaining why the shoot would have to go on hold for a while. He was sympathetic and understanding, and she was beginning to feel a lot better by the time she hung up.

She tried to call Ross, but he hadn't arrived at his office and she was reluctant to bother Eve at that early hour. She'd nursed a faint hope that Vic might call again, but by the time Slade had returned to drive her to the airport, she knew it was a false hope.

Vic was going to make her pay in the worst way he knew how. He was going to make her sweat it out, not knowing when, or if, he was going to bring Michael back.

Just don't hurt him, she pleaded silently as Slade drove them to the airport. It was a plea she'd uttered over and over again through the long night.

The flight to Reno seemed endless. They had been lucky to get seats together on the crowded plane, a result of Slade's urgent explanations of an emergency to the sympathetic ticket clerk.

Slade shifted in his seat, his knees drawn up to accommodate his long legs in the narrow space allotted them. His muscles felt stiff after his restless night on the couch.

Kate's apartment had been the last place he'd expected to spend the night, he reflected wryly. It had been the second night in a row he'd lost sleep. He'd spent the night before going over and over what she'd told him about Vic's treatment of Michael.

Even then he'd wanted her as bad as ever. If not more. Eight years ago, when she'd first left him, the pain had helped him through the lonely nights. Whenever the need got too much for him, he'd let the bitterness take over. The pain subsided as he gradually came to terms with what had happened. But the need for her had never faded. No woman had ever been able to set him on fire the way she had.

Finally he'd given up trying to find a replacement. In time he hardly missed having a woman to share his nights with. Until he'd come face-to-face with Kate again.

Ever since then, the need—the hot, burning longing to feel her body merged with his—tormented his nights, driving him to the edge of endurance.

The force of that need scared him. He could not give in to it. He couldn't light those kind of fires again, he didn't have the power to survive the inferno he knew it would create.

He glanced at Kate and saw she was dozing, her lashes fluttering against her cheeks. A wave of tenderness almost overwhelmed him. If it was the last thing he did for her, he swore to himself, he'd bring Michael back to her.

Everything she had ever done, everything she had ever been, had been for his son. He knew that now. How could he blame her for that?

He leaned back and closed his eyes as pain knifed through him. He was the one to blame. He was the one who was scarred, incomplete, and no matter how much he wished otherwise, he couldn't change. God knows he'd tried.

There was one thing he could do. He could help her find their son. Maybe then, in the lonely years ahead, he'd have something to hang on to. The knowledge that there was one time when he hadn't let her down. He squeezed his eyes shut, and tried to sleep.

Kate listened to the drone of the engines, and the subdued voices of the passengers around them, rehearsing in her mind how she was going to approach Gladys. Vic's sister knew what had happened. Leave *them* alone, she had said. The only way she could have known Michael was with Vic was if Vic had called her. If Michael wasn't with her, there was a good chance she knew where he was. Kate was certain of that. It had been in Gladys's voice, in the abrupt way she'd hung up.

Kate tried to remember what she knew about Gladys. She remembered her as a short, dumpy woman with shifting eyes and a high-pitched giggle that had set her teeth on edge. Kate had only met her once, when Gladys had come to Portland for the Rose Parade and stayed overnight with them. Gladys hadn't spoken more than two words to her, Kate thought, remembering how nervous the woman had seemed.

She wondered if Gladys had known her brother was unstable, and had been scared of him. Maybe she was scared of him now, Kate thought, and that was why she wasn't telling them anything.

It gave her a small measure of hope to cling to. One thing she was certain of, if Gladys knew anything, anything at all, she and Slade would worm it out of her. Vic wasn't the only one who could be frightening.

She lifted her lashes and stole a look at Slade. His head leaned back against the headrest, his eyes tightly shut. She knew he wasn't sleeping, but the relentless expression on his face didn't encourage conversation, and she closed her eyes again.

She wasn't sure what she wanted to say to him, anyway. She had felt awkward that morning, alone in the apartment with him. She'd avoided looking at him whenever possible, afraid that her face would give away the hunger that had tormented her during the long night. Whatever she did, she could not let him know that in spite of everything, she still loved him, and probably always would.

She dozed, and awoke with a start when the captain announced over the intercom that they would be landing in five minutes.

Kate peered out the window, conscious of Slade stirring next to her. His arm pressed against hers, and she felt a piercing urge to reach for his hand. She resisted it, and kept her eyes glued on the swirling beige and browns of the Nevada desert. Far below them she could see the city of Reno shimmering in the summer heat.

On the ground, the hot, dry desert wind fanned Kate's skin as she stood waiting outside the busy airport. Slade had left her in charge of the luggage while he'd gone to see about renting a car.

All around her people poured in a steady stream in and out of the doors, some excitedly hailing cabs, while others dragged suitcases into the terminal. They all looked like people with normal lives, people with homes to go to, families waiting. She wondered if she'd ever feel normal again.

She rubbed her arms; even the fierce heat couldn't seem to warm her skin now. Where was Michael? Was he hurt? Frightened? She couldn't bear the thought of the long night he must have suffered. She could only hope and pray he knew she would be looking for him.

He needed something to hold on to. She knew only too well what it was like to suffer without hope. She closed her eyes, willing him to hear her as she vowed again to find him. Soon.

The insistent blaring of a car horn jerked her eyes open again. Slade was across the street, leaning from the window of a dilapidated-looking compact, his arms waving furiously.

Kate picked up the bags and struggled across the road, dodging slow-moving buses and cabs to reach him. Slade met her halfway across and took the bags from her.

"I didn't want to leave it double-parked," he said as he threw the bags through the open rear window. "The last thing we need is to get held up with a traffic ticket now."

Kate scrambled in the front seat, wishing she'd had time to change into shorts. Her cotton slacks were already sticking to her legs, and the collar of her shirt felt damp on her neck.

She eyed Slade as he pulled the small car into the traffic, and knew he had to be uncomfortable, too. He'd unbuttoned his shirt halfway down, and she could see sweat glistening beneath his collarbone.

"How do you turn on the air conditioner?" she asked examining the row of switches on the dashboard.

"It's broken." Slade swore as a car swerved out from the curb, narrowly missing his front bumper. "Sorry about that, but it was the only car I could get on short notice. This is the height of the tourist season."

Kate sighed and adjusted her sunglasses on her nose. "I guess we're lucky to get one at all."

She felt him send her a swift look. "It's going to be hot, but with the windows down you should be all right."

She nodded. Coping with the heat was the last of her worries. She glanced at her watch. "How far is it from here?"

"About an hour's drive. We should be there shortly after noon."

Her stomach twisted in knots when it occurred to her that Michael could be less than an hour away. She made herself put the thought out of her mind. She could not hope for too much, and the disappointment if she was wrong would be unbearable.

At least she was doing something, she thought. Anything was better than sitting around, helplessly waiting. She stared out of the window at the low buildings that lined the highway. It looked so dry, so desolate. And so vast.

So many places for someone to hide a small boy. They could search for years and never find him. She reined in the panic before it could take hold. She would not allow herself to consider defeat, she thought fiercely.

In an attempt to keep her mind off such undermining speculation, she turned to Slade. He was staring at the road, a slight frown drawing his brows together.

"Don't you have any sunglasses?" she asked in a fragile attempt to start a conversation.

"I've never worn them." He sent her a quick glance. "It's a little tough to keep them on your nose when a bull's doing its best to grind you into the dirt."

"I guess it is." She looked back at the road, watching dust devils whirl and dance across the shimmering pavement. They had left the town behind now and were speeding across the open desert. The buildings gradually dwindled to an occasional shack or two, then they, too, disappeared, leaving a vast emptiness of dust, sand and heat.

The road lay ahead, an endless, flat ribbon of reddish gray, narrowing to a thin thread in the hazy distance. The far horizon scarred the hot blue sky with a smudge of blue mountains, so far away they looked no bigger than molehills.

Kate blinked as puddles of water seemed to spread across the road in front of the car, disappearing as they drew nearer, only to reappear further ahead. The wind, rushing through the window, ruffled her hair, but failed to cool her burning cheeks. She seemed to be breathing fire—and dust.

She fanned herself with her purse, and heard Slade ask, "How are you doing?"

"All right. It seems so lonely out here, as if we're the only living things in the entire desert. I can't even see any birds."

"Most likely we are the only humans on the road. No one is crazy enough to drive this road at midday in mid-July. There's plenty of rattlesnakes, though, if you want company."

Kate shuddered. "No thanks, I'd rather have the loneliness." She felt a deep sense of gratitude that he hadn't even suggested they wait for the cooler temperature of evening. "I can't imagine anyone living out here," she added, looking at the acres of barren land.

"Well, people do. There are a few towns on this road before you hit Las Vegas, though a lot of them you can't call towns. They're mostly just a few buildings on the side of the highway."

"Why would anyone want to bury themselves out here?" Kate murmured.

"Some people are born in desert towns; they can't imagine living anywhere else. Then there are those who'd like to escape, but can't find the will to do it."

He leaned back, holding the wheel with one hand while he pulled his shirt free of his jeans. "Then there are the ones who go looking for a place to hide, to escape a world they can no longer deal with."

She watched him undo the rest of his shirt buttons, and allow the wind to flap the material free of his chest. Something deep inside her stirred, and she looked away.

Wishing she could be as casual with her own shirt, she eased away from the seat. She felt as if she were melting; all her clothes were stuck to her, and her eyes felt gritty behind her sunglasses.

She took them off, and was almost blinded by the harsh glare. She wondered how Slade could see in that glinting, searing light that sent dazzling waves of heat off the hood of the car. She could have wept with relief when he pointed to what looked like a pile of toy building blocks in the distance.

"That's Gold Canyon up ahead," he told her. "We'll be there in about ten minutes."

In spite of herself, she couldn't stop the surge of excited hope. "Do you think Gladys's address will be listed in the phone book?" she asked, slipping her sunglasses back on her nose.

"If not, it's a small town. Someone's bound to know where she lives." He lifted a hand to brush strands of hair up from his forehead. The wind caught them and blew them back again. "Does she live alone?"

"Yes." Kate wondered briefly what she must look like. Sweaty, dusty and windblown most likely. She wished she could clean up before confronting Gladys, then reflected that it really didn't matter. Nothing seemed to matter much anymore. Nothing except getting Michael back, safe and unhurt.

Give her that, she thought fervently, and she'd never ask for another thing.

She realized Slade had said something else and turned to him with a start. "I'm sorry. What did you say?"

"I asked you if she'd ever married, or is her name Wheeler, too?"

"She was married once," Kate said vaguely. "I think he died. Her last name is Scott."

"Okay." He hesitated, as if he knew she wasn't going to like what he was going to say next. "I'd better go in there alone," he said at last. "There's no telling what Vic is likely to do, if he's there."

"No," she said sharply. "You can't do that. If Vic sees you I'm afraid of what he might do."

She still couldn't bring herself to voice the fear that Vic might actually hurt Michael. She had to avoid thinking about the possibility, she told herself, or she'd go out of her mind.

She was surprised when Slade didn't argue. He must know it would be a waste of time.

She tried to relax her shoulders as Slade pulled up in front of a pair of sun-bleached gas pumps. The heat seemed to pour into the car without the rush of wind to slow it down.

Kate felt the perspiration trickling down her back when she leaned forward to watch Slade stride over to the weathered shack that served as an office. He disappeared inside, and when he came out, he was followed by a wizened old man in filthy overalls and a battered, oil-stained hat jammed down on his head.

Unable to stand the heat any longer, Kate pushed the door open and climbed out. The sun attacked her bare arms, scorching her skin as she watched the old man pump gas into the compact.

"On vacation then, are ya?" the old man asked in a voice as dry as the desert.

"Yeah." Slade fished a handkerchief out of his back pocket and wiped at his forehead. "Thought we'd stop by and visit a friend of ours. Gladys Scott. You know her?"

"Old Gladys? Sure. She lives just down the road. You can see her place from the highway. Big, old yeller house. Falling apart, it is, but she won't let no one touch it."

"Perhaps her brother will fix it up," Slade said casually.

So casually it took Kate a moment to realize what he'd said. She held her breath as the old man frowned up at Slade.

"Don't know nothing about a brother," he said, shaking his shriveled head. "Far as I know, Gladys ain't got no one but herself."

Kate tried not to let her disappointment get the better of her as Slade paid the station owner and climbed back in the

IT'S A WILD, WILD, WONDERFUL
FREE OFFER!
HERE'S WHAT YOU GET:

1. *Four New Silhouette Intimate Moments® Novels—FREE!* Everything comes up hearts and diamonds with four exciting romances—yours FREE from Silhouette Reader Service™. Each of these brand-new novels brings you the passion and tenderness of today's greatest love stories.

2. *A Practical and Elegant Bracelet Watch—FREE!* As a free gift simply to thank you for accepting four free books, we'll send you a stylish bracelet watch. This classic LCD quartz watch is a perfect expression of your style and good taste, and it's yours FREE as an added thanks for giving our Reader Service a try.

3. *An Exciting Mystery Bonus—FREE!* You'll go wild over this surprise gift. It is attractive as well as practical.

4. *Free Home Delivery!* Join Silhouette Reader Service™ and enjoy the convenience of previewing four new books every month, delivered to your home. Each book is yours for $2.74*—21 cents less than the cover price. And there is *no* extra charge for postage and handling! If you're not fully satisfied, you can cancel at any time, just by sending us a note or a shipping statement marked "cancel" or by returning any shipment to us at our cost. Great savings and total convenience are the name of the game at Silhouette!

5. *Free Newsletter!* It makes you feel like a partner to the world's most popular authors . . . tells about their upcoming books . . . even gives you their recipes!

6. *More Mystery Gifts Throughout the Year!* No Joke! Because home subscribers are our most valued readers, we'll be sending you additional free gifts from time to time with your monthly shipments—as a token of our appreciation!

GO WILD
WITH SILHOUETTE®TODAY—
JUST COMPLETE, DETACH AND
MAIL YOUR FREE-OFFER CARD!

*Terms and prices subject to change without notice. NY and Iowa residents subject to sales tax.

GET YOUR GIFTS FROM SILHOUETTE®
ABSOLUTELY FREE!

Mail this card today!

PLACE
JOKER
STICKER
HERE

PLAY THIS CARD RIGHT!

YES! Please send me my 4 Silhouette Intimate Moments® novels FREE along with my free Bracelet Watch and free mystery gift. I wish to receive all the benefits of the Silhouette Reader Service™ as explained on the opposite page.

(U-S-IM-12/89) 240 CIS YAEN

NAME _____
(PLEASE PRINT)

ADDRESS _____ APT. _____

CITY _____

STATE _____ ZIP CODE _____

Offer limited to one per household and not valid to current Silhouette Intimate Moments subscribers. All orders subject to approval.

SILHOUETTE BOOKS
"NO RISK" GUARANTEE

- There's no obligation to buy—and the free books remain yours to keep.
- You pay the low members-only price and receive books before they appear in stores.
- You may end your subscription anytime—just write and let us know or return any shipment to us at our cost.

IT'S NO JOKE!

**MAIL THE POSTPAID CARD AND
GET FREE GIFTS AND $11.80 WORTH
OF SILHOUETTE NOVELS—FREE!**

If offer card is missing, write to:
Silhouette Reader Service, P.O. Box 1867, Buffalo, NY 14269-1867

car. She closed her mouth against the dusty heat as she slid back inside and closed the door.

She would not accept defeat, she told herself. Even if Vic wasn't there, Gladys knew where he was. She had to. *She had to.* The air moving past her face brought a slight breath of relief as Slade drove down the road to where the old man had indicated Gladys lived.

They reached a long, low building with beer signs in the windows and a lone pickup parked outside. Slade pulled onto the parking strip and cut the engine. He ignored Kate's questioning glance and peered at the tavern. A sign declaring the establishment was open hung in the curtained window.

He braced himself for the impending argument and looked at Kate. Her hair was a mass of windblown curls. Her face, flushed a dull red by the heat, was streaked with dust. He couldn't see her eyes behind the sunglasses, but he knew by the set of her mouth that she was in no mood to be reasonable.

She bore no resemblance to the cool, urbane-looking woman who'd walked into the rodeo arena nearly two weeks earlier. He felt an intense desire to pull her into his arms and kiss away the worry and the fear that marked her face.

It wouldn't help his purpose one bit, he thought ruefully. He knew what his chances were of persuading her to let him go on alone, but he had to give it a shot.

He nodded his head at the building. "In there," he said evenly, "is a long, cold beer and a bathroom with cool running water. By the time I come back you should be feeling a whole lot better."

"Really. Well, I'm quite sure that Gladys has a bathroom, and I can live without a beer."

She took off her sunglasses and looked at him. She'd spoken calmly, but he recognized the resolution gleaming in her eyes. That disheveled appearance might have softened the way she looked, but there was no mistaking the determination behind that expression.

He sighed in defeat. "All right. I don't think Vic will be there, but if he is, let's play it cool. We don't want to antagonize him any more than we have to."

She gave him a measuring look. "Exactly. Which is why I have to go on alone and talk to Gladys while you go for the beer."

He softened his refusal with a half smile. "Not a chance."

"I don't want to argue about it."

His smile faded as her gaze locked with his. "Then don't. I'm not going to back down on this so you might as well save your breath." He wanted to say something else, but whatever it was on his mind, it wouldn't form into words.

When she offered no further objection he looked back at the road and started the engine. "Let's go do it," he muttered, backed the car away from the tavern and drove off.

He parked the car some distance from the house, figuring that Gladys would have less chance to see them if they approached on foot.

Kate felt her lungs growing tight as they neared the ramshackle porch. There was no garage next to the house, and no car. Unless it was parked around the back out of sight.

In spite of her reservations, she was grateful to have Slade with her. Although Vic's warning was still prominent in her mind, she wasn't sure she'd be able to handle Vic on her own.

Maybe he'd back down, she thought when faced with Slade's formidable presence. Her fingernails dug into her palms as she climbed the rickety steps behind Slade, repeating the same words over and over in her mind. *Please let him be there.*

She'd slung the strap of her purse over her shoulder, and she gripped it with both hands while Slade rang the doorbell, then, after a long wait, pounded on the door with his fist.

The sound seemed to echo all around them, then drifted into silence. A silence so still, so profound, Kate could hear her own heartbeat in her ears.

"I'm going to look around the back," Slade said, his voice making her jump. "You stay here."

"I'm coming with you."

He accepted that without comment and she trod carefully behind him, feeling the ground burning through the thin soles of her sandals.

The smell of burned grass wafted up to greet them as they stepped across what remained of a lawn. Amazed that any vegetation could survive in that harsh climate, Kate kept as close to the house as she could, taking advantage of the shade to escape the searing power of the sun's rays. Ahead of her Slade rounded the weathered wall and stopped dead. Coming up alongside of him, Kate looked to see what had halted him, and her breath stilled in her throat.

A short row of splintered wooden steps led to a door. Poking through a hole in the broken window pane, aimed straight at Slade's head, was the long, black barrel of a shotgun.

Kate gasped as Slade shot out an arm and shoved her roughly behind him. "Wheeler?" he said loudly. "I want to talk to you."

"He ain't here."

Kate's knees sagged as she recognized Gladys's voice. Peering around Slade's back she called out, "Gladys, it's me. Kate. We just want to talk to you. Please?"

The gun wavered. "Who's he?"

Had Vic told her about Slade? Kate wondered. Probably not. He wouldn't want Gladys to know he wasn't Michael's father. "He's a friend of mine," she said, pushing past Slade's restraining arm. "He won't hurt you, Gladys. We just want to talk to you."

"Go away."

The gun steadied and Slade caught Kate's shoulder. She sent him a swift warning look and shook him off. "I'm coming in, Gladys," she said steadily. "I really don't think you want to shoot me."

She took a step forward and heard Slade's hiss behind her. For agonizing seconds she stared at the barrel of the gun. Then with a muttered curse from behind the door, the rifle was slowly withdrawn.

Kate let out a rush of breath as the shadow behind the window moved and the door opened an inch or two. Gladys's face appeared in the gap.

"I told you, Vic ain't here."

"I know." Kate heard Slade moving forward and waved her hand at him in warning. "I just want to ask you a couple of questions, that's all."

"So ask."

Kate held out her hands in appeal. "Gladys, we've been driving for over an hour in this heat. Could we come in for just a minute or two? I don't feel too good, I could really use a glass of water."

Gladys's eyes were blurred behind thick-rimmed glasses, and Kate found it impossible to gauge what she was thinking. "Please?" she added, wiping a feeble hand across her brow for good measure.

Several more seconds ticked by, then the door opened abruptly and Gladys emerged. "Come on, then," she said ungraciously, "but only for a minute. You can have a drink, then you be on your way."

Pouring out her thanks, Kate climbed the wobbly steps. For a moment she thought Gladys would refuse to let Slade in, but he gave the stout woman a smile that would have melted an Ice Maiden, and she stepped back to let him pass.

Kate looked around the cluttered kitchen, her eyes desperately searching for any signs a small boy might have left behind. The counters were strewn with cooking pots, dishes and a variety of containers with dubious contents. Dishtowels hung from the backs of three metal chairs set at a Formica-topped table. The table was clear, except for the pages of a newspaper scattered across it, and a pile of opened mail.

Gladys swept the mail and newspaper off the table with one hand and motioned for them to sit down. Kate did so, aware of Slade's searching glance around the room.

Hoping he'd see something she'd missed, Kate made an attempt to capture Gladys's attention. "It's been a long time, Gladys," she said, endeavoring to put some warmth into her voice. "You're looking well."

Gladys still held the shotgun, and Slade said pleasantly, "Perhaps you'd better put the gun down. You wouldn't want it to go off and hurt someone."

"It ain't loaded," she said gruffly, but leaned the gun against the wall before shuffling over to the sink. She opened a cupboard, took down two glasses and filled them with water. "Ain't got no beer," she said, giving a glass to Slade. "This'll have to do."

"This will do just fine," Slade said with another of his devastating smiles. "Thank you, Gladys."

Gladys made a harsh noise in her throat and slapped the other glass down on the table.

Kate noticed the faint pink in Gladys's cheeks and silently applauded Slade. He was a better actor even than she'd given him credit for.

She gulped down half her water, then looked at Vic's sister. She could see the woman was nervous, but then she'd never been anything else as far as Kate remembered.

Deciding the best approach was the direct one, she leaned back in her chair. "Did Vic tell you where he was taking Michael?" she said, taking care to keep her tone casual.

Hope bounded in her as Gladys shook her head. "Nope. He said he was taking him for a holiday, but he didn't say where to."

"Then he was here," Slade said quickly.

Gladys shook her head again in a violent motion from side to side. "No, he wasn't. I talked to him on the phone."

Kate leaned forward, abandoning all attempts at detachment. "What did he say? Is Michael all right? Didn't he say anything about where they were going?"

"No, I told you." Gladys folded her arms across her breasts and glared down at Kate. "He just wants to spend time with the boy, that's all. Without you interfering. Vic said you didn't want him to see the boy. That ain't right, stopping a man from seeing his son."

Kate's shoulders slumped. She'd been right about Vic not telling his sister the truth. And there didn't seem any point in trying to convince Gladys otherwise. It was obvious she wouldn't believe her, any more than she'd believe Michael could be in danger from her brother.

She stared down at the glass in her hands, and felt all her energy slowly drain away. Maybe she was overreacting, she thought wearily. Maybe Vic had been rehabilitated. He could even be feeling sorry for what he did to Michael, and wanted to make up for it. He was probably still in Portland, and would call her any day to bring Michael back.

She drank the rest of the water, though it was now lukewarm and did nothing to refresh her. Setting down the empty glass, she faced the harsh reality. She was all out of options. Vic had won.

Chapter 7

"Are you all right?" Slade asked quietly.

Kate felt his hand on her shoulder and looked up. She saw in his eyes the same despair that engulfed her. "Yes. I guess we'd better leave." She pushed away from the table and stood. The room seemed to tilt, then steadied again.

Holding on to the table for support she looked across at Gladys. "I'd like to use the bathroom first, if you don't mind?"

Slade gripped her under the elbow. "Are you sure you're all right?"

"I'm fine." She managed a weak smile. "Or I will be, once I've used the bathroom."

Gladys led her to a door that opened into a dark hallway. "Down here," she said, waving a pudgy hand. "At the end of the hall."

Kate smiled her thanks and concentrated on keeping her balance as she felt her way down the musty-smelling hallway. She opened the door, but when she looked inside she saw a double bed, still unmade, pushed up against the wall under a window.

A pair of slippers, with the toes worn through, lay at the foot of the bed. Next to them, almost under the bed, lay a crumpled article of clothing, the vivid yellow fabric a glaring contrast to the dark unpolished floorboards. Like a ray of sunshine, Kate thought, grimacing at her whimsy.

The door at the end refused her first attempt to open it, but gave after she pushed it with her shoulder. The bathroom was cleaner than she'd expected and she stood for several minutes scooping handfuls of cool water to dash over her face.

Heedless of the splashes down her shirt she dabbed her skin dry, then fished in her purse for a comb. Feeling a little better she emerged several minutes later, squinting at the darkness in the hallway.

It would feel good to be outside in the fresh air again, she thought, closing the door behind her. Even the heat of the sun was preferable to this. Sliding the strap of her purse over her shoulder, she started up the passage. She glanced at the open door to the bedroom as she passed, remembering her stray thought about the ray of sunshine.

It looked like a T-shirt, she reflected, then halted, one hand against the wall for support. She was visualizing Michael the last time she'd seen him—was it only yesterday?

She could see him clearly, his scrubbed face smiling up at her, his arms stretched out for her hug. He was wearing his favorite T-shirt, with a stenciled likeness of his favorite cartoon character on the front. *A bright yellow T-shirt.*

She spun around so quickly she had to wait for the dizziness to pass before stepping back to the bedroom. She tiptoed across the floor and stooped to pick up the tiny bundle of yellow fabric. Shaking it out, she held it up. A striped cat with bulging yellow eyes grinned back at her.

She stood for a moment, the shirt crushed to her breast. Michael. He was here.

She didn't know how she felt. She'd almost convinced herself that Vic would bring him back, but she knew now that it had been no more than wishful thinking.

If Vic had brought him this far, he had no intention of bringing him back. She buried her face in the soft fabric. At least she knew now that Gladys was lying. Vic had been here. How long ago had they left?

Turning, she hurried down the hall, bumping into the wall as the floating feeling in her head intensified. She heard Slade say something to Gladys and the woman answered. Kate couldn't hear the words. She didn't care. She wanted to hear one thing and one thing only.

Anger, so intense it almost blinded her, propelled her forward. She crashed through the door, and was vaguely aware of Slade's muttered oath as she stumbled toward Gladys.

The older woman took a startled step backward as Kate advanced, brandishing the T-shirt in her clenched fist. "You lied to me," she said, her voice trembling with fury. "You deliberately lied to me. He was here, wasn't he?" She put her face up close to Gladys's and yelled, "Wasn't he?"

Behind her Slade said sharply. "Kate. Ease up. Let me talk to her."

"There's no point in talking to her," Kate shouted. "She lies. She's been lying all along. This is Michael's shirt, and if she doesn't tell me the truth I'm going to throttle her with it."

Gladys's face blanched and she threw one hand to her throat. Her eyes flew to Slade, who crossed the room in two strides.

"Kate," he said gently. "Sit down. You're upset. Let me handle this."

"No, I'm not upset," Kate said, shooting a furious glance at him. "I'm mad as hell. And I'm going to get madder if she doesn't tell me where they are." She heard her own voice rise on an hysterical note and dropped her hand. She was out of control, she thought desperately.

Slade's hands descended on her shoulders and guided her to a chair. "Sit," he ordered.

Unable to resist the slight pressure of his hands she dropped onto the chair. The slight floating sensation bothered her and she shook her head trying to dispel it. The motion only made things worse.

From a long way off she heard Slade say, "I'll take care of this. You stay in that chair."

She couldn't do anything else, she thought, trying to focus on him. Nothing seemed to be working right. Her arms felt like lead, her legs like melted rubber, and she was hot. So damn hot.

Giving in to the lassitude creeping over her, she laid her arms on the table and rested her forehead on them. She heard Slade move away, and made an effort to concentrate on what he was saying.

"All right. Now you can either tell us where Vic has taken Michael, or we can call the police and you can tell them."

"The police?"

Kate got a grim satisfaction out of the fear in Gladys's voice. The woman obviously didn't know the police had refused to help. Vic probably knew they couldn't touch him, but he hadn't informed his sister of that. Kate closed her eyes. Slade knew what he was doing, after all.

"I don't want no police 'round here," Gladys spluttered. "You got no call to bring the police in. Vic ain't done nothing wrong. He just wanted to have some time with his son; you can't blame him for that."

Eyes closed, Kate listened to the short silence.

"When did Vic get here?" Slade said, his voice deceptively calm.

"Last night. Came in on the late plane. I picked them up at the airport in Reno."

Gladys sounded sullen, but at least she was answering, Kate thought. Warily she lifted her head. The room seemed steady enough and she sat back in her chair.

Slade stood with his arms crossed, his face a formidable mask. Gladys was still backed up against the wall. She looked confused and very frightened.

"In your car?" Slade asked.

Kate frowned, wondering where all this was leading.

"Yeah, in my car." Gladys sniffed loudly.

"So where is your car now?"

Kate's eyes darted to the other woman, who lifted a hand to rub at her nose.

"He's not going to hurt him," Gladys wailed, sending a chill down Kate's spine. "He swore he wouldn't hurt him."

Kate ran the tip of her tongue over her dry lips. "He's hurt him before, Gladys," she said clearly. "You know that. You can't be sure he won't do it again. Michael is only a little boy, he can't defend himself, he can't . . ." To her dismay her voice broke on a sob.

She struggled for control while the silence hung thick and heavy in the suffocating heat of the kitchen. Somewhere in the depths of the house a cat mewed. Someone say something, Kate pleaded silently. She was beyond it.

"He took my car," Gladys said, her words dropping like stones into the silence. "They took off this morning. He didn't say where, but he was heading south when he turned onto the highway."

"What make is your car?" Slade asked, his voice quickening.

"One of them Chevs. Impala. Four door, powder blue. It's a '72."

He crouched down and scooped up a page of the newspaper. "Do you have a pencil?"

Gladys shook her head.

"I do." Kate reached for her purse. Her hands were shaking so much she fumbled for several seconds with the catch without success.

"Here," she said, pushing it over to Slade. "You get it." She couldn't seem to think straight. Only one fact seemed clear in her mind. Michael had been here. Just a few short hours ago, Michael had been in this very room. She wanted to cry, but her eyes remained dry. She didn't seem able to feel anything. No emotion.

She wondered if this was how Slade felt all the time, and knew she wasn't being fair. Even he couldn't feel this empty inside.

She heard Gladys give him the number of the car. She saw him scribble it down on the scrap of newspaper and stuff it in his pocket. She heard him fire a dozen questions at Gladys who steadfastly maintained she knew nothing more.

Vic had called her the day he'd been released from the hospital, she told Slade. He'd told her he was coming to visit, but she had no idea Michael would be with him until he'd arrived at the airport.

Kate felt as if she were watching an old movie with a fuzzy picture and muffled sound. She felt Slade's hand under her elbow and rose obediently when he exerted pressure. Gladys stood by the door, looking ready to burst into tears at any second. Kate almost envied her ability to feel emotion.

"Mikey's all right," Gladys said as Kate passed her. "He'll be all right, you'll see."

Even the effort to nod was too much for her. Kate dragged her lips into a farce of a smile, instead.

The air outside was no cooler, though it smelled considerably fresher. Kate stumbled around the corner of the house, supported by Slade's firm grasp. He ordered her to wait while he got the car.

He was back in a few minutes, and helped her into the front seat. She sat as if in a trance while he climbed in next to her and started the engine.

When they reached the highway and turned north, she finally struggled back to awareness. "Where are you going?" she demanded weakly. "Gladys said south."

"I'm taking you back to the tavern," Slade said with a sideways glance. "You're in no shape to go anywhere until you've eaten something."

He cut off her protest with a low curse. "Look at you, Kate. You can't stand up by yourself. When was the last time you ate anything more substantial than cereal?"

She tried to think. "Lunch yesterday." A small lunch at that. It was the only thing she'd eaten all day. No wonder she was feeling so awful. She leaned back against the seat and closed her eyes. It felt good, having someone to take care of her, she thought, letting her body relax.

It had been a long time since anyone had taken care of her. She'd had to fend for herself and for Michael for so very long. It wasn't permanent, she warned herself. It wouldn't do to get used to it. But for a little while she could at least enjoy it.

The tavern was air-conditioned, and she was quite sure nothing had ever felt so good. She used the bathroom to change into shorts and a tank top, for some reason feeling a little self-conscious when she returned to the bar and met Slade's approving gaze.

He'd picked a booth in a dark corner, away from the windows. Beer wasn't one of her favorite beverages, but the cool, refreshing liquid soothed her dry throat. Even the greasy hamburgers Slade ordered tasted better than they looked. Kate smiled at him gratefully when she'd finished the last crumb on her plate.

"Feeling better?" His gaze took in her face, as if to reassure himself when she nodded.

"Much better. I'm ready to go on now."

His eyes flickered, and she braced herself for the argument she guessed was coming. "I think it would be better if you flew back to Portland," he said, "and let me carry on from here."

She met his dark gaze with an unshakable resolve. "You know very well I'm not going to do that."

"Kate, you're in no shape to go on. You can't take this heat. I'm used to it, you're not."

"I was hungry and upset. That's all. I'm fine now."

"It could get a lot worse before we're through."

"I don't care." She glared at him, angry that he couldn't understand. "How can you imagine that I could go calmly back home when my son is out there somewhere in this desert, with a man who may or may not be a dangerous psychopath?"

"You've got to stop thinking like that," Slade said sharply. "Vic is not going to hurt him. You said yourself that the hospital released him because he was well again."

"I said they thought he was well again." She took a sip of the beer, more to give herself time to calm down than because she wanted it. She set the glass on the table. "I'm not going home without Michael."

"There are no guarantees that we'll find him. If someone really wants to disappear it's easy enough to do."

She knew his words weren't meant to hurt. He was trying to be realistic. She drew in a shaky breath. "I know that. But you're forgetting one thing. Michael doesn't want to disappear. Sooner or later, he'll find a way to trip up Vic. And I want to be there when he does."

"That's asking an awful lot of a little boy," Slade said slowly.

"Damn you, Slade, quit arguing about it. I'm going and that's the end of it. You can either like it or lump it, but at least shut up reminding me how difficult it's going to be."

Where the anger had come from she had no idea. Slade was simply trying to save her a lot of heartache and pain. She knew that. But all she had left was hope. If he took that away from her she would buckle under the strain.

She sent him a look of apology, but his face betrayed no emotion. Just once, she thought fiercely, she'd like to smash through that tough shell of his and shake him to the roots of his foundation.

"I'm sorry," she said, trying to sound it. "I didn't mean to yell at you."

"I know." He lifted his glass and drained his beer. "I guess I know when I'm beaten." He set his glass down with a thud. "We'd better get going."

She followed him out to the car, wincing when the heat enveloped her once more. The lighter clothes helped, and she managed to bear the burning touch of the upholstery without flinching. Once they were on the way, the wind made it bearable.

"Where do we start?" she asked Slade as he increased their speed on the highway.

"There's not much between here and Las Vegas. If Vic wants to hide, my guess is he'll go all the way."

Kate thought about the sprawling city with its vast swarm of tourists. She refused to admit that Slade's doubts had been justified. They would find Michael somehow, if they had to search for a year.

She didn't let herself wonder how long Slade was prepared to search. She had to believe they'd find Michael long before Slade was ready to give up. As for her, she vowed silently, she'd never give up. No matter how long it took.

"He'll have to stop for gas before he gets there," Slade said, breaking into her thoughts. "And that car drinks gas. There's a good chance someone at a gas station will remember a car like that."

"You're going to check out every gas station between here and Las Vegas?" Kate asked.

"We shouldn't have to. Vic must know you called Gladys, that's why he took off again. He's in a hurry. He'll stop at a roadside station to fill up. Some attendant may have talked to him or Michael. It's worth looking into."

She didn't agree, but didn't say so. She would much rather have gone straight into Las Vegas. The longer start they gave Vic, the tougher he would be to find. She knew it would be pointless to argue with Slade, and she didn't want another argument. She closed her mouth and leaned back, letting the wind blow the dust across her face.

Several minutes later she opened her eyes with a start as Slade cursed quietly. "What's wrong?" She sat up and looked at him, heart thumping in apprehension.

"I'm not sure." He tilted his head on one side. "Hear that noise?"

She listened, hearing only the sound of the engine. Puzzled, she shook her head. "I can't hear anything."

"It's a knocking. In the engine."

Now that he'd pointed it out, she could hear the tapping noise. "What is it?"

"I don't know. I just hope it's not serious. We've still got a few miles to go to the next town."

Kate stared ahead at the road baking under the white-hot heat. She tried not to imagine herself walking along that searing strip of pavement.

Slade drove in silence for the next few minutes, then cursed again. "Steam," he said shortly. "I think we've got trouble." The words were hardly out of his mouth when the engine started rattling and steam hissed up from the hood. Muttering something under his breath he pulled the car onto the shoulder and coasted to a stop.

Kate watched anxiously while he climbed out and lifted up the hood. Another cloud of steam boiled up in his face and he retreated until it had cleared.

He seemed to be bent over the engine for ages before he straightened. Kate opened the door and stepped onto the heated road. "Can you fix it?" she asked hopefully.

"No." He lifted his head and dropped the hood back in place. "The water pump's gone."

Kate sagged against the side of the car. "What do we do now?"

"We walk." Slade shaded his eyes with his hand and peered up the road. "It's just over that rise. About a mile." He looked back at her. "You could wait in the car till I get back with a tow truck."

She shook her head. The thought of sitting alone in that furnace of a vehicle worried her far more than walking. "I'll make it," she said, wishing she could be sure of that.

"Did you bring a hat?" Slade said, casting an eye at the sun.

"No. I never wear one."

Instead of answering he reached in the back of the car and pulled his bag toward him. After unzipping it, he eased out his black hat. "Never go anywhere without it," he said, catching sight of her surprised expression.

He dropped it on her head, and she tilted it back with her hand to look up at him. "Don't you need it?"

"I've got a tougher head than you. Ready?"

She leaned into the car and grabbed her purse. "Now I am."

Together they started up the road, with Slade setting an easy pace so that Kate didn't lag behind. Even so, she felt her feet beginning to drag by the time they'd reached the brow of the rise.

The road sloped down gently to a small cluster of buildings scattered on both sides of the highway. They looked so close, yet it seemed to Kate that the farther they walked, the farther the buildings slipped away. She could feel the sun scorching her shoulders, and wished she'd worn a blouse instead of the tank top. She was grateful when Slade unbuttoned his shirt and pulled it off.

"Here," he said, throwing it over her shoulders, "you're beginning to burn."

Touched by his consideration she smiled up at him. "Thanks. But what about you?"

"I'm burned already."

He was, she saw as she ran her gaze over his tanned chest and shoulders. She looked back at his face and found him watching her. She felt as if she'd been caught invading his privacy, and looked away embarrassed, hoping her sudden spasm of awareness had escaped his notice.

It wasn't as if she hadn't seen his bare chest before, she reminded herself, or everything else for that matter. The memory seemed to heat her insides even more than the desert sun. Somehow the man trudging along at her side was a far different proposition from the man she'd made love with eight years ago. Slade Montana was like a stranger to her now.

It didn't change the way she felt about him, she reflected wryly, and marveled that even in the midst of all that discomfort and worry, he could still arouse such strong sensations.

She was past feeling anything, though, when she finally dragged her feet into the first gas station on the edge of town. It was actually no more than a sparsely populated community, Kate discovered when she'd recovered enough to take notice of her surroundings. Little more than a scattering of buildings along both sides of the highway.

Sitting in the stuffy office, she was vaguely aware of Slade's heated discussion on the phone with the owner of the car-rental agency. He snorted with disgust as he slammed down the receiver. "They don't deserve the business," he muttered.

"What did they say?" Kate asked, already expecting the worst.

Striding to the door, Slade paused to look at her. "They can't get another car to us. They want us to get this one fixed and send them the bill." He lifted his hands in helpless frustration. "We could be stuck here all night."

She watched him go out to look for the attendant, and wondered how many more obstacles she would have to face before she could hold Michael in her arms again.

The attendant promised to send his tow truck out to the car. The matter of a new water pump was something else. They would have to send to the next town for one, the young man explained to Slade. It was impossible to get it done before the next day.

Kate swallowed her intense disappointment as Slade handed the car keys over.

"Is there anywhere we can stay for the night?" Slade asked the attendant climbing into the tow truck.

"The Red Barn down the road," the young man said, pointing into the sun. "They've got a room upstairs."

When Kate and Slade got there, she was not in the least surprised to discover that the Red Barn was a tavern. It seemed as if there were some things even a small community could not exist without. The tavern owner, a huge man with a mop of curly red hair and a bulging belly, showed them up a narrow staircase to a dingy room that looked as if it hadn't been occupied in the last century.

The dark brown furniture was drab but serviceable, and although the drapes and coverlet on the bed were shabby, they were reasonably clean, Kate determined on inspection. She took off Slade's hat and laid it on the bed before slipping his shirt from her shoulders.

It was the only room in town, the man assured them when Slade questioned him. They didn't get many visitors. She could understand why, Kate reflected as she stared through the smeared window at the highway below. At least the room had a private bathroom. That was something.

It wasn't until after the man had left that it dawned on her she would be spending the night in the same room with Slade.

She turned and saw him sitting on the bed, his back toward her. The sharp, intense longing she'd felt earlier stabbed through her body, destroying her breath. The heat seemed to be pressing down on her, suffocating her. She couldn't take her eyes from his bare back. She watched the muscles rippling in his shoulders as he lifted his feet one at a time to pull off his boots. The movements seemed so intimate, so personal. She wiped her damp palms on her hips as the memory of his kiss pulsed through her mind.

A stranger's kiss, yet so dearly familiar. She wanted his kiss again, she acknowledged as need ran hot through her veins. She wanted the comfort of his arms, the security of his touch. She wanted, just for a little while, to forget her fears and her worries. She wanted him to take her in his arms and drive everything out of her mind except the need to satisfy the primal urges building in her body.

Where had all this passion come from? she wondered, dazed by the force of her emotions. Even when they'd been together all those years ago, she'd never felt this earthshaking need, this intense desperation clamoring at her senses.

For the past twenty-four hours she'd been through a nightmare of agonizing distress. It had destroyed all her confidence, and with it, her self-control. She was hurting, and she wanted to be comforted. She wanted to be *loved*.

She stared at Slade's back, fighting the urge to go to him, to wrap her arms around his chest, and press her lips to the smooth, tanned skin. She wanted to run her fingers down the length of his spine, that long indentation that reached down to his jeans and beyond.

She had actually taken a step forward when he pushed himself off the bed and turned. Startled, she jerked her gaze to his face, hot guilt flooding her cheeks.

His eyes widened when he looked at her, and he went very still. His lips formed one soft word. "Kate."

She was shaking, as if she were bitterly cold. But she wasn't cold. She was hot—burning, on fire—like the desert floor beneath the merciless sun. She wanted to say something, to do something to bring him to her, yet she couldn't move, couldn't speak.

She knew he was fighting his own desire. She could see it in his eyes. She could see it in the way the muscle in his jaw jerked in a spasm of tension. She watched his chest rise and fall with his effort to breathe, then lowered her gaze down over his flat belly....

Slade called on every ounce of his willpower, balling his hands into fists at his sides. He had to make allowances, he warned himself urgently. She was in a fragile state, distraught, scared. Hell, he was scared himself; he knew how she felt. That look on her face didn't mean what he thought it meant.

She was simply reaching out to another human being for comfort and reassurance. And he couldn't give it to her. So help him, he dare not touch her now. All his senses kicked into high gear as he willed himself not to drag her down on the bed. He could feel every hair on his body, as if an electric current flowed through each one.

Perspiration beaded on his brow, on his chest and down his back. The pain in his groin was becoming unbearable and he knew if he didn't get out of there, she was going to know the full extent of his problem.

"I'm going down to the bar," he said hoarsely. "Maybe the barman knows something."

She stared at him while seconds fraught with tension ticked by. Her voice sounded tired when she said, "I'm coming, too."

"No." He softened his tone as she sent him a sharp look. "Why don't you have a shower first and cool down?" He reached for his shirt and dragged it on. "I'll order a beer for you. It will be waiting when you get down there."

"I'm coming with you." She picked up her purse and thrust her arm through the strap. "I can have a shower later."

He knew better than to try to change her mind. Shrugging, he sat down again and pulled on his boots, then reached for his hat. He opened the door and she brushed past him without looking at him. He led the way down the steep staircase, every inch of his skin conscious of her close behind him.

The smell of beer and stagnant smoke almost overwhelmed Kate as she stepped into the gloomy bar. One long counter dominated half the room, running down the length of one wall. Several stools lined the bar and the ginger-haired tavern owner sat on one of them. He was talking to a long, lean man with stringy hair and a mustache who had perched his hip on the stool next to him.

Two pairs of curious eyes swept over Kate as she approached the two men and she wished she'd changed back into her slacks and shirt. Slade ordered two beers, though she would have preferred water. She kept close to his side, resisting the impulse to slip her hand through his arm while he talked to the men.

Neither of the men had seen the car. Slade described Vic and Michael, but the tavern owner was quite sure no one like that had stopped in town.

"There were a few cars went by this morning," he said in answer to Slade's questions. "We get most of the traffic through here early morning or evening. The trucks usually come through at night."

He gave Kate a smile from his rubber lips that made her cringe inside. "They make quite a racket going through. Hope you're not a light sleeper."

"We'll manage," Slade said shortly. "Is there anyone else who might have seen them?"

The man's eyes slid reluctantly back to Slade. "You might try old Silas, down the road aways. Got the old barn on the other side of the road. Does a bit of horse breeding. He's usually out back somewheres. If anyone's seen 'em, it'll be old Silas.'' He gave Kate another curious scrutiny. ''Why are you looking for 'em?''

Ignoring the question Slade drained his beer, then touched his hat in a brief salute and made for the door. Kate hurried after him, anxious to be out in the fresh air.

The sun was succumbing to the approaching night, and the breeze felt cooler on her hot skin. She had to practically run to keep up with Slade but she kept her protests to herself.

Ever since that pregnant moment in the room, when they'd stared at each other across the bed, she'd had the distinct impression that he was angry about something. Was he angry at her? she wondered. If so, why? What had she done? He couldn't have known what she was thinking. Even if he had, why would he be angry?

For one wild moment she had even believed he'd felt the same erotic sensations coursing through his body. Until he'd broken the spell and rushed down to the bar, as if he couldn't wait to get away from her.

Maybe he thought she was going to start something he didn't want to finish, she thought. She almost had.

Well, he needn't worry. She couldn't believe now that she'd actually come close to letting him know how she felt. That would have been the ultimate humiliation. It would be a cold day in hell before she gave in to those crazy notions again.

She was out of breath by the time they found Silas. He was a wiry little man and seemed anxious to please, but he wasn't any more helpful than the others had been. Although they questioned several more people on the way back to the tavern, no one remembered seeing a powder-blue Chevrolet, or a man with a small boy.

They found a tiny coffee shop on the back street behind the tavern and ordered two plates of spaghetti, though Kate didn't have much of an appetite.

She gave up trying to hold a conversation with Slade when he gave her one-word answers, and she was glad when the meal was over and they could go back to the room.

Slade collected their bags from the car, and she half expected him to stay down in the bar, which now held a few men at the counter, but he followed her up the stairs.

Once inside the room, she wished he had chosen to stay in the bar. The room seemed smaller and hotter than it had before, in spite of the cooler night air.

"We should have hitched a ride to the next town," Slade said, sinking onto the bed and burying his face in his hands. "We probably could have had separate rooms, at least."

The last words were muffled, but Kate heard them. "Don't worry, I can sleep in the bathtub." She hadn't meant to sound so shrewish. She scraped her hair back with one hand, trying to think of something to say that wouldn't sound defensive.

"I'll take the bathtub." Slade's voice held a dry note that grated on her raw nerves.

"You had the couch last night," she said crossly. "You can have the bed tonight."

"I'm used to sleeping rough."

"Well, I'm shorter than you, I'll fit in it better."

He lifted his head to look at her over his shoulder. "Don't argue with me, Kate. I'm in no mood for an argument."

His warning only aggravated her temper. "I'm trying to be helpful," she retorted, "but of course you're too pig-headed to see that. If you want to sleep in the bathtub, go ahead, but don't complain to me in the morning if you can't sleep."

"I haven't so far," he said evenly.

She flung her purse on the bed, feeling ashamed of her outburst. She was tired and hot, and her nerves were shattered. Still she had no right to take it out on him.

She sat on the edge of the bed with her back to him and tried to maintain some kind of control. "Did they say when the car would be ready?" she asked, unable to keep the exasperation out of her voice.

"No. I imagine it will be around noon."

She jutted her bottom lip and puffed at her face to cool it. "That means another trip in this damned heat."

"I told you to go back to Portland."

"I know you did." She gritted her teeth. "And you know I can't do that. As long as my son is out there I'm going to keep looking for him."

"*Our* son."

She heard the anger in his voice and tensed. "He's only been your son for a few days," she said, giving in to her resentment. "He's been my son all his life."

"Whose fault was that?" The bed jerked as Slade shoved to his feet.

Kate jumped up, too. Whirling to face him she met his stormy gaze. "It certainly wasn't mine. If you'd stuck around you might have had the chance to see him born, to hold him in your arms and to watch him grow."

"You told me to get lost."

"And you didn't waste any time doing it." She jammed her fists into her hips. "It was your decision to stay away, to reject him. You have no right to call him your son."

His face told her she'd gone too far. She was past caring. Angry with him, furious at herself, all she wanted to do was get away from him and to be alone.

She snatched up her bag from the floor and muttered, "I'm going to have a shower." Flinging herself into the bathroom, she slammed the door behind her. At least she had put a wall between them, she thought as she dumped her bag on the floor and opened it.

She found her cotton nightgown and hung it on the towel rail. If he wants to play the martyr and sleep in the bathtub, let him, she thought, scowling at herself in the mirror. Lord, she looked a mess. Not that it mattered. She could look like a fashion plate and he wouldn't notice.

Kate stared at her furious image, and admitted the truth. That was what this was all about—his total unconcern for her existence. He'd even tried to get rid of her, to send her back to Portland.

Why she let his attitude bother her when she had so much more to worry about she couldn't imagine, but she was sure of one thing. She leaned her hands on the sink and glared at her reflection. No more. She'd had enough. From now on, Slade Montana could go sleep in a pigsty for all she cared. Feeling no better, she pulled off her clothes and turned on the faucet.

Slade stared at the bathroom door, fighting the anger surging through him. Where the hell did she come off? he fumed silently. He was doing his best to help, and that was the thanks he got. Did she really imagine he was enjoying this lousy situation?

He sat down on the bed and slammed his fist into the hard mattress. Did she think that because he hadn't seen his son grow up he was any less concerned and worried about him than she was?

He shot to his feet again, unable to sit still. What the hell did she think he was doing here? Would he be chasing all over this stinking desert if he wasn't every bit as anxious as she was to find Michael?

He thumped his fists on the dresser, rattling the ashtray that sat on top of it. They needed to pull together, not tear each other apart. Hell, they'd be better off sleeping together, instead of fighting about who was sleeping where.

He stood for several seconds, staring down at his balled fists. Then very slowly he turned and looked at the bathroom door. He could hear the water rushing from the shower head. A mental vision of Kate standing naked beneath it seared his mind.

He hesitated for a moment longer, then with a low growl deep in his throat, he strode to the bathroom door and crashed his boot into it, slamming it open against the wall.

Chapter 8

Kate gasped. She sent one startled look at Slade standing in the doorway, then grabbed at the shower curtain to hold it in front of her.

"What the hell do you think you're doing?" she spluttered, backing out of the spray of cool water. It might just as well have been hot water, she thought, the way her body was heating up.

Slade didn't answer. His eyes burned into hers as he slowly stretched out one hand and leaned it against the wall. Lifting his foot, he dragged off first one boot, then the other.

Kate felt her lungs constrict. "Slade," she said sharply. "Get out of here. Now."

Without taking his eyes from her face he began unbuttoning his shirt.

She watched his fingers, mesmerized, as the buttons came undone one by one. The tingling began, low in her stomach, and she struggled to control it. She watched him tug his arms out of his shirt and drop it to the floor. Then his hands went to his belt. She jerked her gaze back to his face. He looked grim—and very determined. Kate's mouth went dry.

He unclasped the oversize silver buckle and pulled his belt open. Kate felt the tingling reach the tips of her breasts and gave a soft moan. She was beyond words now, her body sending confused signals in all directions.

His gaze locked with hers, Slade unbuttoned his jeans, then eased them down his legs and stepped out of them. He hooked his thumbs into the waistband of his briefs and said quietly, "You just say the word and I'll walk out of here."

She formed her lips to say "No." She wasn't too surprised when "Yes" came out instead.

He slid the briefs down past his knees and kicked them off. He took a step toward her and she clenched the curtain between her fingers.

"Just to make sure," he said softly. "Yes, you want me to leave, or yes, you want me to stay?"

She fought for breath. "Yes, I want you to stay."

He grinned then, a slow, mind-destroying grin that sent spurts of hot desire rippling through her body. "Then move over, lady," he murmured and stepped into the tub.

She shifted backward, away from him. He stuck his head under the streaming water, letting it cascade down over his body, then stepped out of the spray and shook his head. Drops of water flew in all directions, splattering the walls and her face.

She still held the curtain in front of her. She could feel the drumming of her heartbeat against her ribs as he reached out and pulled the fabric from her grasp, letting it drop behind her.

His gaze moved over her, scorching where it touched like a physical caress. She'd dropped the soap when he'd kicked the door open, and he stooped to pick it up, his gaze searing up her body as he straightened.

He held it out to her, unsmiling, his eyes smoldering with his hunger. "You first."

She took the soap with nervous fingers and almost dropped it. He turned his back on her and she gazed at his smooth skin. It was broken by a faint scar that sliced across his back just below his shoulder blade. She remembered him telling her he'd been gored by a bull. It had healed well, she thought. She hadn't noticed it until now. She reached out a trembling hand and began to slide the soap over his back.

He lifted his chin sharply at her touch, but said nothing as she soaped his back, moving lower and lower until she reached his lean, hard buttocks.

She heard him catch his breath when she soaped her hands and smoothed them down over the firm curves to his thighs. Excitement had her in its grip now, tingling, coiling, tightening in every inch of her body.

She touched the back of his knee and his leg buckled slightly, giving her immense satisfaction. He had always had remarkable control; it felt good to know she could still sabotage it.

She straightened, feeling the tremendous sense of power that came from the ability to arouse a man. "Turn around," she said, her pulse leaping in response when he did what she asked.

His chest expanded as he struggled to draw breath. His eyes blazed down at her and his nostrils flared, fueling her excitement. Slowly he raised his hands above his head.

She reached for the soap, turning it over and over in her hands before replacing it on the ledge of the tub. She spread the foam over his chest, working it across his shoulders, and down over his taut nipples to his hard, flat stomach.

She took her time, pausing to add more foam to her hands, before continuing down. She felt him tremble beneath her touch as she drew her palms over his belly to the thatch of curls below his navel.

Her own rasping breath matched his when she touched him, and she felt the shudder rack his body as he muttered, "Oh, God." He lowered his arms around her, crushing her against him, his mouth finding hers in a hard, demanding kiss that robbed her legs of any remaining strength.

She sagged against him, whimpering as the length of his wet, soapy body fitted against hers. He moved backward, pulling them both under the streaming water, holding her away from him just long enough to rinse the soap from his torso before dragging her back again, his mouth searching for hers.

She clung to him, her hands roaming his back and shoulders, her hips straining against his, her skin tingling as his rough body hair teased her vulnerable flesh, and the swollen, throbbing evidence of his need nudged her belly.

She was moaning, soft little cries that came from somewhere in the depths of her being. His mouth left hers and traveled to her ear, where his tongue teased the sensitive folds until she pressed her teeth lightly into his shoulder to stop the exquisite torture.

He cupped her breast, his fingers creating new and fiercer flames of desire that intensified when he lowered his mouth to torment her swollen peaks. She gave a sharp moan as excitement stimulated her body, building the craving to an unbearable pitch. Her fingers dug into the muscled flesh of his shoulders as he moved his hand lower, his fingers finding the source of an explosive need that drove all the breath from her body.

He moved suddenly, taking her by surprise. He reached down and turned off the faucet. Then in one swift motion he scooped her up in his arms and stepped out of the tub. Dripping water all the way, he carried her to the bed and lowered her onto it.

For one brief moment she thought about their wet bodies on the covers, then forgot everything as his damp flesh descended and his mouth captured hers. His tongue plundered her mouth as he eased her thighs apart with his knee. Supporting himself on his hands he raised his shoulders up from her and looked into her eyes.

She stared into his burning gaze. She had forgotten how he could make her feel. Had she ever felt like this before? Had she ever felt this raw, aching need to take him inside her?

He moved against her, caressing her with his lower body, a powerful reminder of his own hunger. The fragrance of soap blended with the exciting, disturbing male smell of him. It filled her mind, blotting out all memory of the past, leaving only now, this moment, this gnawing, agonizing need.

She whispered his name, and as his throbbing flesh slid into her, she jerked her head back and closed her eyes. He filled her, pausing for a second or two before beginning the slow rhythm that began the path to euphoria.

She lifted her legs and crossed her ankles behind his hips, hearing his guttural groan. His movements quickened, his deep, measured thrusts becoming more and more urgent. The pressure built, and she strained against him, taking him deeper. His gasp mingled with her cry as his shuddering body took them both to the crest of endurance and beyond, leaving her weak and trembling, and utterly, incredibly content.

It couldn't last—that warm, soothing sensation spreading throughout her body, she knew that. Sooner or later she would have to face the anxiety and the terror again. But right now, just for the moment, she wanted to hold on to the incredible sensation of Slade's hard body lying on hers, his mouth buried in her neck.

Except for that one brief exclamation, he hadn't spoken one word while he was making love to her, she realized. Now that she came to think about it, he never had. Not that he needed to. He could create more excitement with his mouth, his hands and his body than a thousand words could achieve.

He made love the way he did everything else, with a slow deliberation and a total command of concentration. Until the final moments, when he abandoned all his control and gave himself up to the ultimate culmination, taking her with him.

She stirred, and he shifted his weight off her, his arm still holding her as he cuddled against her side. She turned her head and looked at him. His eyes were closed, his mouth relaxed and content. Still, she thought, just once, she would have liked to know what he'd been thinking during the heat of their passion. She let out her breath on a soft sigh. Nothing had really changed.

They had made love eight years ago, but it hadn't been enough to hold him. She was realistic enough to know that it was no more likely to hold him now. Less perhaps, with Michael in the picture.

I would have made a lousy father. He'd admitted his limitations. She would have to accept the fact that sooner or later she would lose him again. She could only hope that he'd stay long enough to find Michael. She winced as pain stabbed through her.

Slade must have felt the subtle movement. He opened his eyes and looked at her. "You okay?"

She smiled. "More than okay. How about you?"

"Mmm." He lifted her hand and brought it to his mouth. "Fantastic." His lips moved against her fingers. "Know what I'd like to do now?"

She traced the outline of his mouth with a gentle finger. "Tell me."

"I'd like to take a walk outside. Have you ever seen the stars in a desert sky?"

"No." She caught her breath as he opened his mouth and captured her fingers with his teeth. "I've never been in the desert before."

"Well, you've never lived." He sat up and swung his legs off the bed. "Just wait till you see those stars."

He reached for his bag and stood, looking down at her for a long moment before saying, "I'll get dressed and we'll go.

It'll be cooler out there now. You'll see the desert at its best.''

She watched him walk into the bathroom, admiring the long, lean length of his body before he closed the door behind him. His love of the open sky had echoed in his voice. He loved the desert at night, and he wanted her to see it, too. At least he was willing to share something with her, she thought ruefully.

When he was finished with the bathroom she dressed quickly in clean slacks and shirt, and ran a comb through her damp hair. Her reflection looked back at her, looking so much calmer than it had earlier. She felt a moment's guilt that she could feel so tranquil inside, in spite of her worry over Michael.

Tomorrow, she promised him silently. We will find you tomorrow. She closed her eyes briefly, then hurried out of the bathroom to join Slade.

The night breezes drifted across her face and arms as they walked without touching to the edge of town. They reached the vacant highway, and began walking along it, facing the open desert.

The moon cast a pale light over the landscape, revealing the vast, flat plain. Huge cactus plants were scattered across the terrain, looking like strange, fat aliens surrendering to an unseen enemy. Kate tilted her chin to look at the stars, amazed to discover there were far more than she ever imagined. The clear desert air made many more of them visible to the naked eye, and she caught her breath at the glittering carpet spread out above her head to the far mountains and beyond.

"It's so beautiful," she whispered. "And so still. It's like we're the only ones on earth."

"I know. That feeling is rare. Make the most of it."

She lowered her face and found him watching her, his face somber in the moonlight. "It's important to you," she said. "Being alone, I mean."

He gave her a half smile that barely moved his lips. "Yes. It's the only way I can find peace."

Her pulse quickened. He seemed different. An air of expectancy seemed to hover around him. She sensed that he wanted to talk—really talk—and was waiting for encouragement.

She decided to give it to him. Treading warily she said, "Peace comes from inside ourselves, not our surroundings."

He made a slight sound of skepticism. "Do you really believe that? How many people do you know who are totally at peace with themselves?"

"I don't know anyone who is as much at war with himself as you are," she said quietly.

He looked at her for a moment longer, then shrugged and turned away. Jamming his thumbs into his pockets he lifted his gaze to the sky. "There are some things we can never escape, no matter how badly we want to."

"Now that's something I don't believe." She found a patch of coarse grass and sat down. Crossing her legs and resting her elbows on her knees, she said casually, "We all have the power to change, if we have the desire to make the effort."

He glanced down at her. "That's easy for you to say."

"Sometimes talking about it helps."

She waited, watching the struggle going on inside him. Something warm squeezed at her heart when he appeared to make up his mind and came to sit down beside her.

He reached out and wound a long stem of the grass around his finger. Tugging at it gently, he said in a hushed voice, "Something happened a long time ago that will always haunt me."

She studied his face and knew how difficult he was finding it to tell her. "Do you want to talk about it?" she asked, managing to sound far more composed than she felt.

"Yes, I think I do." He kept his gaze on the grass he was winding around his finger. "If you're willing to listen."

If she was willing! She's spent nights longing for him to open up to her. It was ironic that he should want to now. Now that it was too late for them.

"Of course I want to listen," she said softly.

He let go of the grass and wound his arms around his knees. "I was fourteen years old," he said in a low, dry voice that twisted at her heart. "My father was a mean-tempered man. He'd been beating on me since I could remember, with anything that was handy—his belt most of the time. It had a heavy metal buckle. It was years before I could wear a belt with a buckle."

She felt sick. Michael was in the hands of someone who had done the very same thing. She looked at Slade's face, shadowed in the moonlight. This was the first time he'd ever spoken to her of his past. It was probably the first time he'd ever spoken of it to anyone. "Go on," she said quietly.

"I came home from school one day." He paused, as if searching for the right words. "He was beating on my younger sister. Something exploded in my head. I'd taken it from him all those years, and I couldn't take him hurting Nancy."

His breath shuddered in his throat. "I took the belt away from him and I hit him with it. Again and again. I couldn't stop. It was like there was a stranger inside my head, urging me on."

He buried his face in his hands. "He was yelling, but I kept on hitting him. I wanted to kill him," he said so quietly she barely heard the words. "I wanted him dead."

She felt frozen with disbelief. The one thing she had never associated him with was violence. She had seen him angry more than once, but he had always held his temper in check. She had always admired his control.

She stared at him, trying to deal with the last statement. How it must have tortured him, for him to have kept it to himself for so long.

She struggled to find something to say, afraid to lose the slender thread of communication. Her mind refused to cooperate and she waited in silence for him to go on.

"My mother called in a neighbor and between them they pulled me away," he said, finally lifting his head. "When my father came out of the hospital he had me arrested. I was underage, and was put in a reform school for four years."

Kate's shocked gasp seemed to echo around them. "But what about your mother, your sister? Surely they—"

"They didn't." He let out his breath as if he'd been holding it for a long time. "My mother refused to say anything. Maybe she was afraid of him, I don't know. It was a small town; the local newspaper made a big deal of it. My sister denied he'd beaten her. She blamed me for the publicity. She said she'd never forgive me for embarrassing her in front of her friends."

Slade reached for a blade of grass and tugged at it viciously. "She was only twelve, I thought she'd get over it. But I never heard from her in all the time I was at the home. I never heard from any of them. When I was released, I changed my name, left town and moved to Prineville. You know the rest."

Kate blinked back tears as she stared at him. She wanted to touch him, to hold him and try to blot out the painful memories. Something held her back, some instinct that told her there was more to come. She waited.

"I've told you all this," Slade said, still not looking at her, "because I wanted you to understand. I couldn't go on letting you think I rejected my son. I stayed away for the same reason I let you send me away."

He looked at her then, and she was shocked by the pain in his eyes, clearly visible in the moonlight. "I can't trust myself," he said quietly. "I can't be sure I can keep my temper under control. If I ever hurt someone I loved, I could never live with myself."

"Oh, God, Slade." At last she understood. He was so afraid of losing control again that he wouldn't allow himself to let anyone close to him. Anger boiled in her heart, so fierce it shook her to the core. How could his family have done this to him? They were all guilty. Between them they had ruined his life. And hers.

She sought for the words. "Slade, that was so long ago. And you had a damn good reason for what you did. You can't go on blaming yourself for something that happened twenty years ago. You have to learn to trust yourself, to realize you're a different person now."

"I don't know that I am." He uncurled his body and stood, brushing the sand from his jeans. "It's still there, Kate. The anger, the blind fury. Sometimes I feel it bottled up inside me, waiting to explode."

"But you would never hurt someone you love." She jumped to her feet, and laid her hand on his arm. "You must know that, Slade, in your heart."

He looked down at her fingers, as if surprised to see them there. "I wish I *could* know that," he said, and the pain in his voice echoed inside her. "You know what my father told the woman who came to take me away? He said he'd disciplined me because he loved me. He wanted to make a man of me."

He raised his face to the sky and closed his eyes. "Can't you see, Kate? What is in him, is in me, too, and I'm afraid that one day it could turn me into what he is."

He looked back at her, and she was shocked to see tears in his eyes. "You know what hurts the most? It's knowing that even with all that pain, all that sacrifice, my son still had to endure the very thing I fought so hard to protect him from. So help me, Kate, if Vic has hurt that boy again, I'm afraid of what I'll do."

She felt cold fingers touch her spine. He was seeing his father again in Vic. And himself in Michael. Was it possible that he would try to vindicate his son by destroying the person who represented his father? She didn't want to believe that.

She shivered, and Slade put his arms around her, pulling her close. "You're cold. It's time we went back. But there's something else I must say before we do."

She slipped her arms around his waist, hugging him to her as if to shut out what he was going to say next. Instinct told her what his words would be.

"Nothing's changed, much as I wish it could. When this is over, I have to leave. You know that, don't you?"

She fought to get the words out past the lump in her throat. "I know that you have to do what you think is best. I can't hold you against your will. I wouldn't want to."

She wanted to tell him. She wanted him to know that the love she'd had for him all those years ago hadn't died. That she loved him as much now, if not more, than she had then. But it wouldn't solve anything. Nothing she said would make any difference, she knew that now.

He had to find his own peace, in his own way. She could only make him stay if he learned to love her, and she knew now that was impossible. She would have to love him enough to let him go when the time came.

They walked back to the tavern in silence, while Kate fought the depression threatening to smother her. She couldn't give in to it now, she told herself. She had Michael to think about. At least Slade was willing to help her find him.

And they would find him. She had to believe that. Once they did, she vowed silently, she would pick up the pieces and go on with her life without Slade. She had done it before, she could do it again. And this time, she wouldn't look back. She and Michael would make it alone, as long as they had each other's love to depend on.

She managed to sleep that night, in spite of Slade's body lying next to her, and the gnawing ache of what might have been.

By eleven o'clock the next morning, the car was ready. Feeling more rested, and determined to keep a positive attitude, Kate waited anxiously to reach the next town. The tension that had vibrated between her and Slade had settled into a wary truce that, if not what she wanted, was at least bearable.

She was relieved when they were on the road again and their objective once again took precedence. They made three stops before they finally got lucky.

Slade pulled into the gas station at the midsize town that was bigger than anyplace they'd stopped at so far. When he described the Chevy Vic was driving, the fresh-faced attendant nodded his head.

"Sure," he said with a nonchalance that seemed ludicrous to Kate. "He was in here yesterday morning getting gas. Had a kid with him, little blond fella. Real bright for his age. I remember thinking it was strange his daddy wouldn't let him go to the bathroom by himself."

Kate saw the anger flash across Slade's face and tensed. She could only guess how he felt to hear Vic referred to as Michael's "daddy."

Slade seemed passive enough as he asked casually, "He didn't say where he was going, I suppose?"

The attendant nodded. "As a matter of fact he did. Said he was on the way to Las Vegas." He stopped, and peered up at Slade with suspicious eyes. "You're not after him for anything, are you?"

Slade gave a good imitation of a laugh. "No, of course not. They're friends of ours and we were hoping to catch up with them before they got into town. We wanted to surprise them."

"Ah." The young man's face cleared. "Well, I guess you'll have to hunt for them. I mentioned that the boy wasn't old enough to gamble, and his father said something about staying with a friend in a trailer park outside of town. He didn't say which one, though.''

Kate's heart leaped with hope. How many trailer parks could there be? Surely it shouldn't be too difficult to track them down? When she voiced her hopes to Slade, he was a little more cautious.

''It depends how determined Vic is to stay hidden,'' he said as they sped on their last leg into Las Vegas. ''And who he has helping him. This friend of his, for instance. Do you know who that might be?''

''No.'' Kate kept her eyes glued to the dark blur on the horizon that Slade had assured her was the famous gambling town. ''I didn't think Vic knew anyone in Nevada except his sister. Of course, it could be a friend of hers.''

''I thought of that, too,'' Slade said, ''but I don't think she's going to tell us any more than she has. She's more frightened of Vic than she is of us.''

Kate nodded. ''That was the impression I got. Do you think she does know where he is?''

''She may have known where he was headed. That doesn't mean he'll still be there.''

She looked at him in alarm. ''You don't think he'll leave town and go somewhere else?''

''That depends on how much Gladys tells him. If she's smart, she'll tell him we went back to Portland. She won't want him to think she told us where to look for him. It can't be easy being on the run with a small boy. I imagine as long as Vic thinks he's safe, he'll stay put.''

Kate leaned back and closed her eyes. How was Michael holding up in all this? she wondered. He had made such large strides in his recovery, this was bound to set him back again, and destroy all the confidence he'd built up over the past couple of years.

She'd have to start all over again, she thought, refusing to give in to the tiny doubt that said she might not get the chance. She would not allow any negative thinking to creep into her mind. She had to believe they would succeed in finding Michael, unharmed. It was the only way she found the strength to keep going.

She opened her eyes, her pulse jumping when she saw the blur had spread out on either side of the road. The cactus were giving way to spindly palm trees, sparse at first, then becoming more prevalent as the dark puddle of buildings expanded to a lake, then grew and spread until the faint zigzag of the skyline became visible.

Soon they were speeding along the main highway into town, and finally the gaudy, glittering buildings with their noisy casinos came into view as they entered the Strip.

Any other time Kate would have been fascinated by the sights and sounds that erupted on either side of her as Slade drove carefully through the main street.

Most of the revelry slid by unnoticed as her gaze scoured the bustling sidewalks for the sight of a small blond head. She leaned forward, hands gripping the dashboard, but nowhere in all that boisterous crowd could she see a child, let alone Michael.

"Relax, Kate. You're not likely to see him on the Strip."

Kate leaned back and sent Slade a rueful smile. "I know. I just had to look, though."

"We'll find a motel farther out of town. It will be less noisy."

She nodded, wondering if he would book separate rooms. He'd refused to let her pay the tavern owner for the room, saying the car-rental company would have to take care of it. She couldn't let him foot the bill at the motel. She'd brought her credit cards with her, aware that it could be days before they found Michael.

The motel Slade chose was unpretentious, tucked away on a back street at the edge of town, close to the residential section of the city.

He booked two rooms, each in their own names. Kate didn't know whether to feel relieved or miserable about the arrangement. After showering and changing her clothes, she decided the next priority was to do laundry. She had just found a launderette in the Yellow Pages when Slade tapped on the door.

He'd changed, too, into light pants and a yellow knit shirt. He looked cool and comfortable, and very much in command as he took the book from her and thumbed through it for the listings on trailer parks.

While she gathered up her laundry he began making calls, but Kate soon realized he was getting nowhere as his exasperation became more and more pronounced in his voice. She emerged from the bathroom as he slammed the receiver down for the fourth time. "You really didn't expect to find them on the first go, did you?" she asked as she emptied her holdall to make room for the laundry.

"No, but I did expect these people to be a little more helpful. That's the fourth person who's told me they can't remember everyone they talk to."

Kate stuffed her blouse inside the bag. "Surely they have a listing of who their tenants are?"

"Of course they do. But if you were Vic, would you use your real name?"

She looked at him in dismay. "Oh, no. I hadn't thought of that."

His eyes were sympathetic when he looked at her. "It's not going to be quite that easy, Kate. I'm sorry."

She sat down on the edge of the bed, since he was sitting in the only armchair. "So what do you suggest?"

"Those pictures you brought with you. You said you had one of Vic."

She nodded and reached for her purse. "I kept it because it was such a good one of Michael when he was baby." She pulled out a couple of photographs. "Here they are."

Slade took them and looked at them. One of them was of Vic holding an eight-month-old Michael. The other was Michael's last school picture.

"He'd had one tooth missing in the front and had refused to smile," Kate said as Slade looked at the school picture.

He made no comment, turning to the baby picture. He studied it for a long time, then said quietly, "He was a beautiful baby."

Her heart ached for him, knowing how much it must hurt to think about what he'd missed.

"We'll take the pictures with us," Slade said, tearing pages from the phone book. "We'll hit every trailer park in the area. If they're in one of them, we'll find them."

More hopeful, she followed him out the door.

It was dark by the time they gave up for the night. The long car trip and the heat had taken its toll, and Kate felt like a damp sponge by the time Slade suggested they get something to eat.

Over the late meal she brought up the subject of financing. "I can't let you pay for everything," she protested when Slade refused to discuss it.

"We can settle it all when we get back to Portland," he said shortly, putting an effective end to the topic.

As well as his salary, Kate thought, her depression deepening as she remembered the hitched trailer. If Michael hadn't been kidnapped Slade would have been long gone. She would have to replace him when this was over. That was if she still had a contract when she got back.

She shelved the thought, concentrating on more urgent matters. "How many more trailer parks are there?" she asked, watching Slade stir sugar into his coffee.

He pulled the pages from his pants pocket and spread them out on the table. "Thirteen," he counted, "and two more where the managers weren't there. We'll go back to those tomorrow."

"If we draw a blank at all of them, we'll start again. And this time we'll ask around all the trailers. We can't assume that all the managers are telling us the truth. One of them could be protecting Vic."

"And we could still draw a blank." His shoulders lifted in a weary shrug.

She was disheartened by his words. No doubt he was trying to be realistic, but she needed a boost for her morale, even if they both knew it was unfounded.

What she needed, she admitted ruefully, was the comforting presence of his arms holding her through the long night. She dreaded the thought of spending those demoralizing hours alone.

All the time she was doing something, even if it proved fruitless, she could hang on to her conviction that soon they would catch up with Vic, and Michael would be safe again. Alone in the dark shadows of the night, she knew it wouldn't be so easy to dispel the clawing fear that could plunge her into a dark pit of despair.

She glanced at Slade, who seemed preoccupied with stirring his coffee. It was hard to believe now that it was the same man who had banished that fear so effectively the night before. When she closed her eyes she could still feel the excitement of his body close to hers. The intense ferment of passion that had thrust them both out of the pain and anxiety and, for a few, brief moments in time, had united them.

She wanted that feeling again. She needed it, craved it. She opened her eyes and found him watching her, a sad, still expression on his face.

Her pulse leaped, but as she moved her hand to touch him, he shoved his chair back and stood. "We'd better get some sleep," he muttered. "I want an early start in the morning."

Disappointed, she got slowly to her feet. "I need to do some laundry before I go to bed," she said. "There's a launderette a couple of blocks from the motel. If you have anything you need washed you'd better give it to me."

He shook his head. "I'll take care of it myself later."

His refusal of her offer hurt, and she gave herself a silent rebuke. She couldn't let herself be affected by his attitude. She had to start building her defenses again. She would need them when he was no longer around.

He hesitated at her door and for a fleeting instant Kate allowed a flare of hope, but he muttered a short "Good night," and left her. She stared after him, fighting the urge to call him back and beg him to stay with her.

It took her the best part of an hour to take care of her laundry. As late as it was, she found it difficult to fall asleep. She fidgeted restlessly for what seemed like hours, struggling to keep the demons of fear and anxiety from invading her mind.

The night was softening into dawn before she fell into an uneasy sleep, disturbed by shadowy nightmares and undisclosed horror.

Slade greeted her the next morning with a studied casualness. They set off after breakfast, arriving at the first trailer park just as the manager was leaving.

He looked at the pictures, then shook his head. "Sorry. Haven't seen anyone like that around. Have you tried the Sunset Park?"

It was on their list, Slade told him, and thanked him. But they had no better luck at the Sunset Park, or the five parks that followed it on the list.

Trying not to give in to her despondency, Kate faced Slade across the table at the restaurant they'd picked for dinner that evening. The waitress slapped hamburgers down in front of them and moved off.

Slade lifted his Coke and drank deeply. His dark eyes studied her for a moment, then he reached over and covered her hand with his. "Hang in there, Kate. We're not done yet. We still have the two managers we missed yesterday."

It shook her that the simple touch of his fingers could give her so much strength. She managed a weak smile. "Never say die, huh?"

"Something like that."

She sighed. "I don't know if I can wait through another night."

"We don't have to. Neither of them are far from here. We can visit both of them tonight."

She nodded. If they had no better luck at the remaining parks, the trail would be cold. She wasn't sure she could handle the defeat. She made a halfhearted attempt to eat her hamburger, but couldn't finish it, in spite of Slade's comment that she needed to keep up her strength.

By the time they entered the first trailer park, the sun had already dipped below the horizon. Kate stepped out of the car, breathing in the cooler air with appreciation. The aroma of barbecued meat and wood smoke hung in the air as they walked toward the darkened office.

Kate's spirits sunk when she saw the note on the door. "He's left again," she said, without even bothering to read the note.

"Not for long," Slade said, peering at the door. "It says here he'll be back at nine. It's almost that now." He lowered himself on the step and looked up at her. "We'll wait for him."

She sank down beside him, and released a heavy sigh. Her lips trembled and she made an effort to steady them. In the shadowed light she saw his eyes burning with his intensity.

She felt a tear fall, and she heard his agonized breath.

"Don't, Kate," he whispered. "You have more guts, more determination, than any woman I've ever met. You deserve to win, and you will. I swear to you that if we have to search the entire country, I'll see you get Michael back." He leaned forward, and she tilted her face for his kiss. Before his mouth could touch hers they were caught in the beam of powerful headlights as a car swept down toward them.

Scrambling to his feet Slade waited for the driver to get out before greeting him. He introduced himself and offered his hand, which the park manager took, giving his name as Martin Ramsey.

It was a ritual Kate had seen repeated so many times over the past two days. She barely took notice when the manager unlocked the door to his office and turned on the light. She listened as Slade repeated his story of trying to track down the brother of his best friend. She watched Martin Ramsey take the pictures and study them, waiting for him to shake his balding head.

She was too stunned to speak when the burly man lifted his face and said, "Yeah, I know this man. He came in two days ago with the boy. I remember the boy's name. Mikey, wasn't it?"

Chapter 9

Kate bit back a cry of relief as Slade said sharply, "Where are they now?"

The manager shrugged. "I don't know. They only stayed the one night. The guy said he was looking for a friend, but the friend had moved. I gave them a place to sleep that night and they left yesterday morning."

Slade swallowed his frustration with a silent curse. If the damn car hadn't gone out from under him, they would have been there a day earlier.

He sent a quick glance at Kate, who was staring at Ramsey. He put a hand lightly on her shoulder. "They give you any idea where they were headed?"

The manager shook his head. "They must be staying in town. The guy said he'd got a job at a restaurant here."

Slade felt the jerk of Kate's shoulder under his hand. "Did he say which one?"

"Nope. Sorry I can't help you on that." Ramsey glanced at Kate before looking back at him. "Where are you staying? If I run into them again I'll give you a call."

Slade gave Kate a light squeeze and let her go. He pulled the torn telephone pages from his pocket and ripped off a corner. "Where's your pencil?" he asked Kate, and waited for her to find it in her purse.

Her movements were slow, as if she were doing everything in her sleep. He gave her a worried glance before scribbling down the name of their motel, and his own name.

"Here." He handed the scrap of paper to Ramsey. "I'd appreciate a call. We'll be around for a few more days."

Ramsey tucked the paper into his shirt pocket without looking at it. "Sure," he said. "Sorry you missed them."

"So am I," Slade said grimly. He lifted his hand in a brief farewell, then took Kate's arm and led her back to the car. She didn't speak when he opened the door for her and stood back to let her climb in.

He walked around the hood to the other side of the car, and saw Martin Ramsey watching them from the doorway of his office. He was still watching them when Slade backed out, then pulled onto the road that led to the highway. Slade had the distinct impression that the manager watched the car until the headlights had faded from his view.

He worried about that as he drove back to the motel. Something about Martin Ramsey bothered him. Maybe it was the way he'd asked about their motel, then stuck the paper in his pocket without reading it.

Slade narrowed his eyes against the onslaught of dazzling lights that greeted them as they drove onto the Strip. Or maybe, he thought, it was the look the manager had given Kate, just before he'd asked for the name of their motel. He was getting paranoid, he told himself, impatient with his suspicions. If he went around suspecting everyone they spoke to, he'd be a basket case before this was over.

He glanced at Kate, and immediately forgot his preoccupation with Ramsey. She sat slumped in her seat, looking as fragile as a sugar ornament.

"You okay?" he said, cursing when she appeared not to hear him. He increased pressure on the accelerator, weaving in and out of the heavy traffic amid a blare of horns, finally clearing the main streets with squealing tires.

He pulled into the parking lot of the motel, slammed on the brake and cut the engine. "Kate?" he said gently. When she didn't answer him, he touched her shoulder.

Very slowly she turned her head to look at him. He could see her face in the light from the street lamps, and her expression shocked him.

She stared at him as if he were an apparition, transparent, without substance. Her face looked as if it had been drawn in charcoal, all stark lines and slashes.

He had promised himself he wouldn't touch her again. He couldn't trust himself to hold her and not do what his body demanded of him. He would not take advantage of her vulnerability again, he'd vowed during the long night he'd lain awake desperate with his need for her.

But he could no more see that look on her face and ignore it than he could fly. Without a word he held out his arms and, with a sob that tore at his heart, she leaned into him.

He held her until the storm of weeping had passed, one hand stroking her hair, the other lightly massaging her back. The shuddering eased, and with a final gasping sob she pulled back out of his arms.

He felt a strange emptiness in his chest where her head had rested. He said nothing, waiting for her to speak.

"I'm sorry," she said shakily. "I promised myself I wouldn't do that."

He'd made promises, too. Promises he wasn't sure he could keep. He nodded gravely. "It's understandable, under the circumstances. It probably did you good."

She drew a trembling breath. "It was just...we'd been so close, so damn close."

"I know." He sighed, and rested his fingers on the steering wheel, drumming them quietly against the spokes. "We're not done yet. Tomorrow we start on the restaurants. Someone somewhere is going to give us another lead. I'm sure of it."

She made a small sound that could have been a laugh. He turned his head and looked at her. Tears still sparkled in her eyelashes. He wanted to wipe them away with his thumb. A nerve coiled in his belly and he knew he couldn't touch her again.

"It seems as if the tables are turned," she said, her voice sounding stronger. "Now you're the one with all the optimism."

"Because you gave it to me." He clenched his fingers on the wheel. "You made me believe that you could get Michael back, and I'm not going to let you lose that faith. That's what's going to see you through this thing."

She smiled. "That, and you. Thank you, Slade, for being here. I wouldn't make it without you, I know that now."

"Yes you would," he said gruffly. He didn't want her depending on him. He'd already warned her she couldn't rely on him. He couldn't rely on himself.

"We'd better get inside," he said, pushing his door open before his arms could obey the messages his body sent to them. "We'll get an early start in the morning."

He walked her to her door and stood looking down at her. Her hair glowed almost silver in the light from the lamps. She gazed up at him, and his stomach contracted when he read the message in her expressive blue eyes.

Cursing his weakness he curled his hands into fists. "I'm going to find that launderette before I turn in," he said quickly.

She lowered her head, but not before he'd seen the disappointment cloud her face. God, he thought desperately, it would be so easy to give in. It was what they both wanted, there was no denying that. But it wouldn't be fair. Not to her, and not to himself. He had to forget he'd ever held her in his arms again. He had to blot out all memory of her body under his, warm and eager and so full of giving.

He had nothing to give her in return. Knowing that, he had no right to accept what she offered. It took a formidable effort to say lightly, "Get some sleep. Tomorrow's another day."

She nodded, and slipped her key in the lock. "Good night, Slade," she said quietly, and then she was gone from him. The door she closed between them might just as well have been a fortress, shutting him out forever.

Kate threw her purse on the bed and kicked off her sandals. She felt like crying again, but had no tears left to shed. Perhaps once she had Michael back, she thought wistfully, this awful ache she felt for Slade would eventually sift away.

She felt as if she had lost something very fragile, very special. It was like a captured bird; for a short time she'd held it in her hand, then she'd spread out her fingers and it had flown, before she'd really had time to examine it.

There were times when she wished with all her heart she hadn't gone to see Slade that day, that she'd never thought of asking him to pose for her. Yet how could she deny herself the beautiful night she'd spent in his arms, and the memory that would be hers to cherish for always?

She walked slowly into the bathroom and turned on the faucet. The sound of the rushing water soothed her jagged nerves, and she pulled off her clothes and stepped under the cooling spray.

She washed quickly, unable to bear the memory of Slade's naked body, slick with soap, rubbing sensuously against hers in a cascade of streaming water. Stepping out of the tub she reached for a towel and began to pat her face dry. Her skin smarted with the effects of the sun, and she made a mental note to buy suntan lotion in the morning.

She hooked the towel under her arms and secured it, then wandered back into the bedroom to retrieve her nightgown from under the pillow. She was reaching for it when the silence was shattered by the shrill tone of the telephone. Her frayed nerves jolted her entire body as she swung around to stare at the jangling phone.

It had to be Slade, she thought, her pulse leaping in expectation. Though why would he call her? Breathless with hope she rushed forward and grabbed the receiver to press it against her ear.

Her "Hello?" shivered in the silent room. She waited for an answer that was much too long in coming.

"Kate. How nice to hear your voice."

The wheezing cough that followed set her teeth on edge. She leaned a hand on the dresser for support and tried to collect her scattered thoughts.

"Vic? Where are you?"

She sounded ridiculously calm. Her whole body shook with the force of her apprehension, yet she'd managed to sound so damn calm. Slade would be proud of her, she thought irrationally, and in the next instant wondered if he was still next door.

"You really don't expect me to tell you that, do you?"

"Is Michael with you? Is he all right?" She tried not to panic at the obvious satisfaction in Vic's voice. He intended to milk every ounce of enjoyment out of her anxiety, she didn't doubt that. She could not afford to let him think he was winning.

"He's fine—for the present."

The ominous pause drew cold shivers across her back. "Can I speak to him?"

Vic's laugh tightened her nerves. "You know it's past his bedtime. What kind of daddy do you think I am?"

"I don't know, Vic," Kate said bitterly. "What kind of daddy would take a small boy away from his mom and scare him like that?"

"Michael's not scared, he's having a ball. He's enjoying his vacation with his daddy."

If that was meant to reassure her, Kate thought savagely, it wasn't working.

"I told you not to come after me, Kate," Vic said softly. "That was a stupid thing to do. You make me cross when you don't do what you're told."

"How did you know I was here?" Kate said, trying not to let his insidious tone destroy the fragile hold on her reasoning. She couldn't seem to think straight. Something wasn't adding up.

"Gladys told me you paid her a little visit. She said she hadn't told you where I was, but I know my sister. She never knew when to keep her mouth shut."

Kate let that go, deciding Gladys would have to fend for herself. She waited until she felt she had control of her voice.

"I got anxious about Michael," she said, striving for a casual tone. "I thought he might miss me. I guessed you'd gone to see Gladys; I thought we might have a nice time all together. Like we used to."

She closed her eyes. She had never been a good liar. She prayed Gladys hadn't mentioned Slade.

Her hopes were dashed when Vic gave a menacing chuckle. "Well, that would have been cozy, wouldn't it? You, me and the bastard rodeo drifter."

"Vic—" she began, but his roar deafened her.

"Now get this, you bitch. You get that no-good bum outta here and back to the bullring where he belongs. As long as he's hanging around you there's no way you're gonna get your precious son back. You got that?"

The click in her ear was cold and final. She stared at the receiver, unable to believe what had happened. She'd actually had him on the line, and he'd escaped again. She gave an agonized cry of frustration and slammed the phone down, rattling the dresser.

Slade. She had to tell him now. She dragged on clothes in a frenzy of impatience and then ran out the door, leaving it open behind her. She pounded on the door next to hers until her hands were sore, collapsing against it when she realized he wasn't there. The car had gone; he had to be at the launderette.

She started running across the parking lot and out into the street, racing along the sidewalk under the pale gleam of the lamps. One block, two. Her breath sobbed in her throat as she darted across the second set of lights without waiting for the walk signal. She saw the lighted sign of the launderette and had reached the door before she realized the compact was not in the parking area.

Bursting in she ignored the startled gazes of the two young women standing by the machines. One swift glance around was enough to tell her he wasn't there.

She backed out, and stood for a moment or two, regaining control of her breath. Anger flooded her, swift and consuming. Why wasn't he there? She needed him and, damn him, *he wasn't there*.

She began to walk back, with quick, short strides, her teeth gritted in anger. She knew she was being unreasonable. She knew she had no right to expect him to be where she wanted him. He had no way of knowing that Vic would call, she reminded herself.

It didn't help one bit. She was remembering the times she had needed him, eight years ago. The car accident, when they'd taken her to the hospital for observation. Shaken and hurting, she'd called all over town to find him. He'd taken a backpack and gone into the mountains without telling her. By the time he came back her bruises had healed, but not her heart.

Kate swung into the parking lot and started across it at a fast clip. Then there was the time her cat had been hit by a car. It was the only family she'd had, and she was devastated. Once again she'd tried to find Slade. He'd turned up two days later. She didn't even ask him where he'd been.

It had been like that throughout their entire relationship. He would simply disappear, sometimes for a day, sometimes a week, always turning up without explanation, expecting to carry on as if nothing had happened.

She'd finally given up trying to hold him. She'd let him go, unaware that she was carrying his son—until it was too late.

He was right, Kate fumed as she approached the still-open door to her room. Nothing had changed. Even now, in the midst of all this anxiety and fear, he had simply taken off somewhere and heaven knew when he would turn up again.

Light flooded the area in front of her room from the open door. It blinded her for an instant, and she didn't see him until she had stepped into the room.

He was sitting on the bed, his expression as hard as granite. He rose as she halted in surprise, and said harshly, "Where in the hell have you been?"

Wondering why she hadn't noticed the car parked outside, Kate lifted her chin. "I was looking for you," she said, resentment trembling on every word.

"You were in that much of a hurry you couldn't close the door behind you?" He jerked his hand at the door. "Do you have any idea how I felt when I came back and saw the door hanging open and you gone? I thought . . ." His throat worked, and he muttered a low curse.

"You thought what?" She knew the dangers of losing her temper, yet she couldn't seem to control it. "That I'd run out on you? Is that what you thought? Well, welcome to the club. I spent a great deal of my time thinking the same thing eight years ago. It didn't seem to bother you then. Now the boot is on the other foot. Maybe you'll have just a little inkling of how I used to feel."

He blinked. "What the hell are you talking about? Why are you bringing all that up now? What has it got to do with this?"

Nothing, she thought wearily. She had no idea why she'd blurted all that out. He was right; this had nothing to do with the way he'd treated her in the past, except for one thing. If she'd harbored any hopes that things could work out for them, he had just destroyed the last vestige of them.

"I went to the launderette," she said, brushing past him. "I thought you might be interested in knowing that Vic called me."

"When?" His voice cracked across the room.

"A few minutes ago. That's why I went looking for you." She felt so tired. "Where were you, anyway?" It was an automatic question; she really didn't care anymore.

"I picked up some beer on the way back." He gestured at the bed, and she saw the six-pack on the covers. She remembered passing the small general store. She'd been too preoccupied to notice the car outside.

"Tell me, what did Vic say? Is Michael all right?"

She sat on the edge of the bed, trying to think. "He was mad because you were here. He said as long as you were with me, I wouldn't get Michael back."

"Did he say where he was?"

She shook her head. "He was enjoying himself," she said bitterly. "He knew what he was doing to me, and he was enjoying it." She shuddered, remembering the sly tone in Vic's voice.

Slade swore. "I had a feeling Ramsey knew more than he was saying."

Kate jerked her head up. "What do you mean?"

His dark gaze still held traces of anger as he looked at her. "Hasn't it occurred to you to wonder how Vic knew you were here?"

"Well, yes, but—"

"Ramsey. He's the only one who knew the name of the motel where we're staying. He must have called Vic."

Kate's eyes widened as she took in this new development. "Then he does know where Vic is."

Slade swung around to the door. "You bet he does. And this time he's going to tell me if I have to beat it out of him."

"Slade, wait!" Kate's voice rung out as she jumped up from the bed.

He hesitated, and looked back at her. The expression in his eyes worried her.

"You can't go back there," she said urgently. "If he's a friend of Vic's, he'll tell him you're still with me. Vic could take off with Michael and we'll never catch up with the man again."

"He won't have time. By the time Ramsey is in any fit state to talk to anyone, I'll be on Vic's trail."

"No." She leaped across the room and grabbed at Slade's arm. "Listen to me. Let me go and talk to him. Vic has probably told him a bunch of lies. I'll tell him what's really going on and explain about Vic. He'll have to tell me where they are."

"He doesn't have to tell you anything." Slade stared down at her, his face hard and unyielding. "He could send you on a wild-goose chase, tell you anything."

"He could just as easily lie to you," Kate argued. "What if I tell him that if he doesn't tell me the truth, I'll have the police question him?"

She waited, watching the indecision gradually wear away the anger in his eyes. "All right," he said quietly. "We'll play it your way. But I'm driving you out there." He held up his hand as she started to protest. "You can drop me off at the end of the road. I'll wait for you there."

"All right." She would have agreed to just about anything at that point. Snatching up her purse she followed him outside, closing the door firmly behind her.

He was silent on the way back to the trailer park, and she was glad. She had been frightened that he would goad Vic into taking off again. And scared that he would carry out his threat and beat up Martin Ramsey.

His words still haunted her. *I couldn't stop. I wanted him dead.* Never once in all the hours they'd spent together had she ever suspected he'd concealed such a painful secret. She wondered if he'd ever thought about telling her, and what it had cost him to tell her now.

She understood so much more now. Why he was the way he was. Why he was afraid to let himself love anyone. Why he had denied himself his son.

Knowing didn't make it any easier. It still hurt that he couldn't trust her enough to let go of the past. That in spite of all they'd shared together, it wasn't enough. It would never be enough.

Slade parked the car at the end of the road beneath a stand of tall palm trees. He opened the door, then looked at Kate, his face shadowy in the darkness.

"Be careful. I don't think he'd hurt you, but just watch yourself. I'll be close by, in case you need me."

"I won't need you, but thanks." She waited for him to slide out, then climbed into the seat behind the wheel. The words had sounded more bitter than she'd intended. She gave him the ghost of a smile. "I'll pick you up on the way out."

She saw his hand lift, then he stepped back. She could feel the tension tying knots in her back as she put the gearshift in Drive and let out the brake. Slowly she crept forward, her eyes on the twin beams of her headlights. The lights had been dimmed in the trailers along the roadside, and when she reached the office, the windows were dark.

She and Slade had assumed Ramsey lived in the trailer office. If he didn't, Kate thought worriedly, she would have to try and find someone who knew which one he did live in.

She parked the car and climbed out. The stars provided a glittering backdrop to the full moon, though they lacked the luster of the stars in the open desert. The air, freshened by the night breeze, still smelled faintly of wood smoke.

Kate took a steadying breath and stepped up to the office door. Las Vegas was a city that ignored the distinction between night and day, and she could hear the hum of traffic from the highway. A phrase popped into her mind. The city that didn't sleep.

Whereas Martin Ramsey could be sound asleep by now. She rapped lightly on the door, then waited several long seconds before rapping again, louder this time. If he'd told them the truth earlier, Kate thought grimly as she pounded the door, she wouldn't be here now, disturbing the entire park.

As if to echo her thoughts, lights sprang on in the trailer next to the office. A voice yelled something, muffled by the walls of the vehicle. Kate waited guiltily until the door swung open to reveal a thickset man wearing the bottom half of a dark track suit.

The light fell across his face and Kate felt a rush of relief when she recognized Martin Ramsey. His mouth fell open when he saw her, and he shut it with a snap, his eyes shifting away from her to stare into the darkness.

"He's not here," Kate stated clearly, guessing Ramsey was looking for Slade.

The manager smoothed what was left of his hair back over his head. "So what do you want?"

"I'd like to come in. I need to talk to you." It was the last thing she wanted, but she couldn't take the chance of his slamming the door in her face.

She thought at first he was going to refuse, then he shrugged and stepped back. Wishing she didn't have to do this alone, Kate stepped up inside the trailer.

Ramsey had not been in bed, she saw with relief. The trailer was much bigger than the one Slade lived in. There was enough space for two small armchairs, instead of the narrow bench that lined Slade's walls. Newspapers were strewn at the foot of one chair, and a portable television set flickered in front of it.

Ramsey leaned over to switch off the television and waved her into the vacant chair, seating himself in the other one. "So, what can I do for you?"

"You can tell me where to find my ex-husband," Kate said clearly.

Ramsey pretended to look surprised. "Do I know him?"

"The man we were asking about this morning. Vic Wheeler."

The manager's gray eyes studied her in silence. "I don't remember you saying he was your ex-husband," he said finally.

"I didn't have to. Apparently you already knew that." Kate leaned forward. "Mr. Ramsey, I don't know what Vic has told you. Two days ago he kidnapped my son and is holding him against his will—"

"Hold it a second, hold it." Ramsey held up his hand. "I don't know anything about a kidnapping. Seems to me, if Vic is the boy's father, that's a strong word to use."

"Not if he was taken without my approval, and against my son's will."

"Well, now. That's not what I heard." Ramsey reached for a pack of cigarettes lying on a table at his elbow. "Vic told me they were on a vacation together. He was catching up on the time he'd spent away from him."

"Did he tell you where he'd spent that time?" She waited while Ramsey shook a cigarette out of the pack and captured it with his lips.

"He mentioned a spell in the hospital, if I remember rightly."

"Well, he told you half of it," Kate said. "Until a week or so ago, he *was* in a hospital. A mental hospital. He was sent there three years ago for beating up his son." She saw no reason to elaborate on that point.

Ramsey blew a spiral of smoke through his nose. When he didn't say anything she continued, "I was given custody of Michael. Two days ago Vic met him from school, without my knowledge or consent, then called me to tell me he was keeping Michael for a while, and ordered me not to come after him. I found out he'd brought him here and I followed him.''

"With your boyfriend."

Kate ignored that. "Mr. Ramsey. My ex-husband is a dangerous man. I'm afraid he will harm Michael. He is insanely jealous, and I mean that literally, despite what the hospital might think. I will do anything necessary to get my son back. You know where he is. If I have to call in the police to help me get that information, believe me, I will.''

Ramsey held up his hands. "Whoa, lady. Don't get hostile on me." He took the cigarette out of his mouth and waved it in the air. "I want no truck with the police. Your old man told me you and the boyfriend were planning to steal the boy away from him. He said he didn't want a stranger messing with his kid. I felt sorry for him.''

Kate could understand that. Vic had always been good at soliciting sympathy. "So he told you to call him if we showed up?''

"Yeah. He said to find out where you were staying and then call him. So I did." He got up and went to the door. "I don't want any trouble. None of this has got anything to do with me.''

"Then tell me where they are and I'll leave," Kate said, getting to her feet.

Ramsey hesitated. "You won't tell him I told you? I don't want no loony coming after me.''

Kate gave him a wry smile. "I won't tell him.''

Ramsey pushed the door open. "He's at the Windmill, just off the Strip. Anyone can tell you where it is.''

She felt a surge of triumph. "Thank you." She stepped past him into the darkness, then turned. "Did you see my son, Mr. Ramsey?''

"Yeah." He stuck the cigarette in the corner of his mouth. "He looked fine, Mrs. Wheeler. Quiet, but just fine.''

"Thank you again," Kate said softly, and went down the steps without looking back. She heard the door close as she walked away, her heart singing with hope. Soon now, she told herself. Soon she'd hold Michael's thin body in her arms again. She quickened her footsteps and hurried to the car.

She almost screamed when a dark shadow moved from behind it. Then she heard Slade's voice, quiet and reassuring. "It's only me. Get in."

She scrambled into the passenger side, turning eagerly as Slade eased himself in next to her. "I got it," she said. "The Windmill. Do you know where it is? He said it was off the Strip."

"We'll find it." Slade gunned the motor and nosed the car back onto the road. "Are you sure he was being straight with you?"

She felt a moment's uneasiness, then dismissed it. "Yes, I am. He didn't know about Vic's...illness. And as soon as I mentioned the police he told me where to find them."

Slade refrained from answering, and she sensed he didn't share her conviction. She leaned back in her seat, praying her instincts had been right.

It took them over half an hour to find the Windmill. Ramsey had been wrong about one thing—no one seemed to know where it was. By the time they finally tracked it down, her uneasiness had returned, and intensified.

It was a shabby-looking building, in a back street a long way off the Strip. Slade looked at his watch as he cut the engine. "Almost midnight. I hope they've got a clerk on duty." He held out his hand. "Give me the photos; I'll hunt someone down."

"No." She took a tight grip on her purse. "I'm going in alone."

"I'm not going to argue about this," Slade said evenly. "From everything you've said, you've convinced me that

Vic is unstable and unpredictable. It could take two of us to get Michael out of there unharmed."

"I'm pretty sure Vic wouldn't hurt him as long as I'm alone. I can't be sure what he'd do if he saw you with me." In the reflection of the streetlight she saw the resolution on his face and reached out to clasp his hand. "Please, Slade. I have to do this alone."

He stared at her for several seconds, then let out a long breath. "All right. But tread very carefully."

"I will," she promised, and with apprehension quivering in every pore, she stepped out of the car.

She could see a light shining in the office, which was a tiny room on the end of the L-shaped building. She walked quickly, aware of the soft, flapping noise her sandals made on the pavement.

She passed several windows, and it took all her willpower not to stop and try to look in each one. Somewhere, in one of these rooms, Michael lay sleeping. Was Vic with him? Or had Vic left the boy on his own while he pursued his own enjoyment out on the town?

She wondered what Vic had said or done to prevent Michael from running away. Whatever it was, it probably wasn't pleasant. So far Slade hadn't brought the subject up, but she knew he must have considered the question. She pushed the thought from her mind before it became unbearable.

She ran the last few steps, bringing herself to a halt when she reached the door. It swung open when she touched it, and somewhere inside a bell jangled loudly.

She could see no one behind the desk, and she sent a quick glance around, noticing a door in the far wall. It opened almost at once, and she realized it must lead into the motel room next door.

A thin, untidy-looking woman stood in the doorway, rubbing at her eyes. "Double or single?" she murmured, and shuffled toward the desk.

"No. I'm looking…" Kate hesitated. "I was supposed to meet my husband and son here," she said, fishing in her purse for the photos. "Can you tell me what room they're in?"

"Name?" The woman shuffled the pages of a grubby registration book.

Kate felt a sinking sensation in the pit of her stomach. Had Vic used his real name? If not, her story was going to sound more than a little suspicious. Taking a chance she said, "Wheeler. Vic Wheeler."

Her heart leaped when the woman muttered, "Oh, yeah. Here it is." She pointed a jagged fingernail at a signature, then peered closer and frowned.

Kate took a nervous step forward. "What room is it?"

The woman closed the book with a thump and stared at Kate with narrowed eyes. "Well, they *were* in room 56."

The sense of impending disaster gripped tight as Kate repeated faintly, "Were?"

"Yeah." Curiosity flickered in her dark-ringed eyes. "They checked outta here."

Kate jumped as the bell jangled again. Slade's voice spoke behind her, sharp with urgency. "When?"

She reached out to him and he took her hand in a comforting grasp.

"What is this?" said the woman, her voice loaded with suspicion. "Who are you?"

"A friend of mine," Kate said quickly. He'd ignored her request that he stay in the car, but for the moment she was glad he was there. "He's helping me locate my son." She looked helplessly at Slade. "And my husband," she added as an afterthought.

"What time did he check out?" Slade repeated.

"Couple of hours ago. I'd just come on."

"Did he say where they were going?"

"Nope. He didn't say much at all, that one. Too busy keeping an eye on the boy."

"Was Michael...?" Kate swallowed, and tried again. "Did he look all right? My son, I mean?"

The woman shrugged. "Fine. Stood there quiet and as good as gold. That's why I wondered why his father seemed so worried about him." She leaned forward and peered closer at Kate. "Is everything all right?"

Realizing her devastation must show on her face, Kate managed a faint smile. "Thank you. I'm sorry to bother you." She had to get out of there, she thought suddenly, before she fell apart. She turned, grabbing at Slade's arm for support as her head spun.

He held her arms and looked across at the woman. "He didn't give you any idea where they might be going?"

Kate's shoulders slumped. They had been so close. Just one step behind all the way.

"Sorry," the woman muttered behind her.

She felt Slade's arm around her, supporting her as they moved to the door. It felt so good to lean on him.

They had the door open, and were passing through when the woman called out to them.

Slade paused, one arm still holding Kate, and looked back.

"There's just one thing," the woman said, pulling open a drawer in the desk. "Mr. Wheeler paid me with a salary check; I remember 'cause I had to give him the extra back in cash. Hold on."

Kate's heart began a slow pumping as she waited, hardly daring to breathe.

"Yeah, here it is." The woman held the slip of paper up in triumph. "The Lonesome Wagon Steak House. On West Sahara. You can't miss it, it's got a big ol' covered wagon on the roof. How they got the damned thing up there I'll never know."

"Thank you," Kate said shakily.

For the first time a smile crinkled the woman's face. "Hope you catch up with your son, honey."

"So do I," Kate whispered fervently. "Oh, God, so do I."

Chapter 10

Kate was surprised to find herself shivering when she seated herself in the car. She rubbed her arms as Slade started the engine. He sent her a quick glance. "How're you doing?"

She flashed him a quick smile. "Fine. I'm cold, though."

"The desert cools off at night. You're noticing the contrast. You should have brought a sweater."

She felt her teeth begin to chatter and clenched them. Her whole body felt jittery. It was like coming off a roller coaster. She'd gone from hope to despair so many times in the past couple of days.

"Can you find the restaurant?" she asked as Slade turned onto the main street.

"I know where it is. I remember seeing it when we came into town."

She sat tense and silent, hardly aware of her surroundings as Slade drove through the glittering lights of the town. She was afraid to hope for too much; yet without hope she wouldn't have the strength to go on.

She caught her breath when the car slowed and turned onto a wide, tree-lined street. Small shops and businesses bordered the sidewalks on either side, and once they had passed over the expressway, she could see the restaurant with its covered wagon on the roof.

Even before they reached it she could see it was in darkness.

"I was afraid of that," Slade muttered. "It looks as if it's closed." He pulled into a small shopping center across the road and parked the car. "You wait here," he said, and was gone before she could utter a protest.

Within a few minutes he was back, shaking his head as he climbed in beside her. "Nobody's there. We'll have to wait till morning."

She closed her eyes as a spasm of frustration shook her. Another night to get through. Alone. How much more could she take of this? How much more could Michael take?

Not a second longer than he had to, she answered herself savagely. Vic was only one step ahead of them. Sooner or later their luck would break, and they would close the gap.

She tried not to think about what would happen when they did. All she cared about was getting Michael back, safe and unhurt. That was all she asked. What happened to Vic after that she really didn't care, as long as he left them alone.

If it meant moving to another town, another part of the country, she would do it. She might as well, she thought, feeling fatigue draining her strength away. She had no ties in Oregon. Nothing to keep her there. Only the memories, which would be best forgotten.

She dragged herself out of the car when they reached the motel. In answer to Slade's question she assured him she was fine. Nothing a good night's sleep wouldn't take care of.

He gave her a searching look but offered no comment, and she let herself into her room and collapsed on the bed. A long time later she pulled off her clothes and crept between the covers, hugging her misery to herself until she fell into a troubled sleep.

The phone woke her the next morning, and she stumbled across the room to answer it, angry with herself for sleeping late. It was Slade, telling her to be ready in half an hour.

The sky looked washed out when they left the motel, a thin cover of haze robbing it of its brilliance. The wind had died, leaving a heated stillness in the air. Kate pushed the sleeves of her peach top higher up her arms and wished she'd worn shorts.

Slade drove quickly, the collar of his partly unbuttoned shirt flapping against his neck in the draft from the open window. His bronzed arms beneath the rolled-up sleeves looked even darker against the pale coffee fabric.

He hadn't spoken more than a half dozen words to her since he'd tapped on her door, and she sent him a quick glance, wondering what he was thinking. He looked preoccupied, refusing to acknowledge her questioning look, though he must have seen it. She wondered if his stomach was rolling the way hers was.

He's suggested breakfast first, but she couldn't face the thought of food. When she'd told him to eat without her he'd merely shaken his head.

Once more Slade parked the car in the small shopping center across the street from the steak house. He turned to her, and her heart skipped a beat when she saw his grave expression.

"Do you want me to come with you?" he asked, and she knew by his tone that he didn't expect her to find Vic in the restaurant.

She wasn't really expecting to find him there herself. She wasn't sure what she did expect. It was as if Vic knew exactly what she was doing all the time, every move she made. It was a game, a tormenting, cruel game, and Michael was the ultimate loser.

"No," she said, and gathered up her purse. "There's a chance Vic will be there, and I want him to think you've gone back to Oregon. Maybe then I can talk him into taking me to Michael."

"You know I can't let you do that alone."

"Slade." She laid her hand on his arm. "If he is there, and he agrees to take me, you will have to let me go alone. It's the only chance we have. He will not let you near Michael. It's what set him off in the first place, seeing the two of you together."

Her voice shook and she paused, drawing a deep breath. "We are dealing with an unpredictable man, you agreed with me on that. There is no telling what lengths he'll take to keep you from Michael. Don't you see? He's punishing me; he blames me for everything that's happened to him. He wants me under his control; as long as I do everything he says, he'll be fine. If I don't—"

She stopped, swallowed and made herself go on. "I won't take that chance with Michael. You have to let me do this alone."

He looked down at her hand and lifted it from his arm. He held it for a moment or two, then let her go. "I can't make you any promises, Kate."

It would have to be enough. She nodded, and opened the door, sliding out into the sunshine. Without looking back she walked quickly down the block to the restaurant.

They were open for business, with a dozen or so customers already seated at the round tables. A reed-thin waitress with a startling red punk hairdo bustled around brandishing a notepad and exchanging jokes in the way of someone greeting regular customers. Kate stood for a moment in the doorway, scanning the room for Vic's bulky figure. If he was there at all, she thought, he would most likely be in the kitchen.

The waitress bounded across to her with a determined smile pinned to her face. She looked much too young to be wearing so much makeup, Kate thought, allowing herself to be showed to a table.

The smell of coffee had succeeded in seducing her taste buds and she ordered a cup. Slade would have to wait a few extra minutes for her. She waited until the girl had placed a steaming cup in front of her, then said casually, "Is Vic here by the way?"

"Vic? You mean Vic Wheeler?"

The high-pitched voice seemed to echo around the room and Kate winced. "Yes. Is he here?"

"Nope." Her heavily mascaraed eyes stared unblinkingly into Kate's. "He quit. Came by for his check last night. You just missed him."

Surprise, surprise, Kate thought. She waited for the letdown. When it didn't materialize she realized she'd become immune. She'd been disappointed so often she was expecting it.

"Too bad," the girl went on. "I was getting real attached to his kid."

Kate's head shot up. "He had his son with him?"

"Yeah. Mikey. I kinda kept an eye on him while Vic was working. Sat right there—" she waved a badly manicured hand at a corner table "—like a little angel all day. Not many kids would sit like that. I bought him some comics and a coloring book to keep him occupied. Nice kid." She looked thoughtful. "Real quiet, though. You a friend of theirs?"

Kate hesitated. To admit she was Michael's mother would arouse curiosity, and could prevent her from finding out what she needed to know. She managed to smile. "An old friend."

"Oh." The waitress regarded her with a serious expression. "He seemed awful sad. I was wondering what happened to his mom."

Kate's breath caught in her throat. "He didn't say anything?"

"The kid? Uh-uh. I asked him, but he wouldn't talk about it. I reckon it had to be something bad. Maybe that's why Vic took off all of a sudden like that. He only worked here two days. I was surprised when Sam said he'd picked up his check."

"Sam?"

"The owner." Her smile suggested she had more than a professional interest in her boss. "It must have been late when Vic came by," she added. "I was here till around nine-thirty."

"Is Sam here now?" Kate asked without much hope.

The red spikes quivered as the waitress shook her head. "He don't know anything, anyway. He told me Vic didn't say why he was quitting."

Kate fished in her purse for her wallet and took out a ten-dollar bill. "What's your name?"

"Me?" The girl looked surprised. "Jeannie."

"Well, Jeannie, I'd really like to get in touch with Vic. Would you give me a call if you should hear where he went?" She held up the bill.

"Sure!" The painted face broke into a grin. "You got a number?" She flipped her pad open and poised her pen above it.

Kate gave her the name of her motel. "My name is Kate Templeton," she said, handing over the bill. "And thanks."

"Thank you." The waitress pocketed the bill, and stood back to let Kate get up.

"There's one more thing," Kate said casually. "I'd like to surprise them, so don't mention you saw me. Okay?"

Jeannie winked. "You got it." She caught Kate's arm as she turned to leave. "I don't suppose you know what happened to Mikey's mom?"

"I know, wherever she is," Kate said quietly, "she's thinking about her son."

"Yeah." The girl's face looked sad. "Nice kid. I hope it works out for them."

"So do I." Kate smiled. "Thanks, Jeannie." She turned and hurried across the shabby carpeting to the door. She didn't expect to hear from the waitress again, but Jeannie had been nice to Michael. Kate hoped the ten dollars covered what she'd spent on the comics.

Slade must have been watching for her. He waited until she was halfway across the street before climbing out of the car.

She recited everything Jeannie had said as soon as she was settled. "I can't believe we keep missing him by such a close margin," she said when Slade had heard her out without commenting. "I feel so damn helpless. It's as if he's watching us, playing cat and mouse with us."

"Not really." Slade pulled out onto the highway. "It makes sense if you think about it. We talked to Ramsey around nine last night. He waited till we had left, then he called Vic. He must have told him I was with you; Vic got mad and called you. Then realizing we would figure out how he knew where you were, he guessed we'd go back to Ramsey and talk to him."

"So he had to get out of the motel." Kate frowned. "He probably decided he couldn't take a chance on Ramsey telling us where to find him."

"So he went to the steak house to get his check, then came back and checked out of the motel." Slade pulled off the road again and parked in front of a restaurant that resembled a Swiss cottage. "I don't know about you," he said, silencing the engine, "but I could go for a stack of pancakes and coffee."

Kate nodded guiltily, remembering the coffee she'd had in the Lonesome Wagon. "There's one thing I don't understand," she said when they were seated by the window waiting for their order. "Why would Vic quit his job? If he hadn't paid with his salary check, we wouldn't have found out about the restaurant."

"He probably needed the money," Slade said. He smiled up at the blushing waitress who poured coffee into his waiting cup. He took a sip and closed his eyes in appreciation.

"Think about it," he went on when the waitress hurried off. "The fact that Vic had to work in the first place means he doesn't have any money. When he knew he had to check out of the motel, the only money he had was what he'd earned at the steak house. The only way he could get it last night was to quit. He was lucky he was working for a private owner and not a chain, or he'd have had to wait for his money."

Kate sipped thoughtfully at her coffee. "Put like that it sounds reasonable," she said. "But I can't shake the feeling that Vic is manipulating me, like some damn robot that's under his control."

"You're letting this get to you," Slade said. "Don't let him do that to you. It's what he wants to do. As long as you stay in control, he can't win. Remember that."

Her cup clattered in the saucer when she put it down. "I hope you're right," she said shakily. "I'm more certain than ever now that he doesn't intend to bring Michael back. I'm terrified he'll make a run for it, and we'll never catch up with him again."

She looked up and caught the doubt in Slade's eyes before he erased it. Her hands felt cold and she wrapped them around the cup to warm them. Slade shared her fears, she knew. He hadn't said so, but he didn't have to. That look on his face had been enough.

Her misgivings were confirmed when Slade said, "Today is Saturday. We'll give it three more days. If we haven't caught up with them again by then, I suggest we go back to Portland and hire a PI."

She wanted to cry, but her eyes felt dry. She looked across at him, and said quietly, "You think they've left town."

"I think it's possible. I'm sorry, Kate."

The sympathy in his gaze did more to destroy her wavering courage than anything he said.

She caught her lip with her teeth as the waitress brought the pancakes and placed an assortment of flavored syrups on the table between them. By the time she left them alone, Kate had her emotions under control.

She managed to eat half her pancakes, and let Slade finish them up for her. Three days, she thought in despair. Would she be able to admit defeat and go back as he suggested? It was the most sensible thing to do, she knew, and yet she couldn't give up trying.

She sipped her coffee, deep in thought. When she put her cup down, more carefully this time, she'd made up her mind. Slade would have to go back alone. She would hire a PI in Las Vegas, and stay put until he'd tracked Vic down.

With Slade back in Oregon and on the rodeo circuit again, Vic would know she was alone. There was a faint chance he might contact her again. As long as there was a glimmer of hope, she could not give up.

Three days, she promised Slade silently. That's all you have left. "Where do we start looking again?" she asked when Slade finally pushed his plate away with a satisfied sigh.

"We'll make a couple of calls." He looked up as the waitress approached, nodding when she asked it he wanted a refill of the coffee.

Kate shook her head when the waitress offered to refill her cup.

Slade took a couple of mouthfuls of coffee. "Maybe Ramsey has heard from Vic again," he said, "so I suggest you call him when we get back to the motel. And we could call the motel manager. She may have heard something."

Kate nodded. "Then what?"

"If Vic hasn't left town, he's probably looking for another job. We'll check out the want ads and call the restaurants. If we're still drawing a blank, we'll start checking out every restaurant in town. Between us we should be able to cover most of them in three days. Maybe someone, somewhere, will give us a lead."

She gave him a weak smile. "You should have been a PI yourself."

"I don't have the patience," Slade said, signaling to the waitress for his bill.

Kate might have disputed that, but she kept silent. She was grateful for his help. And his support. Without it she might have crumbled at the first setback.

But she couldn't help feeling that it was a mistake for him to be with her. Some little doubt niggled at the back of her mind, some vague idea that Vic knew Slade was still around, and as long as he knew that, he would stay out of sight.

The conviction grew stronger over the next two days as they searched the town. The phone calls proved fruitless, so they took to the streets, showing everyone who would look the pictures of Michael and Vic. By the end of the second day, exhausted and depressed, Kate showered and changed to join Slade at yet another restaurant to eat.

When this was over, she declared silently, she would never set foot in another restaurant again. She said as much to Slade when he came to pick her up.

"You'll change your mind," he said, sitting on her bed to wait while she finished putting on her makeup. "When this is all behind you and forgotten."

Kate dabbed the lipstick on her lips without too much regard for accuracy. "I'm never going to forget." She capped the lipstick and dropped it in her purse. "For as long as I live."

Her voice broke and she forced the tears back. She would not cry, she promised herself fiercely. She'd done enough crying.

She heard the bed creak as Slade stood, then came up behind her. She felt his hands on her shoulders as he said softly, "Hang in there, Kate. You're doing fine; just hold on to that courage."

Maybe if he hadn't touched her, she would have been able to control the desperate need that racked her body. But the pressure of his hands started a spiral of longing that raced through her like a cresting breaker heading for shore.

She turned, uncaring of the emotion she knew had to be naked in her face. "I'm not fine, Slade. I'm hurting, afraid and so incredibly tired."

She saw her desperation mirrored in his eyes the second before he turned away from her. "I'm sorry, Kate. I wish there was something I could do to ease the pain."

There is, she cried silently. *You can hold me, love me, make all this a little more bearable.* She almost said it out loud. She wanted to tell him that she'd take whatever he had to give, even if it was no more than a few brief hours.

Tomorrow she would have to tell him her decision. He had already given up hope of finding Michael in this town, she knew that. He had done all he could and now it was time for him to leave. Without her.

It was a decision that she intended to stand by, no matter what his argument might be. It would have been easier to face if she could have spent the last hours in his arms.

She looked across to where he stood by the door, waiting. The temptation to tell him how she felt was almost too strong to ignore. She made herself smile and say, "I guess I'm ready to eat, if you are."

"Sure." He looked relieved as he pulled the door open, and she went past him, fighting her resentment. It had taken years to build that much immunity to his own emotions. There was nothing she could do but let him go, and do her best to forget how very much she loved him.

She sat in the car, wondering how she was going to get through a meal, as Slade closed the door and started around the hood. He was directly in front of her when she saw him pause and lift his head. Then she heard it, too. The distant sound of a telephone ringing. It was coming from her room.

Kate was out of the car and at the door before Slade had time to turn around. She hunted through her purse for the key, letting out a cry of exasperation when she couldn't find it.

Turning her purse upside down she emptied it on the ground and snatched up the key. Her hand shook as she tried to fit it in the lock.

"Here, let me," Slade said behind her, but the key finally slid in and turned.

She stepped over the scattered contents of her purse and lunged for the phone. "Hello," she shouted.

A woman's voice answered with a nervous, "Mrs. Templeton?"

Crushing disappointment robbed her of breath. She didn't know who she had been expecting. Vic, perhaps, even Michael. She hadn't given up on a miracle after all.

"Hello?"

The voice sounded even more hesitant, and Kate dragged in a breath. "Yes, I'm sorry. This is Mrs. Templeton."

"Oh, hi! This is Jeannie."

It took her a moment or two to remember the red-headed waitress. "Hello, Jeannie." Kate looked up and saw Slade watching her, his eyes alert and questioning.

The waitress, she mouthed at him silently while Jeannie said in her ear, "You asked me to call if I heard from Vic."

Kate's fingers tensed on the receiver. She signaled her excitement at Slade with her eyes. He frowned back in puzzlement. "You heard from him?" Kate said, still not quite daring to believe the young voice on the phone.

"Well, not directly." There was a pause on while Jeannie muttered something to an unseen person. "Sorry," she said, coming back on the line. "It's getting busy here."

Kate made an effort to contain her impatience. "What did you hear, Jeannie?"

"Oh, right. Well, I got a call from the manager of Sailor's Wharf. It's a seafood place out on Flamingo Road. He wanted a reference on Vic. I don't know why he called me instead of Sam, unless Vic thought I'd be kinder on him than Sam after he walked out on him like that."

"Vic's working there?" Kate asked, watching Slade's expression brighten with hope.

"Yeah, I guess so. On a trial basis. I tried to call you yesterday, but you're always out."

"Jeannie, you are wonderful," Kate said warmly. "Thanks a lot."

"You're welcome. Hope you find them. Mikey needs cheering up." Kate heard a muffled shout somewhere in the distance. "Gotta go," Jeannie said hurriedly. "Good luck, Mrs. Templeton."

"I'm going to need it," Kate said softly as she replaced the receiver. She looked up at Slade's expectant face. "Sailor's Wharf," she said, raising her crossed fingers. "A seafood restaurant on Flamingo."

Slade lifted his closed fists in triumph. "Let's go." He helped her gather the contents of her purse, then strode to the car and was already gunning the engine when she slid into the seat.

The streets were crowded with rush-hour traffic, and it took them several minutes to reach Flamingo Road, then another few minutes to locate the restaurant. Kate let out a cry as they drew level with the parking lot. There in the shadows drawn by the setting sun sat a large, four-door, powder-blue car.

Slade had seen it, too. His breath came out sharply, but he kept on driving past the restaurant and into the next side street, out of view. He parked in front of a real-estate office and turned the ignition key to shut off the engine.

Kate looked at him, and he knew by her face what she was about to say. "I'll let you go in alone," he said, "on one condition. That you give me your solemn promise you will not go anywhere with Vic without letting me know. I have to have that promise, Kate, and I'll hold you to it."

He watched her face carefully as she hesitated. It went against every instinct to let her walk into that place, knowing Vic was in there. The only consolation he had was that it would be difficult for Vic to pull anything in the restaurant. What he was most afraid of was that Vic would promise Kate to take her to Michael. And she would go, with no thought about what she might be walking into.

"I promise," Kate said with obvious reluctance. "It may not be necessary. What if Michael is there in the restaurant?"

"Then you take his hand and lead him out of there," Slade said. "I'll be waiting for you across the street."

He knew she wasn't happy for him to be that close by, but he was adamant, and she finally gave in. He watched her hurry away, and gave her a full two-minute start before climbing out of the car to follow her.

He hoped with all his heart and soul that this would be the end of it. Not only for Kate and Michael's sake, but for his own sanity. He could no longer be alone with Kate. Every time she looked at him, every time she brushed past him, leaving that faint, evocative fragrance she wore wafting around him, he was tortured by the longing to take her in his arms.

He knew that he was reaching the end of his endurance. One more helpless look from those sea-blue eyes, one more touch of her fingers on his arm, and he would have to answer the urges gnawing at every nerve in his body.

There was only so much a man could tolerate, and he'd used up all of his willpower. This had to be the end of it, he told himself passionately as he walked to the end of the street and turned the corner. If not, he would not be accountable for his actions.

He crossed the street, and worked his way to a spot opposite the restaurant, which would give him a clear view of the entrance. Standing in the doorway of a small appliance store, he waited for Kate to reappear.

Kate had slowed her pace as she approached the building, trying to decide on her next move. It was just possible that Michael could be seated at one of the tables, as he had been in the steak house with Jeannie. If so, all she had to do was walk in, grab him by the hand and get him out of there.

The thought that it could be that easy almost suffocated her with excitement. She had to caution herself to calm down. She had to be prepared for all the alternatives, including the fact that this could be yet another disappointment.

Steeling herself, she reached the parking lot and looked at the side of the building, half expecting the car to have disappeared. It was still there. She wanted to be sure. It could be a coincidence; she wanted to make absolutely sure that it wasn't someone else's car she was staring at.

She walked toward it until she could read the license plate. She had to get quite close, the figures were almost invisible beneath the dirt and dust. Her heart leaped when she recognized the numbers. It was Gladys's car all right. She couldn't resist a peek in the windows.

There was nothing to indicate that Michael had been inside the vehicle. No clothing, no comics, nothing that could have belonged to him. A creased map lay on the dashboard, a baseball cap and a pair of men's socks had been tossed on the back seat. An empty Coke can lay on the floor in front of the driver's seat, and that was it. Kate suppressed the squirming stab of anxiety and turned toward the restaurant.

Be there, Michael, she urged silently, and walked toward the door. A tall, thin woman with graying hair confronted her the minute she was inside. The waitress looked harassed and impatient as she thrust a folded sheet of paper at Kate.

"Here," she said. "I was told to give you this. You have to read it now."

"Who gave you this?" Kate said sharply.

"Read it, that's all I'm supposed to say. Though why he can't do his own dirty work I have no idea."

The waitress scurried off and Kate moved out of the way of customers entering behind her. She found a corner by the rest rooms an backed into it. Her desperate scrutiny of the restaurant told her what she'd already expected. Michael wasn't at any of the tables.

With a trembling hand she unfolded the note. "Michael isn't here," it read in Vic's bold scrawl. "If you want to see him, meet me tomorrow in Fools Gallows. We'll be waiting outside the general store at 9:00 a.m."

The rest of it was printed in block letters. "COME ALONE, KATE, OR· YOU CAN SAY GOODBYE TO MICHAEL FOREVER."

She crumpled the note in her hand and shoved it in the pocket of her pants. She didn't know what Vic wanted. She really didn't care. She would agree to anything, promise anything, as long as she had Michael back safe and sound.

The waitress hurried past her with two loaded plates of fish and chips. Kate waited for her to return and grabbed her arm. "Where is Fools Gallows?" she asked as the waitress shot her an impatient look.

"Highway 95 to Beatty, follow the signs to Death Valley. You'll see the turnoff for Fools Gallows." She turned away, then looked back over her shoulder. "Don't go up there now," she said. "It's hotter than hell. The Valley is the hottest place on earth."

Kate watched her plunge back into the crowded dining room and disappear through the swinging doors at the back. She was tempted to follow and confront Vic if he was there. Common sense told her she would achieve nothing by doing that. She would have to wait one more night. Just one more night.

She pushed past the line of waiting customers and reached the door. She would not tell Slade about the note, she decided. He would insist on going with her. She couldn't risk that, not now that she was so close. Somehow she would have to give him the slip.

She would leave the motel early in the morning, hire a cab to take her to Fools Gallows and drop her off there. She hated having to lie to him, but it was the only way. She could only hope he would understand.

She stepped outside, taking a moment or two to catch her breath. The words of her promise echoed in her head. *Promise you will not go anywhere with Vic without letting me know.*

"I'm sorry, Slade," she whispered as she began walking down the street. "Please forgive me."

She didn't know the reason for Vic's change of heart. Perhaps he was tired of the game, tired of having to worry about a small boy who must be giving him a hard time. Whatever the reason, she would not take a chance on Vic's changing his mind again. From now on she would play it his way.

Slade caught up with her before she'd reached the corner. "What happened?" he asked impatiently as she gave him a wan smile.

"Nothing. I didn't see Michael or Vic."

"But what about the car? That was the car, wasn't it?"

She looked away, struggling with her conscience. "Yes," she said finally. "It was Vic's car. But he sold it to one of the waitresses. She doesn't know where he went."

Slade swore. "How the hell does he do it?" he demanded to no one in particular. "I'm beginning to think the guy is a mind reader."

Kate waited until she was seated in the car with Slade beside her. "I guess you're right," she said, putting just the right amount of dejection in her voice. "We might as well hand this over to a detective. We're certainly not getting anywhere on our own."

She felt him glance at her, but could not meet his eyes. She hated the necessity for lies, but there was no other way. She only wished that she didn't have to leave him with deceit between them.

"I'm sorry, Kate. I tried."

"I know you did," she said, hurrying to reassure him. "We both did our best. It just wasn't enough. Maybe an expert will have better luck than we did."

"Maybe."

She heard the suspicion in his voice and tensed.

"I guess we'll start back in the morning, then," he said quietly.

"I guess so." She didn't have to fake dejection when she said, "I couldn't have made it through all this without you. I'm glad you came with me." It hit her then—the realization that after this night, Slade would be gone out of her life forever. The pain sliced through her.

"Are you?"

This time his voice was heavy with doubt, and she risked a look at him. He was staring straight ahead, his hands on the wheel, making no attempt to start the engine.

She guessed he was thinking of the night they'd spent together. It was on her mind, too, a bittersweet memory that would never fade, no matter how hard she tried to erase it.

"Yes, I am." She stirred, anxious to get it all over with. "I guess we might as well have some dinner," she suggested, relieved when he nodded in agreement.

The last thing she needed now was to dwell on what might have been. Tomorrow would be the end of this chapter in her life. Tomorrow she would be reunited with Michael, and all being well, she would be able to carry on where she left off, before her reunion with Slade had ripped her life apart.

The thought helped her get through the meal. She even managed to carry on a normal, if slightly disjointed, conversation. She stuck to the safe topics, asking Slade about the rodeo, telling him about her different promotions, all the while carefully avoiding the subject of Michael.

Slade seemed preoccupied, but answered her questions readily enough, smiling in the right places when she talked about her work.

They left the restaurant and drove back to the motel without talking, both lost in their own thoughts. Kate felt uneasy, wondering if Slade's lapse into silence was disappointment over their failure, or if he had an inkling that she had more on her mind than she was telling him.

She knew she could not hide the agony on her face when they paused at the door to her room. She could only hope he would attribute her misery to her having given up hope of finding Michael.

Perhaps he did, because to her surprise, instead of wishing her good-night and leaving, he caught her face between his hands. "This may be the last chance I have to do this," he said softly, "so let's make it one to remember."

She caught her breath as he lowered his head and captured her mouth. He folded his arms around her and pulled her into him, and the fire that had never been quite extinguished sparked to life.

She opened her mouth hungrily, fiercely, as he deepened the kiss. The delicious trembling that his touch always invoked invaded her body when he lifted his head. In the shadowed light from the street lamp she saw the answering flame in his dark eyes, and her heart began a steady throb of anticipation.

He lifted his hands and placed them on her shoulders, his thumbs caressing her throat. "I've said a lot of things over the past few days," he said quietly. "I wish I could tell you what you want to hear. I want you to know that there will never be anyone else. I'm sorry I can't be what you want me to be. I guess it's just not in me."

She felt tears prickling at her eyes and blinked them back. "I know. I'm sorry, too."

"It doesn't stop me wanting you." He brushed her mouth with his thumbs.

She knew what it would mean if she let him in. She knew the kind of pain she'd have to deal with in the morning. She knew it would be much more difficult, both physically and mentally, to slip away and leave him.

Knowing all that, she smiled up at him. Her key was already in her hand. Without a word she held it up and offered it to him.

Chapter 11

Slade took the key from her fingers and fitted it into the lock. He didn't have to speak. Words were unnecessary.

The door closed behind them, shutting out the world, postponing all thought and deed that didn't belong in the intimacy of their time together.

They undressed each other slowly, savoring each moment with the intensity of knowing it was for the last time. Only when they lay naked in each other's arms did their patience turn to something more demanding.

There was an urgency about Slade's touch that fired Kate's own fierce need. She searched his body with her hands and mouth, imprinting each curve, each indentation, on her mind. She concentrated on every facet of his being—his hair, soft and silky beneath her hands, the scratchy sensation of his jaw on the tender skin of her stomach.

She explored the contours of his shoulders, his arms, feeling the muscles flex under her fingers as his mouth roamed over her tingling flesh. She committed it all to memory—the exciting male, musky smell of him, the harsh sound of his breathing, the vibration of his heartbeat when he crushed her breasts with the weight of his chest.

She would remember, she told herself, everything about him. The salty taste of his skin, the rough pressure of his legs entwined with hers, the sensation of naked flesh against naked flesh, rubbing, stroking, caressing. She locked it all away in a safe, secret part of her mind.

Then his fingers found her, launching her on a dizzying journey, and he joined her to him in a final frenzy of pure, agonizing pleasure, until they drifted together on a gentle plane of contentment.

She listened to the even sound of his breathing long after he'd fallen asleep. Her hand rested on his forearm as it lay across her stomach, the soft hairs caressing her palm. His head lay close to hers on the pillow, so close she could feel the faint stir of breath on her cheek. He'd flung one leg possessively across her thighs, and she could feel the rhythmic movement of his belly against her hip.

She was determined to stay awake, and make the most of the precious minutes as they ticked relentlessly by, eating up the time she had left in his arms. She would have to leave early, she told herself, before he was ready to wake up. It wouldn't be easy to slip away without waking him.

She sighed in the darkness. She would get word to him, she decided, once this was all over and Michael was safe. She hated leaving him to worry, but she couldn't take the chance of his waking up and insisting on going with her to Fools Gallows.

She felt her eyes closing and snapped them open again. In an effort to keep them open she started thinking about Michael. She had no way of knowing how well he was holding up under all the trauma. She wondered if he knew she was coming for him in the morning, and hoped Vic had spared him the agony of another night of despair.

When she opened her eyes again it was to see a faint edging of light around the window. With a jolt of apprehension she looked at her watch. It was after six-thirty; she'd slept after all.

Turning her head an inch at a time she saw Slade had twisted away from her in his sleep. She sent one last, longing glance at his smooth, bronzed back, then very slowly inched her feet to the floor.

Her clothes lay in a heap and, after a moment's hesitation she left them there. Stepping lightly over them she moved to the dresser and eased open the top drawer. There was barely enough light to see, but she found some underwear, a pair of shorts and a shirt. Pulling them on quickly, she felt around the top of the dresser for her purse. She had a bad moment when she couldn't find it, then remembered she'd dropped it by the bed the night before. Holding her breath, she crept back to the bed and bent her knees, one hand groping the floor.

On the bed Slade stirred and uttered a quiet groan. Kate froze as he turned, throwing his arm across her empty pillow. She waited, heart pounding, while he mumbled something, then resumed the deep, rhythmic breathing of deep sleep.

Making herself relax, she ran her hand over her pile of clothes, tensing again as something rattled against her fingers. It was the car keys, she discovered; she must have shaken them out of Slade's pocket.

She was about to put them down when a new idea struck her. She didn't know how long it would take her to get to Death Valley. She'd planned on asking the cabdriver to drop her off so that she could walk the last half mile. She wasn't sure now if she had the time to find a cab.

Come alone, Vic had said. She held the car keys in her hand. If she took the car she would be alone. Slade would understand, she assured herself, once she explained everything to him.

She folded her fingers around the keys and prodded the floor until she found her purse and her sandals. She allowed herself one more glance at Slade.

His face was hidden by the curve of his arm. She let her gaze dwell for a moment on the outline of his naked body, then with pain twisting at her heart, she rose and crept silently to the door. It opened without a sound and she slipped through, closing it quietly behind her.

The clear, bright morning spread warmth over her as she slid her feet into her sandals and walked to the car. She winced as she pulled the door shut with a thud that seemed to vibrate down the length of the motel.

It took her no more than a couple of seconds to turn the ignition and fire the engine. She backed the car out and then threw the gear into Drive, heading for the highway out of town.

Slade threw the door open just in time to see her disappear behind the buildings, leaving a trail of dust in her wake. He swore loudly and violently, cursing himself for being such a complete fool.

He'd known ever since she'd come out of the seafood restaurant that she was up to something. He hadn't believed that story about Vic selling the car, but he'd known it would be useless trying to question her further. He'd had no alternative but to stay close to her, even if it meant spending the night with her.

The fact that he'd been longing to do just that made the decision even more desirable. He finally had an excuse to give in to the hunger gnawing at him, and he'd intended to make the most of it. He was infuriated to realize he'd blown it. He hadn't expected her to take the car.

Slade went back inside and jerked the drapes open. He'd suspected she'd agreed to meet Vic somewhere but he thought she'd go on foot, or pick up a cab. He'd intended to follow her, at a reasonable distance, until he'd decided it was safe to move in.

The minute she'd closed the door he'd pulled his pants on, but then he'd heard the engine revving, and it was too late to stop her. He kicked at the heap of clothes on the floor in disgust. What the hell was he going to do now?

He sat down on the bed and buried his face in his hands. Maybe he was overreacting, he told himself. Kate knew what she was doing. Maybe Vic did want to hand Michael back, and had simply wanted to give her a bad time for a while.

He lowered his hands and stared moodily at the floor. There was nothing he could do now, except wait. And hope. He leaned over and fished up his shirt from the heap of clothes. If only Kate had confided in him. She might have known he wouldn't jeopardize Michael's safety.

He dragged on his shirt, then bent over to pick up the rest of the clothes, automatically sorting Kate's from his. He folded her shirt, and was folding her pants when he heard the rustle of paper in one of the pockets.

Curious, he pulled it out, and smoothed the crumpled note. He read it quickly, repeating the name out loud. "Fools Gallows." He'd never heard of it.

He shook his head, staring at the scrawled words. At least now he knew where she'd gone. He could follow her, except by the time he got to this Fools Gallows, wherever it was, she and Vic, and Michael, too, he presumed, would be long gone.

He had to suppose that she would call him, once she was through negotiating with Vic. He had to trust her, he told himself. She was a sensible, intelligent woman. According to the note, Vic was willing to meet her out in the open, outside on the street. As long as she kept it that way she should be all right.

Slade folded the note and slipped it in the pocket of his jeans. Much as he hated to admit it, she had probably done the right thing. He would have insisted on going with her, and might have ended up antagonizing Vic even more.

He got to his feet and rubbed his stubbled chin. He would just have to wait for her to call him. The idea didn't appeal to him one bit, but he didn't seem to have any alternative.

A shower and shave helped to revive his flagging spirits, and he risked a quick visit to the fast-food restaurant nearby to pick up coffee and doughnuts. He paid the smiling woman behind the counter, then as she handed him his change, he asked casually, "Have you heard of a place called Fools Gallows?"

"Sure," she said. "Not thinking of setting up business there, are you?"

He smiled. "Not exactly. Where is it?"

"It's up by Death Valley." She gave him a curious look. "Not much up there. It used to be a mining town in the old days, but there's no one there now. I reckon it got too hot for comfort. It can be miserable there in the summer."

Slade felt a knot form in his stomach as he stared at the woman's round, cheerful face. "Are you saying that Fools Gallows is a ghost town?" he asked slowly.

"Yeah." She nodded her had vigorously. "Deader than a shed snakeskin. Last I heard they cut if off from tourists. Said it was dangerous, what with the mines caving in."

She turned away, shrugging. "Can't imagine why anyone would want to go up there. It's as hot . . ."

Slade didn't wait to hear the rest of her words. Leaving his coffee and doughnuts on the counter, he strode to the door and flung it open. He knew Kate would never have walked into an abandoned town on her own. Even as anxious as she was to see Michael, she wouldn't have been that stupid. Which meant she didn't know.

And Vic would not have suggested meeting there unless he had some kind of malicious intent. Kate was walking into a potential mine field, without suspecting it was there. His face set in a fierce scowl, Slade headed for the motel.

* * *

The drive was taking much longer than Kate had envisioned. Several times she had glanced at her watch, her stomach twisting in knots as the hour hand crept a full circle, and then another one.

She was low on gas by the time she reached Beatty, but the sign to Fools Gallows gave the distance as five miles. She elected not to stop, figuring that she could fill up on the way back.

Her heart bounded in excitement when she thought about Michael being with her on the return trip. She would call Slade from Beatty, she decided, hoping that he would still be at the motel. If not, they would go back and wait for him.

Kate smiled as she envisioned Michael and Slade being together again. At least for a little while. They would have Slade's company for another day, while they traveled back to Portland together. As for what happened after that, there would be time to worry about that later.

She tried not to put too much meaning into the night they'd just spent together. She understood him too well now to expect much from him. Even so, she couldn't suppress the persistent hope that refused to be extinguished.

Kate frowned, stepping on the brake as the road narrowed and became rutted with potholes. It had to be a small town, she thought, peering anxiously ahead. The road was badly in need of repair, though obviously it had been well traveled.

It spite of the lowered windows, the air inside the car threatened to stifle her as she slowed to a crawl. She could feel the heat rising from the pavement, burning her arm when she rested it on the open window frame.

She uttered an exclamation of dismay when she spotted a barrier erected across the width of the road. It was just her luck, she thought with an impatient glance at her watch. Obviously the road was being repaired.

She pulled to a stop and stuck her head out of the window. The smell of scorched grass hung thick in the heated air. She could see no sign of any workmen, and there didn't appear to be a detour. She began to feel a niggling sensation low in her stomach.

Only a few minutes to get to Fools Gallows, she thought. It looked as if she would have to walk. Pushing open the door of the car, she climbed out. Although it wasn't yet nine, the sun attacked her shoulders and head with the intensity of a blazing torch.

Kate thought longingly of Slade's hat, lying somewhere in his motel room. She felt a stab of guilt as she thought about him, certainly awake by now, wondering where she was. She should have called him from Beatty, she thought belatedly. It would have been too late for him to come after her, but at least he would know where she was.

She glanced again at her watch. If she'd had more time, she would have called him. But it was too late now. She figured she had less than half a mile to walk, with just enough time to make it.

She'd tugged the tail of her pink gingham shirt and tied the ends in a knot around her midriff. The hot breeze on her bare skin did little to cool her, but at least she felt less restricted. She stepped carefully over the gouged grooves on the roadway and approached the barrier. The sign that hung on it was barely legible, faded by sun and wind, and scrubbed by the dry dust that swirled around her ankles.

She leaned forward to read it, her stomach contracting as she made out the words. DANGER. UNSTABLE AREA. VISITORS STRICTLY PROHIBITED.

Kate straightened. The suspicion that something wasn't right blossomed into a full-blown certainty. She hesitated, moistening her dry lips with her tongue. She wished now she'd left Slade a note. Or at least had called him.

It was too late, she reminded herself. She had only a few minutes to get to the town, and now that she was aware that

Vic was still playing some kind of game, she couldn't trust him to stick around longer than a few minutes.

She looked around. She had been driving on a gradual incline for some time. She was high in the hills. Below her she could see the town, half hidden by the brow of the reddish-brown earth. Low-lying mountain peaks obscured the view of Death Valley, but she knew it was there.

She could feel the terrible heat simmering up from the floor of the Valley, eased only slightly by the rise of jagged mountains. Above them the sun smoldered in a hazy sky. Nothing breathed, nothing moved, only the endless dust shifting in the hot winds around her feet. Cactus plants and sparse patches of scrub grass were the only survivors of this desolate place. Not even a rattlesnake could exist in this environment, she thought. She felt as if she'd been abandoned on a lonely planet, lost forever in a silent, still, alien world.

She shook herself, and fastened her gaze on the town nestled below her. She had driven through it less than ten minutes ago. There had been people and traffic, with electricity and telephones—an ordinary, everyday, earthly place. Less than ten minutes away.

She made herself concentrate on that thought as she climbed over the barrier and began to walk at a steady pace along the rutted road.

Slade slammed the phone down with a vicious oath. He'd wasted precious minutes talking to the police, who had seemed disturbingly unconcerned in spite of his attempts to explain the situation. They had finally agreed to compromise. If they hadn't heard from him by midday, they would contact Beatty and have them send an officer out to investigate.

He'd wasted several more minutes trying to talk a cab-driver into taking him up to Fools Gallows. Maybe it was the urgency in his voice that had put them off, but they had all refused, saying the town was off-limits to visitors.

Slade checked his watch, cursing again. He knew it was off-limits, that was the whole point. He would have to get hold of a car from somewhere. One of the cabdrivers had told him it was at least a two-hour drive. He grabbed his hat off the bed and jammed it on his head. If he had to steal a car he'd do so, he vowed silently. He couldn't afford to waste any more time.

He had no way of knowing what Vic was planning. He could only go by the gut feeling in his stomach and the few, scrawled, cryptic words. *Come alone, Kate, or you can say goodbye to Michael forever.*

Slade opened the door and stepped outside, slamming it shut behind him. *You can say goodbye to Michael forever.* It could mean Vic intended taking him somewhere, to another state, or even another country.

On the other hand, it could mean something far more ominous. His stride quickened by the sense of urgency that gripped him, Slade moved swiftly across the parking lot.

Kate paused for a moment to catch her breath, wiping her forehead with the back of her hand. She had been climbing steadily now for five minutes, and still hadn't reached any sign of a town. Her lungs ached with the effort to breathe and her legs wobbled with every step she took.

The heat seemed to press down on her, making her body feel heavy and listless, draining her of vital energy. She shaded her eyes with her hand, dazzled by the blinding sun in spite of her sunglasses.

She looked at her watch. Five minutes after the hour; she was late. Spurred on by the thought that Vic might not wait, she trudged several more steps, her breath coming in painful gasps.

Rounding a curve, she let out a cry of thankfulness. Right in front of her a battered structure that had once been a house leaned tiredly on its foundation. A few more steps brought her around yet another curve, and there, sloping away from her on the downside of the mountain, stood the remains of Fools Gallows.

She could see the mine openings now—holes gouged in the heart of the mountains, boarded up with rotting planks of wood. Farther on, abandoned shacks and cabins led down to a deserted street, where wooden buildings rested in solitary silence on a rickety boardwalk.

Kate walked slowly past the shacks, her eyes on the main street. A ghost town. She had half expected it, after reading the warning, yet she had nursed the faint hope that a few people might still be living there.

Outside the general store, Vic had said in his note. It had to be one of the buildings on the street, yet the narrow space between the boardwalks was deserted. Where was he? More important, *where was Michael?*

She hesitated at the point where the street began, raking the buildings with anxious eyes. Most of the signs were broken, or faded so badly they were impossible to read. Across from where she stood, an empty tavern sulked forlornly, its once lavish decor sullied by the ravages of neglect.

Broken windowpanes, the smell of decaying wood and the unearthly silence greeted her as she edged past the dying buildings. She was almost at the end of the street when she saw it. A broken sign, hanging by one corner, with the words GENERAL STORE carved into the bleached wood.

She stepped up onto the boardwalk and hesitated on the first of the three steps that led up to the door. She wondered if Vic was inside, waiting for her, gratified by her timid approach. She could see nothing beyond the dusty glass of the windows. The inside of the store was in darkness, the doors closed against the sunlight.

There were several broken panes in the windows and she climbed the steps to get a closer look. Avoiding broken tiles and glass she moved over to the window and took off her sunglasses. She shaded her eyes with her hand and leaned forward to peer through one of the jagged holes.

The silence was suddenly shattered by a strange, eerie sound that chilled her blood. She jerked upright, swinging around to face the street.

The sound she'd heard was laughter—loud, raucous laughter with a hint of hysteria in the wild, echoing notes. For a crazy moment she wondered if it was the ghost of some hapless miner, forced to wander forever in the town where he'd lost his life.

In the next instant a figure emerged from the building across the street, and her heart plummeted. She almost wished it had been a ghost.

He stood on the other side of the narrow dirt road, his head thrown back as the ghastly sound of his laughter bounced off the decrepit buildings. And he was alone.

Kate waited, willing the panic to subside as she stared at the man who had once been her husband. He had put on weight and lost some more hair since she'd last seen him. Otherwise he looked much the same.

He lowered his head and looked at her. "Well, hello, Kate. It's nice to see you again."

The trite phrase sounded ridiculous and Kate winced. "I wish I could say the same," she said evenly.

Vic chuckled again, a sinister sound that managed to send a chill down her spine in spite of the suffocating heat. "Now is that any way to greet your husband? I'd expected a little more respect."

Kate clenched her hands at her sides and moved down the steps. She halted abruptly as Vic did the same. Only a few paces separated them now. She was close enough to see his pale blue eyes, and she didn't like the fierce light that burned in them. He was sweating profusely; she could see it running in rivulets down his plump face. His dark hair stuck out in damp spikes on either side of his head, as if he'd been running his hands through it. She'd never noticed the cruel twist of his mouth before, though it must have been there all the time.

Her stomach cramped in an agony of apprehension as she said quietly, "Where is Michael?"

Vic pulled his thin lips back in a grin. "He's fine. He's waiting for you."

"Where?" Kate saw the expression of triumph flash across Vic's slack features and bit back a cry of terror. Slade's words came back to her, clear and insistent. *As long as you stay in control, he can't win. Remember that.*

"I'll take you to him," Vic promised, "but first I think we should talk."

"All right." She made herself walk past him to where the buildings threw a shadow across the burning ground. Once out of the ferocious reach of the sun's rays, she steadied herself with a hand against a protruding hitching rail.

"First of all," Vic said, his expression guarded as he watched her, "tell me where your boyfriend is."

Kate's stomach jerked uneasily, but she managed not to betray her reaction. "I sent him back to Oregon. That's what you wanted, isn't it?"

She met his piercing stare without flinching, letting out her breath when he looked away, apparently satisfied.

"Does anyone know you're up here?" He stared down the street, as if expecting someone to be lurking behind the buildings.

Kate hesitated. If she admitted that no one knew, she could be putting herself in extreme danger. On the other hand, if she pretended that she'd told someone, Vic could fly into one of his rages, and she would be helpless against him.

She couldn't afford to upset him, she decided. Not until she knew where he was keeping Michael. "You asked me to come alone," she said, keeping her gaze steadily on his face, "and I did. I told no one. I've done everything you asked. Now I'd like to see Michael."

He stared at her with a strange, brooding expression that intensified her uneasiness. "We could have made a go of it, you know," he said, a note of petulance creeping into his voice. "You shouldn't have called the police. We could have worked it out."

Kate swallowed, knowing he was talking about his attack on Michael. The horror of it was invading her mind again, arousing her loathing and disgust for the man standing in front of her.

She made an effort to curb the emotion surging through her, and searched her mind for the right thing to say. "I had to call the police. Michael was hurt. I couldn't take care of him myself. I needed help."

"They took me away," Vic said plaintively, as if she didn't know what had happened. "They put me in this awful place. I couldn't even get a drink of water without having to ask someone." His cough was a painful, wheezing sound.

Kate felt sick. She didn't want to feel sorry for him, yet there was an element of pathos about him that aroused a twinge of sympathy. "I'm sorry," she said quietly.

He looked at her, his black brows drawing together. "Are you? Are you really sorry?" The poignancy had vanished, leaving a sneering disbelief in its wake.

"I'm sorry that it happened," Kate said carefully.

"So am I," Vic said nastily. "Believe me, so am I."

Suddenly she'd had all she could take. All caution deserting her, she cried, "Where is my son? I demand that you take me to him right now."

"Demand?" Vic's face grew even more flushed as his voice rose. "Demand? Where the hell do you come off demanding anything?"

He took her arm in a grip that made her cry out in pain. "I do all the demanding from now on, lady, and don't you forget it. I'll take you to see your precious son. And then I'll have a few demands of my own.''

He started yanking her down the street and, frightened now, she dug her heels into the sunbaked dirt. "I'll come with you," she said, trying to shake off his hold. "You don't have to drag me."

He gave her a contemptuous look, intensifying her fear. "Oh, I'm not going to let go of you now, sweetheart. It's taken me a long time to get you where I want you, I'm not taking any chances of you running off again."

She would not let the fear demoralize her, she told herself fiercely. She had Michael to consider. She had to stay in control if she was going to get them both out of this.

She let Vic lead her roughly down the street until he reached the vacant tavern at the end. Turning sharply, he shoved her in front of him, still imprisoned by his cruel grip, to the rear of the building.

Stumbling, Kate righted herself and looked across the uneven tract of land that lay behind the main street. She saw the ramshackle remains of a house, with a few broken posts of a fence still marking out the front yard.

A rusty pump leaned at an angle in front of the house next to what looked like a small raft made of boards lashed together. A covered porch still clung to the roof of the house, supported by two thick posts that had managed to survive the relentless onslaught of sun and wind.

Kate blinked, and squinted against the blinding sun. Something was lashed to one of the posts; something that looked like a shapeless bundle of rags. Then the figure moved, and an anguished howl echoed around the hills.

Kate had torn herself free and was racing full tilt toward the house before she realized that the awful sound was coming from her. She heard Vic's footsteps pounding behind her but paid no heed as she flung herself up the rotting steps. She was sobbing Michael's name over and over again as she finally closed her arms around the thin body of her son.

Her tears mingled with his as he looked at her with desperate eyes. "No," he kept repeating in a thin, high voice, "no, go away. He'll kill you. He said he'd kill you."

"Oh, God, Michael." She couldn't seem to stop crying as she tugged frantically at the cruel ropes that held him. Rough hands seized hers from behind, dragging her away from Michael's pleading face.

Like a wild animal she turned, clawing at the callous eyes that glinted at her in triumph. "Let me go," she screamed.

Pain exploded throughout her head as it was jerked viciously backward by the force of Vic's blow. Stunned, she reached out a hand, feeling the rough splinters of the post digging into her palm as she shook her head to clear it.

She tasted blood on her lip and raised her head. She heard Michael scream out, "Mom!" and the terror in his voice penetrated her rage.

"I'm all right, Michael," she said shakily. "It's all right."

He began to cry—huge, dry, helpless sobs that ripped her apart. She moved forward but Vic stepped between them, barring her way.

"Forget it, Kate. You've had all the time you're ever going to have with your bastard son." He reached for her, pinning her arms behind her. She fought him, but she was no match against the formidable strength fueled by his madness.

He had the rope all ready; it took him only a few seconds to tie her securely to the opposite post. He stood back from her, surveying his handiwork, while Michael's sobs subsided to a mournful moaning that sounded far worse to her anxious ears.

"I've got to hand it to you," Vic said with an unpleasant smirk. "You got on my tail pretty damn fast. I was hoping to hang it out a lot longer.

"I set it up, Kate. The whole damn thing. It was all planned, a step at a time, and you followed the trail like a perfect little bloodhound. You made one big mistake. You brought lover boy along."

In a frenzied attempt to free herself she threw her whole weight against the ropes holding her, heedless of the rough fibre biting into her skin.

"You can struggle all you like, Kate. You won't get free. I sat all those long, miserable months, just waiting for this day," he said with grim satisfaction. "I had plenty of time to think about it, plenty of time to plan."

He waved a hand at the silent buildings. "I used to come to this place when I was a boy. Of course, it was before they stopped the tourists from coming up here. I figured it was perfect for what I had in mind."

She stared at him, filled with helpless rage. "You deliberately baited me," she said furiously.

His laugh set her teeth on edge. "That's what I've been telling you. It wasn't that hard. I knew as long as I had Mikey you wouldn't give up looking for me. I figured you'd question Gladys, and I know she can't keep her mouth shut."

He uttered an explosive sound of derision. "She was supposed to tell you about the trailer camp. Can you believe? The one time I wanted her to say something, she kept it to herself."

She had to find some way to break free, Kate thought frantically. She began sawing the rope that bound her wrists against the sharp edge of the post.

"Not that it mattered," Vic said, "you found it, anyway. I told Ramsey where I'd be, and he told you, just like he was supposed to."

"And Jeannie? The waitress at the Lonesome Wagon?"

Vic grinned. "Nice kid. Very accommodating. I figured she'd want to help you, she's the type. I waited till I saw you talking to her, then I called her, making out I was the manager of Sailor's Wharf. She didn't recognize my voice and sure enough, she called you."

Kate drew in a sharp breath. So Vic had been watching them all the time.

She went on sawing as Vic stared at the distant hills. "I wasn't working there, of course," he said. "All I had to do was give the waitress the note and ask her to give it to you. Some people would do anything for a few bucks." He paused, tilting his head to one side as if listening.

Kate froze, holding her breath until she saw him shrug.

"Anyway," he said, "it all worked and here you are." He looked at her with a vacant grin that put fresh terror in her heart. "Leaving my salary check at the Windmill was a stroke of genius, don't you think?"

She said nervously, "What are you going to do now?"

Vic stretched his arms lazily over his head. "I guess for once you told the truth. You didn't tell anyone where you were going or lover boy would have been here by now." He turned toward Michael and pulled a knife from his back pocket.

Kate screamed. "Please, Vic, no!" Her scream died as Vic slashed at the rope that held Michael, allowing him to fall to his knees.

"This will be the final punishment, Kate." Vic leaned over and grabbed Michael's shirt, hauling him to his feet. The boy squirmed, but was helpless in the grip of the deranged man who held him. "I was going to let him live. I figured he'd learn to obey me if you weren't around to baby him. But now you can watch him die."

Vic grinned, a twisting movement of his lips that sickened her. "It will make it all the more satisfying to know you will have the boy's death on your conscience while you speculate about your last hours."

He began dragging Michael toward the pump while Kate stared in helpless horror. She watched Vic kick at the boards with his foot and a new wave of terror overwhelmed her as she realized the wood had covered an old well.

She uttered a low moan. "Oh, God, Vic, please. Do what you want with me, but please, please let him go. He's just a little boy, he's never done you any harm."

"Hasn't he?" Vic's face creased in a vicious scowl of hate. "He took you away from me, that's what he did. And when I tried to punish him for it, you had me shut away. You took my freedom away from me. I had to do what I was told. I don't like that, Kate." He looked down at the well.

Kate felt the ground tilt and sway under her feet, as if every ounce of her lifeblood was draining away from her body. Her lips formed one word. "No."

"Oh, yes," Vic said pleasantly. "Say goodbye to your son."

Chapter 12

The scream seemed to come from the bottom of her soul. It welled up, a crescendo of noise as it burst from her lips in an ear-splitting explosion of agony.

She heard it shriek through the abandoned buildings and off the hills, and then an echo joined the harrowing sound, deep and vibrating with anguish.

Shock cut off her breath and the scream died when she realized the echo was not her own. She stared at Vic, but he'd spun around and, looking past him, she saw what he saw.

Standing a few feet away, on the small hillock that had hidden him from view, Slade stood silhouetted against the sun. The howl had come from him, heart-wrenching and fearful in its intensity. He stepped down, advancing on Vic with a terrible purpose reflected in his blazing eyes. His face was a mask of rage—a blind, impenetrable fury.

Vic seemed frozen in fear as Michael broke free and raced across the rough ground to Kate. Fumbling with the rope, he struggled to untie it while she murmured words of encouragement.

The rope slackened and at long last, Michael was safe in her arms. She held him, tears running unheeded down her face, almost choked by his thin arms wound around her neck. For a moment she couldn't find the breath to speak, then it came out in a rush. "Oh, Michael."

She hugged him to her, rocking back and forth, and kissed his soft cheek. "Are you all right?" she whispered.

He nodded and drew back to give her a shaky smile. Then, over his head, she saw something that brought a fresh wave of horror.

The two men were struggling, battling for the knife Vic held in his hand. It seemed as if Vic, with the intensified strength of a crazed man, would drive the knife into Slade's chest.

Kate stood, pushing Michael behind her, then took two steps toward the battling men.

With a thrust of his shoulder, Slade knocked the other man off balance. One swift uppercut snapped Vic's head back and he fell in a crumpled heap to the ground. Kate's shoulders sagged in relief until she saw Slade raise his arm. She cried out when she saw the sun glittering on the knife held in his hand.

Stumbling toward him, she yelled, "No! Slade, listen to me." She stepped between them, her eyes on the knife. "He's sick, Slade," she said urgently. "He needs help. He doesn't know what he's doing."

She stared up at his face, willing him to hear her. Slowly his dark eyes lost their fearful glitter and shifted to her face. They focused, and with a long sigh, he lowered his arm.

He stared at her for a second or two, then turned abruptly, heading for the porch. He snatched up the rope that had held her, then strode back to Vic's fallen body.

"Is he dead?" Michael asked, looking at Vic's still form with a mixture of dread and fascination.

"No," Slade answered him with a swift look at Kate. "But we'd better make sure he can't do any harm when he does wake up."

He rolled Vic over onto his face and tied his hands securely behind his back. He'd barely finished when Vic let out a soft moan and his eyes flickered open.

Kate felt the tremor that shook Michael's body and drew him closer as Slade helped a dazed Vic to his feet. "It's all right, honey," she said quickly. "He can't hurt us anymore."

"I know," Michael said, but his voice lacked conviction. Kate had to admit she'd feel a lot better when Vic was safely locked away again.

"All right," Slade said, echoing her thoughts. "The sooner we get this jerk back to town and in the hands of the police the better."

"How did you get up here?" Kate said, giving him a guilty look over Michael's head. "How did you know I was here?"

"I rented a car," Slade said, "I'll tell you the rest later."

It was much later before he had the opportunity. They drove back to town in separate cars, Slade taking a scowling but silent Vic with him in the car he'd rented, while Kate drove her sleeping son to the motel.

Michael woke up just long enough to get out of the car and into Kate's room before falling asleep again on the bed. She was content to sit beside him, savoring the inimitable joy of knowing her child was safe and back where he belonged. She was dozing herself when Slade tapped on her door later. Vic was in custody, he told her, and would not trouble them again. Heady with relief, Kate then told him everything that had happened in the ghost town.

Slade said nothing while she recounted the whole experience, though she saw his hands clench. "I was going to kill him," Slade said quietly.

''I know.'' She glanced at his face but he was staring at his feet, his expression as inscrutable as always. Michael stirred on the bed, and she looked down at him, stroking his hair back from his forehead.

He looked peaceful in his sleep, as if the nightmare of the past few days had never happened. She hoped fervently that it wouldn't have a lasting effect on him.

Her stomach cringed as she thought how close she'd come to losing him. ''I know exactly how you felt,'' she said, remembering the moment Vic had pulled her away from her son. ''For a second or two I wanted to kill him myself.''

''But you didn't.''

She heard the odd note in his voice and looked up at him. ''Nor did you,'' she said gently.

He didn't answer and after a moment she murmured, ''What do you think will happen to him now?''

He sent her a swift glance. ''They'll probably put him away for a long time. You'll have to file charges, of course. And there will have to be a court case.''

Kate nodded soberly. ''I hope they'll be able to help him.''

Slade swore. ''How can you waste your pity on him, after everything he's done to your son?''

Kate smiled. ''*Our* son,'' she corrected.

Slade was silent, and Michael stirred on the bed, capturing her attention.

''How are you feeling, honey?'' she asked gently.

He opened his eyes and gave her a smile that made her want to cry. ''Hungry,'' he said, rubbing his tummy for emphasis.

''I bet you are,'' Slade said, getting to his feet. ''I'll just go and wash up, then we'll go and get something to eat.''

Kate nodded. ''I'd like to shower first, and to tidy Michael up. Though I'll have to buy him a shirt before we go home.''

She looked at the shirt Michael was wearing. ''Vic must have got that one from Gladys. It's miles too big.''

"I liked Gladys," Michael said a little sadly. "She was nice to me."

Kate gave him an anxious look. "We don't have to talk about it now, Michael. You can tell us all about it later."

His face brightened. "Can I have a hamburger?"

She felt Slade's hand on her shoulder and looked up at him.

"He's going to be all right," Slade said softly.

"Yes," she said with quiet satisfaction. "I think he is."

He lifted his hand and ran his thumb gently down her cheek. "How about you?"

Smiling, she reassured him. "I'm going to be fine, now."

Seated in the fast-food restaurant later, Michael calmly recounted the events of the past few days. Vic, he told them, had met him from school saying Kate had sent him to pick him up.

"Did you know who he was?" Kate asked, watching her son satisfy a healthy appetite by devouring both his fries and half of hers, too.

"Not at first," Michael said, reaching for his milk shake. "I sort of knew him, like I'd seen him before, but when he said he was my daddy, then I knew who he was. Then I got scared."

Kate flashed a quick glance at Slade, but he seemed preoccupied with stirring his coffee.

Michael went on describing how Vic had told him he was taking him to see his mom, but when he drove to the airport Michael had become really frightened.

"I told him I wanted to go home," he said, "but he told me you were waiting for me in this new place, so I went with him."

He drank down some of his milk shake before going on. "Then we got to Gladys's house, and you weren't there, and I asked where you were and Vic got angry. He kept telling me to call him Daddy, but I didn't want to."

His voice had risen and Kate touched his arm. "It's all right, honey, you can tell us the rest later."

"There's one thing I would like to know," Slade said when Michael had eaten his hamburger. "If you didn't like being with Vic, why didn't you tell someone? Why didn't you ask someone to help you?"

Michael stared at his plate. "He said if I didn't do what I was told, he'd kill me. And Mom, too."

"Oh, God." Kate leaned over and gave him a quick hug. "Well, he can't hurt you now. You're safe now."

"Good." Michael picked up his milk shake. He sucked on the straw, making a loud gurgling noise.

Kate smiled. "Do you want another milk shake?"

Michael shook his head and patted his stomach. "I'm full."

"Then I guess we're ready to go," Slade said, and lifted his hat off the table.

"I wish I had my hat," Michael said, watching Slade settle his on his head.

"You will have by tonight." Slade reached for Michael's hand. "We're flying out of here this afternoon, and you'll be sleeping in your own bed tonight."

Michael creased his forehead in thought. "Do I have to go to school tomorrow?"

"No," said Kate firmly. "You and I are going to have a nice rest for a few days. Then we'll see how you are after that."

Michael looked up at Slade. "Are you going to be there, too?"

Kate waited every bit as anxiously as her son for his answer. When it came, she understood how frustrating those words could be.

"We'll see," Slade said, and marched Michael out of the restaurant.

She was still thinking about that evasive answer when they were settled in their seats on the plane that would take them back to Portland.

Michael was asleep again, his legs curled up under him and his head resting on the window.

Slade pressed the button to lower the back of his seat. Turning his head to look at her, he asked quietly, "How are your wrists?"

"Sore." Kate rubbed them and grimaced.

"That's what you get for not doing what you're told."

Kate shivered. "I hate that phrase."

He reached for her hand and enfolded it in his warm grasp. "Sorry. But I wish you had trusted me a little bit more. If I hadn't been expecting you to take off on your own, and been ready for it, things might not have worked out quite so well."

She looked at him in surprise. "You knew what I'd planned to do?"

"Sure. Though I have to admit, I didn't expect you to take the car. It was lucky you left the note in your pants, or it might have taken me longer to track you down."

She stared at him, suspicion forming in her mind. She had to know, she decided. It was important. "Is that why you stayed with me last night?" she asked carefully. "To keep an eye on me?"

She saw the wariness in his gaze and knew the answer. "I see," she said tightly and withdrew her hand.

"No, you don't—" he began, but she interrupted him with a yawn.

"I'm tired," she said, closing her eyes before he could see the misery reflected in them. "I'm going to try and get some sleep."

She kept her eyes closed tightly the rest of the way, only opening them when the plane circled for a landing. In the flurry of preparing to leave the plane there was no chance for conversation, and when Slade announced he would get a cab back to his trailer, she made no effort to protest.

She watched Michael give him a final hug, and his eyes met hers briefly over the small boy's head. "Take care," he said quietly.

She nodded, her throat tight. "You, too. Thanks for everything." It sounded ridiculous after everything he'd done, but it was all she could manage.

"Sure." Slade gave Michael a gentle slap on the shoulder. "Keep smiling, friend."

Michael looked up, his face solemn. "Don't fall off any more bulls," he said, sounding forlorn.

Slade gave a lopsided grin that sent a shaft of pain through Kate. "I'll try not to," he said huskily.

"Come on, Michael." She tugged on his shirt and picked up her bag. "Say goodbye." Because I can't, she added silently. She kept her back to the cab as she heard it drive off, concentrating on unlocking the door of her car.

It felt so good to be home, to have Michael back unharmed, to be back to normal. She went through the routine of bath and story time, making the most of every second. Never again would she take these moments for granted, she promised herself.

Only when Michael had settled down to sleep, and she was alone in the darkened living room, did she allow herself to dwell on Slade.

He had given no indication when she would see him again, if ever. She seriously doubted that he would finish the photo assignment; he hadn't wanted to do it in the first place.

She wondered now why he had agreed to pose for her. He'd never told her why he'd changed his mind about doing the ad campaign. Whatever his reasons, it was obvious they no longer applied.

Michael hadn't mentioned Slade's name since he'd left. Kate sighed. He'd accepted it, too. That meaningless phrase, "We'll see," was all too familiar.

She made coffee and took it back to the armchair, too restless to go to bed in spite of her exhaustion. She tried to watch television, but the images blurred and she switched it off in disgust.

Finally, for want of something better to do, she went to bed, and lay for hours thinking about Slade's warm body, and the fiery touch of his lips on hers.

She spent the next two days doing her best to erase the bad memories from Michael's mind. His checkup at the clinic proved him physically and mentally fit, for which she was intensely grateful. Her own bruises blossomed into glorious technicolor, much to Michael's concern, and she had to constantly reassure him they didn't hurt.

They visited the zoo, and the science museum, played miniature golf and went swimming. By the end of the second day Kate was tired of the insistent hope that Slade would appear out of the blue. She packed an overnight bag and drove to the beach, where she knew there was no possibility of bumping into him.

By the time they returned to the apartment at the end of the week, where the faint hope that he'd left word proved fruitless, Kate had convinced herself that Slade had rejoined the circuit.

When she picked up her office phone the following Monday morning, she was speechless when she heard his voice.

"I want to talk to you," Slade said in the inflexible tone he'd used when she'd first approached him.

Kate's heart sank. For one wild moment she'd hoped he was going to finish the campaign after all. "Go ahead," she said quietly when she'd found her voice.

"Not on the phone. Can you meet me for lunch?"

Much as she wanted to, she wasn't sure she could handle seeing him again. "I'm pretty busy," she muttered, cursing herself for her irresolution.

"You must have a break sometime. I'll pick you up at twelve."

He hung up before she could argue. She was too miserable to be angry at his high-handed attitude. She wished he'd left town without bothering to contact her, and in the next minute wished she'd worn something a little more interesting than the lavender shirtwaist dress.

She tried to concentrate on work but irrelevant thoughts kept creeping in. She hoped he would take her to a crowded restaurant. If he was going to break her heart she wanted it to be where she couldn't fall apart.

She had no doubt he was going to tell her he couldn't finish the campaign. If he'd intended otherwise he would have been at the studio that morning. She didn't know why he hadn't simply told her over the phone, and made it easier on both of them.

But that wasn't his way. At least he had the decency to tell her to her face, she thought ruefully as she applied lipstick with a shaky hand shortly before noon.

He arrived a few minutes early. In spite of her good intentions, she couldn't help the thrill of excitement that disrupted her stomach when she saw him at the door of her office.

She could tell nothing from his face. He was dressed in jeans and a long-sleeved cream shirt trimmed Western-style with brown edging. He also wore his hat and looked, she thought with increasing depression, every inch the rodeo rider.

He avoided her eyes as he helped her into his run-down car. He asked after Michael, and seemed relieved when she said he was fine. After that he drove without speaking, and she could find nothing to say.

They were back at the beginning, Kate thought help-lessly. It was as if the few days they'd spent together, the wonderful nights they shared, had never been.

Resentment began to grow as she stared at the buildings flashing by. She had tried to understand. He'd told her he was afraid of his temper, but she knew it went deeper than that. He was afraid of love. Afraid to give anything of him-self that really mattered.

After all these years, he was still the same restless drifter he'd always been. And she seriously doubted if there was a person on the entire earth who could change that now. It was sad, she thought moodily, staring out the window at the trees skirting the fields beyond the freeway. Sad, and a ter-rible waste.

She sat up straighter as she realized where they were. "Where are you going?" she demanded. "I don't have time to go out of town for lunch. I have work to do."

"I need someplace where I won't be interrupted," Slade said calmly.

"And where's that?" Kate asked, afraid that she already knew.

He sent her a brief glance. "My trailer."

No, she thought. I can't be alone with him. "Slade, I really don't have time, I have a two o'clock appoint-ment—"

"I'll get you back by two."

She frowned at him but his gaze was on the road again, and with a sigh of resignation she leaned back. Her stom-ach was tying itself in knots when the car bumped across the field to the trailer.

He braked, and shut off the engine. Without a word he opened his door and climbed out, and reluctantly she did the same. She waited, conscious of the warm wind lifting her hair, while he unlocked the door of the trailer. For a pain-ful second or two she was reminded of a hot desert wind on a still, starlit night, then the door swung open and he stood back for her to enter.

The trailer was dark and a little stuffy. She sat on the narrow seat and placed her purse beside her, while Slade went around opening up windows.

When he was done he opened the small fridge and took out two cans of beer. "I don't have much to offer in the way of lunch," he said. "This was kind of a spur of the moment decision."

Wondering where he'd intended to take her, and why he'd changed his mind, Kate said carefully, "It's all right. I'm not that hungry, anyway."

"I was going to suggest a coffee shop," Slade said, answering her silent questions, "but I decided that what I wanted to say needed more privacy." He took off his hat and laid it on the table before turning back to the fridge. "I could make an omelette, or there's a bit of salad—"

"Will you stop talking about food and get on with it," Kate said crossly. "I don't want any lunch. And I don't know why you brought me all the way out here to tell me you're not going to finish the campaign. You could have told me that on the phone. Or in the coffee shop, for that matter. What did you think I was going to do, anyway? Throw a tantrum and embarrass you or something?"

He straightened slowly. "What makes you think I'm not going to finish the campaign?"

She caught her breath, afraid to hope for too much. The slight gleam in his dark eyes affected her pulse. A lock of his dark hair had fallen across his forehead. She wanted desperately to smooth it back. "You hitched up your trailer," she said, switching her gaze to a window to avoid looking at him.

"I did?"

He sounded puzzled and she shrugged. "The night I came and told you Michael had been kidnapped. We took my car because yours was hitched. I assumed you were planning to leave the next morning."

There was a pause. She dared not look at him. She could feel the tension growing between them like a breathing, living thing. Her heart seemed unable to maintain a steady rhythm; it was skipping like a young colt.

"I'd hitched my trailer," Slade said carefully, "because I'd planned to move to a site nearer town. Since I was working at the studio it seemed like a good idea."

"Oh." Kate pressed her lips together. There didn't seem anything to say to that. Her lungs had joined in her body's conspiracy to destroy her composure. She could hardly breathe.

"When I came back the next morning to pack," Slade went on, "I asked the owner of the field for an extension."

Kate cleared her throat. "I see. So that's what you wanted to tell me? That you want to finish the ad campaign?"

"That depends."

"On what?"

"On you. There are a few conditions that go along with it, if I'm going to continue posing for you."

She pulled in a shaky breath. For some reason her fingernails were digging into her palms. She was glad she was sitting down; it seemed quite possible that her legs would not support her if she stood. "Conditions?"

"Yes." He moved to stand in front of her. "Would you look at me?"

She turned her head and excitement shivered down her spine. If only she could believe that look in his eyes. "What conditions?" she said, her voice barely above a whisper.

"I have it all worked out. All you have to do is agree and we have a deal." He stooped to capture her hands in his. With a gentle tug he pulled her to her feet, and she found her legs would work, after all.

"I've decided it's time I settled down in one place. I'm tired of being on the road all the time. I figure if I finish the

ampaign, and maybe take on a couple of those offers you
romised would come my way, I'd have enough money to
ut down on my ranch."

She moistened her dry lips. "Your ranch?" A tiny part of
er mind pointed out she was repeating everything he said.
t didn't seem to matter. Her hands felt so warm and secure
n his clasp. He held them against his chest, she could feel
is heartbeat. It seemed as erratic as her own.

"Well, I was thinking of it more as *our* ranch. Somewhere in eastern Oregon, I thought. We can raise cattle, and
naybe I'll tame a wild horse or two. I was hoping that you'd
onsider working free-lance from home. Lots of people do
hat now with computers and modems and whatever
lse—"

"Slade." It came out on a croak and she tried again.
"Slade?"

He looked down at her and she saw anxiety mirrored in
is eyes. "Could you please get to the point?" she asked,
raying he would say what she longed to hear.

"I thought I was." He took a deep breath. "I guess you
vant me to ask you properly."

Joy and hope mingled with disbelief as she gazed up at
im. "You bet your cowboy boots I do."

He smiled. A wonderful slow smile that warmed his face
nd kindled a flame in his eyes. "I love you, Kate. Would
ou consider marrying me?"

She made a tiny sound in the back of her throat.

He frowned and bent his head to look in her face. "Is that
yes?"

She pulled her hands free and wrapped her arms around
is neck. "You bet it's a yes."

His mouth found hers, warm, insistent and incredibly
atisfying. She could feel the dampness of tears against her
shes, then forgot them as his touch blocked out every-
hing except the two of them, sharing a love that she knew
ould stand the test of time, just as it had always done.

A long time later, curled up in his arms on the narrow seat, she said dreamily, "That's the first time you've eve told me that you loved me."

"It's the first time I've ever said it to anyone."

He looked at her, one eyebrow tilted. "How do you thin Michael will take it?"

"He'll be delighted. He's been waiting for someone to b his daddy for a long time." She studied him thoughtfully "What made you change your mind?"

"About what?"

"Everything. Settling down, getting married, all th things I thought you'd never do."

His answer was so long coming she almost gave up. "I fi nally realized how powerful love could be," he said at last "I watched you battle the fear, the heat, all the frustration and discomfort, and finally, when it came down to it, you put your life on the line for Michael.

"Most people would have given up, but there was neve any doubt in my mind that even if I'd left you alone in th middle of that desert, you would have found some way to get to your son."

"Our son," she corrected quietly. "And you did the same thing."

"I know. That's when I realized I was capable of loving like that, too." He shifted again, wrapping his arms around her as if he were afraid to let her go. "That really shook me It shook me even more to realize that I had gained contro of my temper, that I hadn't done what I was intending to do because of you and Michael. That's when I knew I love you both. Too much to walk away."

He dropped a kiss on her forehead. "With a love like that I knew we could survive anything. Without you and Mi chael, I had nothing."

She stirred, moving so that she could look up at him "Why did you take so long to tell me all this?"

"I wanted to be sure." This time his kiss landed on her mouth, soft and full of promise. "I'd made a mess of so many things in my life. I needed time to really explore my feelings and what I wanted to do. I had to be sure I could make you and Michael happy."

She smiled. "And you're sure now?"

"Never been surer."

"I never had any doubt," she said softly. "I just had to wait and hope you would realize it, too."

He sighed. "I almost blew it again."

"Ah, but you didn't." She traced his mouth with the tip of her finger. "You won't miss the rodeo?"

"Uh-uh. I won't have time. The ranch will keep me busy. What about you? Will you miss working at the studio?"

"No." She sent him a mischievous grin. "The babies will keep me busy."

His eyes widened. "Babies?"

"Sure." She looked at him anxiously. "You do want more babies, don't you?"

His kiss this time took her breath away. "I've never believed in single-child families," he said when he lifted his head. "Especially on a ranch. It can be very lonely."

"That's what I think." She gave a smile of pure satisfaction. "We'll have to make sure Michael's not lonely."

His eyes gleamed. "I think we should get started on that as soon as possible."

The afternoon at the office seemed to drag, but finally it was time to leave. Slade was waiting for her in the outer office, and her heart turned over when she reminded herself that from now on he would always be there for her.

She let Slade walk to the school building to meet Michael. Watching from the car, she heard her son's shout of joy, and felt a prickling of tears when the man she loved swung the small boy off his feet and into his arms.

Michael tumbled into the car, words tripping up on his tongue in his excitement. "Hi, Mom! Isn't it great to see Slade again?"

"It sure is," Kate said unsteadily. "But you'll have to stop calling him Slade."

"How come?" Michael demanded.

"I have a new name," Slade answered for her. He climbed in behind the wheel. "How does 'Dad' sound?"

Michael let out a long sigh of pure contentment. "I guess from now on we're going to be a real family, huh?"

Slade reached for Kate's hand, drawing it to his mouth. His eyes met hers, full of promise and deep, overwhelming love. "Yes, son," he said softly. "From now on, we're going to be a real family."

*   *   *   *   *

You'll flip . . . your pages won't!
Read paperbacks *hands-free* with

Book Mate • I

The perfect "mate" for all your romance paperbacks

Traveling • Vacationing • At Work • In Bed • Studying • Cooking • Eating

Perfect size for all standard paperbacks, this wonderful invention makes reading a pure pleasure! Ingenious design holds paperback books OPEN and FLAT so even wind can't ruffle pages — leaves your hands free to do other things. Reinforced, wipe-clean vinyl-covered holder flexes to let you turn pages without undoing the strap . . . supports paperbacks so well, they have the strength of hardcovers!

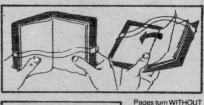

Pages turn WITHOUT opening the strap

SEE-THROUGH STRAP

Reinforced back stays flat

Built in bookmark

BOOK MARK

BACK COVER HOLDING STRIP

10 x 7¼ opened.
Snaps closed for easy carrying, too

Available now. Send your name, address, and zip code, along with a check or money order for just $5.95 + .75¢ for postage & handling (for a total of $6.70) payable to Reader Service to:

Reader Service
Bookmate Offer
901 Fuhrmann Blvd.
P.O. Box 1396
Buffalo, N.Y. 14269-1396

Offer not available in Canada
*New York and Iowa residents add appropriate sales tax.

BM-G